THAT NIGHT

Also by Amy Giles

Now Is Everything

THAT NIGHT

AMY GILES

HARPER TEEN
An Imprint of HarperCollins*Publishers*

For Pat, Maggie, and Julia. Always.

Jess

It's funny, in a tragically not-really-that-funny kind of way, what I *do* remember of that night. Like how warm it was for March and Ethan wouldn't shut up about how that was because of global warming. How the last of those dingy gray mountains of snow piled up in the corners of the parking lots had finally melted, leaving behind puddles as the only evidence of their once-towering existence. How Marissa was wearing Ethan's hoodie because she said she was cold, even though it was warm, and how I realized with the passing of that sweatshirt that my brother and my best friend liked each other.

The earth still feels off-balance without them. Even the weather has shifted: late March seems to think it's winter this year, not spring. Rubbing my arms for warmth, I walk in the opposite direction of school, blowing off first period. Maybe even second. Some mornings it takes a little longer for me to get my act together enough to face another day without them, even a year later.

On my way to the beach, I pass houses crammed so close together one neighbor could pass a cup of sugar to another through a window, which then give way to mom-and-pop shops. Queens never sleeps, but weekday mornings have their own jarring soundtrack. Buses lurch and belch down Mott Avenue, picking up people for work or dropping them off after their night shift. Car horns blare at trucks double-parked to make their deliveries. Planes taking off from JFK roar overhead every couple of minutes. Storekeepers lift their metal security gates with grinding metallic clangs. Inside of Shu's Fish, Shu places whole silver porgies on mounds of fresh ice. The A train passing by rumbles in the air like thunder.

Far Rockaway isn't cool like Manhattan, or stuck-up like Nassau. We're unapologetically Queens but with beaches. For me, that's the best thing about living here, our beaches, the ones that attract day-trippers from Memorial Day through Labor Day. But they're ours all year long.

I turn right on Beach Channel and keep walking until my feet touch the boardwalk. Only die-hard power walkers and joggers brave this early morning chill at the beach. Cold wind, so much sharper here by the water, stings like needles against my exposed skin. I sit down on the sand and watch the swell lines roll in. To the east is the Atlantic Beach Bridge, which we used to take to get to Marissa's family's beach cabana. Marissa, Ethan, and I spent so many summer days there together. Not anymore.

Everyone who survived that night at the Balcony has a story to tell. The movie was sold out by the time they arrived, they were in the bathroom, on the concession line.

Eighteen people didn't get to tell their story.

People think we're lucky, because we survived, because you can't see our scars. But we feel them every day. We're the walking wounded.

At Ethan's funeral Mrs. Alvarez, our next-door neighbor, came over to comfort me, dabbing at her nose with a tissue. Spoiler alert: no one in the history of death and dying has come up with any magical combination of words that can erase the pain of losing someone. Some people do even more damage in their awkwardness.

"God spared you. His hand was on your back guiding you," Mrs. Alvarez said, eyes red and watery from crying. But her faith was unwavering. There wasn't even a hint of doubt in her voice.

It had only been a few days and I was still numb, digging crescent-shaped gouges into my palms with my nails just to make sure I hadn't died that night too. It would be a few more days until the loss really started to kick in. When I didn't have to race Ethan to the bathroom in the morning. And later when my phone went deathly silent without the constant chiming of Marissa's texts after her parents sent her to that private school in Colorado.

If Mrs. Alvarez had told me her theories about God's plan a week later, I would have been furious. "Really? So that's how God works? He chooses favorites? Me over Ethan?"

But I was still in shock at the funeral, so I said, "I was just getting candy."

Sno-Caps, to be specific. This is important because they were for Marissa. She handed me a five without even looking at me. "You know what I like." And I did. I knew Marissa so well that

I could tell she wasn't coming with me to the concession stand because she wanted to stay with Ethan. I also knew that when Marissa was seven, she threw up after eating too many Sno-Caps and hadn't eaten one since.

So while *he* snuck in through one of the emergency exits, I was buying my best friend candy that would make her sick because I was pissed at her.

And *that's* how I was "spared."

LUCAS

Mom's cool hand on my cheek startles me awake. "Wake-up time," she says, like I'm three years old.

I glance over at the alarm clock on my nightstand. 6:58. Two minutes before my alarm is supposed to wake me up.

She pushes my hair away from my face. "I made you an omelet. Hurry up before it gets cold."

Omelets are safe. I can't think of any bottled marinade or packet of artificial seasoning she can add to it to mess it up. Breakfast is actually the one meal here that isn't smothered with synthetic-tasting flavors that cannot possibly come from the natural world.

She reaches overhead to shut off the swooshing ceiling fan. I keep it on all night. The white noise helps me sleep—otherwise every creak of the floorboard, every noise out on the street, makes me jump out of bed.

"That was some cough last night." She reaches her hand to my forehead again and holds it there for a second. Then she replaces her hand with her lips.

"Ma!"

She puts her hand on my cheek to get another reading. "You feel warm."

"I'm fine. I just woke up."

"Are you sure?"

"Positive."

Her eyes are glued to my face looking for signs of illness that don't exist. "I think you're overdue for a visit to see Dr. Patel anyway. Isn't it time for your annual?"

"Pretty sure it hasn't been a year yet." I tread carefully. Cautiously.

She busies herself picking up my dirty laundry off the floor. "I'll call them today. Just to make sure."

I sit up in bed and stretch. "Did you get my text last night?"

She finds a stray sock by my bed. "About your keys?"

"Yeah. Have you seen them? I ended up walking to the gym."

She laughs at that as she gets on her hands and knees to search under my bed for more laundry.

I get it. It sounds weird to complain about walking to the gym when I willingly get up and run five miles every other morning.

I pull my legs out from under the blanket. "I just don't know where they went. I swear I put them on the peg."

She stands back up and adjusts the dirty clothes in her arms, holding them like a baby. "Well, they couldn't have just walked off on their own. I'm sure they'll turn up."

No, they didn't walk off on their own, but my mother has been stooping to new lows lately and I have a bad feeling in my gut.

Mom stops by my window, where my boxing gloves are hanging off the crank, and lifts one glove for a sniff. With a scrunched-up nose from the lingering BO, she says, "I'll pop a couple of dryer sheets in these. That should help."

She heads toward the door, but not before stopping for a few painful heartbeats too long to stare at Jason's Corner: the empty bed, the shelves of trophies and ribbons he collected over the years that she still dutifully dusts every week, the shrine to her spectacular firstborn. She bows her head and leaves before she's overcome by the most God-Awful Thing in the World to Happen to the Rossi Family.

Sometimes I miss the things that used to bug me the most about Jason.

"Wake and bake, bro!" He'd shove his ass in my sleeping face. "Steak and onions last night! Take a good whiff!" He'd wave his hand so I could really enjoy the fine bouquet of his farts.

I never thought Jason's steak-and-onion farts would be something I'd look back on with nostalgia.

The alarm clock goes off exactly at seven. I shut it off. The scent of eggs wafts up the stairs to my room. It's not that different from the stench of Jason's farts, actually.

Jess

Looks like I'm blowing off third period too.

I take a few deep breaths, letting the salt air sink to the bottom of my lungs, before pushing off the sand. I head back to Mott Avenue to look for a job. School can wait today.

The Ponsetis don't need my babysitting services anymore, not since Mrs. Ponseti's mother moved in with them, which stinks because they were the perfect family to work for: they went out all the time (they have more of a social life than I do); they could never break a twenty, so they always rounded up in my favor; and their pantry was a wonderland, chock-full of high-fructose delicacies. They even had Pop-Tarts. *Pop-Tarts!*

I've been looking and applying for weeks. The Laundromat said to try back in a month. Key Food, where Ethan started working after Dad left, didn't have any openings. The woman at the clothing store that had every shade and wash of denim hanging fashionably off emaciated headless mannequins looked me up and down before answering a hard no.

There's one last stretch of stores I haven't hit yet. Squeezed in between the Korean grocer and the comic book store is Food of All Nations. Inside, the scent of spices fills the air; my mouth waters. I walk over to a box of Turkish delights and hold it up to inspect it. I remember reading about them in the Chronicles of Narnia. Edmund betrayed his family for them. I've never had one before, but they must be really something to sell out your family for a box.

"Can I help you?" a woman behind the counter asks, straightening her hijab.

I put the box down exactly as I found it and walk to the counter. "I was wondering if you were hiring?"

She purses her lips. "No. I'm sorry. We're a family-owned business."

"Oh. Okay. Thanks." I try to smile, but weeks of rejections weigh my cheeks down.

"You might want to try Enzo's," she offers.

I thumb to the right. "Enzo's *Hardware*?"

Not as if there is any other Enzo's; it's just that Enzo has terrified me since I was a kid. Always just sitting on a chair behind his counter, grunting, never smiling. I used to cower behind Dad every time we had to run in there for something.

"Are they hiring?" I ask.

She nods. "Ask for Regina, Enzo's niece. Tell her Adab sent you."

I nod, encouraged. *Adab, Regina . . . Enzo . . .* I resist a shudder. I can do this.

I thank her, then point to the Turkish delights. "When I make some money, I'm coming back for those."

She smiles and nods. "I'll keep a box for you until then."

I walk outside and take a steadying breath before marching over to Enzo's.

"Fill out this form."

"Regina," who is actually Reggie Scarpulla, a girl I went to high school with who graduated last year, shoves a piece of paper at me. We weren't friends at school, but I remember seeing her in the bathroom, reapplying her lipstick.

I fill out the form while sitting in an uncomfortable orange plastic chair next to a vending machine on the other side of the Employees Only door. Once I'm done, Reggie brings me into her office and closes the door, trapping the hot, stale air inside with us. A trickle of sweat charts a ticklish course down my spine.

"Jessica Nolan. I remember you." She bounces a pencil eraser across her desk, looking over my paperwork. *Taptaptaptaptaptap*. She glances up. "You turned seventeen last month. That makes you a junior, right?" I nod. "So you're looking for hours after school?"

I nod again. Clear my throat. "Yes."

"Why aren't you in school now?"

"I'm going in late. I have a note." I add the note part so I don't come across as a habitual ditcher, even if I am. I don't mention I wrote the note myself and forged my mother's signature.

Taptaptaptaptaptap.

She exhales. "So, Jessica. Why do you want to work here?"

"Oh. *Why?*" As in why wasn't I prepared to answer this basic fundamental job interview question? She raises her eyebrows, waiting. "I . . . I just really need a job." I feel my cheeks burn.

Judging by the way her head jerks back slightly in surprise, I take it no one's ever answered that way before. Reggie uses the eraser tip to scratch the top of her head, then resumes her tapping. Seconds pass while she thinks my response over.

"A little bit about us." I take that as a sign that I haven't totally bombed the interview yet. "We're small, but we're not that small. We expanded last year. Now we have everything here that the big stores have. Plumbing, heating, cooling, electrical, painting . . . We have lawn and garden, home organization. . . ." She ticks off everything on her fingers, scanning the ceiling for her mental inventory.

She exhales and plants her palms on the desk. "Okay, so . . . we *are* looking to fill a position. But it's not a specific position, you know? Not like customer service or kitchen design." She wiggles her fingers in the air like kitchen design is the fanciest thing she could imagine. "Everyone who works here is expected to pitch in with everything and anything. Except registers. My uncle doesn't let anyone touch the money." She laughs and looks down at my paperwork before adding under her breath, "Not even me."

She glances back up. "That means unloading trucks and restocking shelves. You *have* to be able to lift up to seventy pounds."

Her eyes travel along my shoulders, my arms, everything she can see from where she's sitting. I know what she sees, and it's not much. I wish my clothes weren't so baggy, exaggerating my small size.

"I can lift seventy pounds," I promise.

"It's a *suuuper* unglamorous job, Jessica. The day will come when I'm gonna ask you to unclog the toilet in the bathroom. You would not *be-LIEVE* the presents some customers have left us in there." She rolls her eyes hard.

I force myself not to show my disgust picturing that day. "It's okay. I can do it."

She's trying to scare me off, I can tell. But I'm more afraid of not getting this job than getting it. She stares up at the flickering fluorescent lights, thinking. I count each agonizing second of silence.

"Your brother was at the Balcony, wasn't he?"

There's no need to say more; everyone in our neighborhood knows what that means.

"Yeah," I say. "So was I."

"Oh, I didn't know that. I avoided all the . . ." Her hand twirls in the air. *"Ceremonies."* She makes a face, as if the word leaves a bad taste in her mouth.

I know what she means. The tree planting, the bench dedication, the charity softball game. All intended to honor the people who died that night but ended up making us survivors and our families feel like some kind of freak show on display, people you wouldn't want to trade places with in a million years. But still. Those "ceremonies" were for us, not for her.

"I couldn't," she adds. "I just saw his name on the list." She stands up from her chair. "Wait here."

She leaves the door open, thank God. It lets in a little air, but I'm still sweating. There's a fan in the corner, unplugged. I'm desperate to turn it on, but then I picture all the papers flying off her desk and fluttering around her office like a flock of seagulls.

I tug my shirt away from my skin and shake it around to circulate some air before the sweat stains soak through my shirt.

Watch out for boob sweat. I hear Marissa in my ear. It makes me smile. I can just imagine what she'd say if she saw me here applying for a job unloading trucks.

Don't forget to pick up a jockstrap on the way home from work! Bwahahahaha!

Large pockets of rust consume Reggie's metal desk. The back of a picture frame faces me.

Turn it around! Let's see it. Marissa bosses me and I obey.

It's Reggie with a very tall, very muscular guy. He looks familiar. I can practically feel Marissa leaning over my shoulder. *Wow, he's cute!*

They're at the beach, smiling at the camera, their tanned arms wrapped around each other. He looks like Paul Bunyan next to her, as if he could crush her between his arm and torso if he exerted even the slightest effort.

And HUGE! The guy's a friggin' skyscraper!

Reggie comes back in as I'm still holding the frame.

Nailed!

In a panic, I place the frame back where I found it.

"I'm sorry." I half expect to self-combust of embarrassment right here and now. Cause of death: mortification.

"It's okay," she says, but her eyes are fierce, protective. I crossed a line; not smart on an interview. She exhales, as if to let it go. "He was my fiancé."

Was. That's why she made that comment about the ceremonies.

"He was at the Balcony too. Jason Rossi."

Now I know why he looked familiar. Jason Rossi was a senior when I was a freshman. Homecoming king. Star quarterback. Marissa and I went to all the football games just to watch him play, even though we had zero school spirit and even less interest in football. He was *that* big of a legend.

She tears her eyes off the frame. I recognize her look of pain. No one from the Rockaways is completely immune.

"His brother goes to school with me," I say.

She picks up her pencil and taps it again. There's a shift in her mood, a brightening in her voice at the mention of Jason's brother, Lucas. "You guys know each other? Lucas works here too."

I lean back in my chair, picturing him. A senior. Quiet. Also built like a skyscraper. "Don't mess with Lucas" is a golden rule at school.

He's kind of cute too. Maybe this job won't suck so much after all.

Reggie drops her pencil on the desk. "We pay eleven dollars an hour. Shifts fluctuate week to week, depending on how busy or slow we are. Any problems with that?"

I shake my head no.

"Okay to start next Monday . . ." She squints at a calendar hanging on her wall. "April third? Just come straight after school."

I smile, feeling ridiculously proud of myself for landing this probably pretty crappy job.

"Sounds great."

Halp! What's the answer to ? #3 on the math hw?

I don't know. I haven't gotten to it yet. Ask Siri.

Siri's a jerk.

Bet you didn't know her favorite color is green?

You asked her?!!!

I'm awesome that way.

Your awesomeness never ceases to amaze me.

Shmanks.

I've been rereading my and Marissa's old text messages. I could scroll for hours and still not reach the end. They make my chest ache, but these Marissa fixes keep me going, like the oxygen masks that come down in the airplane when the cabin pressure fails.

I haven't heard from Marissa in months. Boulder Academy for Children and Adolescents with Social and Emotional Challenges doesn't allow their students to have cell phones or any kind of communication with the outside world. Mrs. Connell told me that they have weekly family therapy sessions over Skype with Marissa, but that's limited to immediate family only. Being "practically family" doesn't count for much it turns out.

A lot of kids never came back after that night, like Marissa. The school brought in grief counselors to help the rest of us. The hallways were clogged with people hugging and crying on each other's shoulders. I didn't have a shoulder left to cry on.

I squeeze the hard pebble-sized knot inside my earlobe, the

second piercing that I had to let close after it got infected. Marissa said that putting the needle in the lighter flame would sterilize it. It didn't.

I reach in my locker for my biology text, just as Sarah Ochtera's and Andrew Sarro's bickering escalates across the hall from me. They've been dating for a year now. It got all around school when they first did it, about a month into their relationship. A cautionary tale of the perils of popularity. People really don't care what I do or don't do, or who I do or don't do it with.

"No, please, *enlighten* me. What *wouldn't* I understand?" Andrew throws his arms out by his sides. Andrew wears too much hair product in his thick curly hair. It looks both crispy and greasy, which is only a great combo if you're an egg roll.

Sarah rolls her eyes but won't answer him. When she reaches for a textbook from her locker, Andrew grabs her wrist.

"I'm *talking* to you!"

A few heads turn to watch.

"Get off of me!" she yells back at him, wrenching her wrist away. He slams a hand on either side of the locker, trapping her. There's a bunch of "oh shits" muttered, but no one does anything.

Except for one person.

Lucas Rossi swoops in, grabbing Andrew by the back of his shirt and yanking him away from Sarah, lifting him off the ground and throwing him back several feet.

"She said get off of her," Lucas warns.

Andrew cranes his neck to stare up at him, his anger replaced so quickly by fear I expect to see a puddle of pee pooling around his feet. Lucas is maybe *the* tallest guy at school. Everything about him, from his nose to his feet, seems enlarged 70 percent to fit his enormous scale.

"It's none of your business," Andrew says, a statement, not a threat; he doesn't sound as ballsy as when he was harassing his girlfriend.

"I'm making it my business."

Andrew holds his hands up in surrender and backs away. He looks at Sarah one last time. "We'll talk later."

"Much later," Lucas adds.

Lucas pivots and turns away, and as he does, our eyes connect through the crowd. He looks at me for a beat, long enough that I feel like he's placing me in some catalog of his memories. A smile works its way across my cheeks. My hand goes up to wave. I mean, we're going to work together. I open my mouth to tell him.

"Hey . . ."

Lucas's expression changes, from anger to mild panic. Because of me?

I abort my wave and pretend I was just pushing my hair behind my ear. But he's already speeding down the hallway away from me.

The tingling starts in my fingertips. It's a familiar feeling by now. Everything is too tight: the hallway, my clothes, my throat. I race to the bathroom by the cafeteria. If I'm lucky, Domie or Charmaine will be in there with their stash of weed. A few hits will get me through this. It always does.

Lucas

I meet Pete at his locker seventh period. "I'm heading out early," I say, swinging my backpack over my shoulder.

"How come?"

Before I can answer, Gwen Welch runs between us and tickles Pete under his armpits. He squeals and folds into himself, giggling as she runs away. He points at her retreating back. "When you least expect it . . . expect it!"

"What was *that*?" I ask.

"A tickle streak," he says as if it's so obvious.

"Between you and Gwen?"

Gwen's not someone we usually hang out with, but you wouldn't know it from that tickle. She really got up there.

Pete grabs a sweatshirt from his locker and sniffs. Gagging, he throws it back in. "The whole school."

"No girl's ever come up to me to try and tickle me." I can't believe I'm jealous of Pete for getting his armpits tickled.

"They'd need a stepladder to reach your rank pits."

Maybe it's not just that my pits are so inaccessible though. Maybe I'm putting off some kind of "do not trespass" vibe.

All around me, everyone's moving on with their lives. A year ago, this place was a war zone. People crying everywhere, all the time. Just walking by someone's abandoned locker would be a trigger. For me, walking by the gym, the trophy case, destroys me. Their name . . . *my* name . . . engraved onto plaques, trophies. Photos of my dad in the late eighties, star football player. Then Jason just a few years ago. They were both a big deal here.

People are bouncing back now. Prom was canceled last year, so this year everyone's even more excited about it. Every time I turn around there's another promposal going on. Across the hall, Jim Barnes waits on his unicycle by Grace McCurdy's locker holding up a piece of poster board that says:

WHAT'S MORE FUN THAN RIDING A UNICYCLE? U*N*I @ PROM!

I heard Aisha Malik is making a fortune coming up with promposal ideas for people; she's charging fifteen dollars for each one.

Pete taps me on the shoulder. "Hey. I'm supposed to ask you something."

"What?"

Pete shrugs. "Molly Kane wanted to know if she promposed to you, would you go with her?"

Molly. Long brown hair, blue eyes. Smart, funny, cute.

I wince, as if Pete can convey my apologetic look to Molly.

"No, sorry. I'm not doing prom."

Not everyone's moved on just yet. Definitely not me.

I think about Ethan's sister waving to me this morning. Pretty girl smiles at you and waves and you run away? Smooth, Lucas. Real smooth.

It's not like I thought it through. If I could do it over, I would have at least nodded or said hi back before taking off. But every time I turn around there's another reminder. And sometimes there are just too many of those in one day. Jess Nolan just happened to wave at me when I'd already hit my daily quota.

Pete nods, understanding. "Yeah, that's what I figured." He turns away from me and grabs his econ book from his locker. "So where're you going now anyway?"

My phone buzzes in my back pocket. I know it's Mom even before I check.

I'm here.

"My mom made a doctor's appointment for me. Took the first opening they had available."

"Are you sick?" Pete leans not so subtly away from me.

"No. But she *thinks* I am, sooo . . ."

"Yeah."

"Yeah."

He gets it. Pete's been my closest friend since we were kids. Everyone acted differently around me after that night. Not Pete. I could always count on him to be himself. He never pumped me for information or tried to get me to talk about my feelings . . . that was Dr. Engel's job. Pete didn't hover to make sure I wasn't

20

springing any new leaks . . . that was my mother's job. He just showed up, sometimes to just drive around aimlessly with the music blasting at ear-bleeding decibels.

Pete was even the one who got me into boxing last June.

"Hear me out," he said after suggesting it. His fingers gripped the steering wheel as he tried to explain himself. "I was reading up on this, okay? There's a boxer who had PTSD after coming out of Iraq. During the day, he had all this anger and anxiety. At night, he couldn't sleep; every little noise, he'd be hopping out of bed. He said boxing helped him deal with it."

He may as well have been describing me.

"You read up on it?" I was a little surprised to hear this coming from Pete. My mom, sure. Not Pete.

His ears turned a shade of Got Caught Caring pink, but he laughed it off. "Our bromance is strong."

I snorted, but I went along with it. "Yeah, okay, sure. Why not?"

The boxing academy Pete found on Seagirt Boulevard was hard-core. The stench of unwashed socks and cheap cologne assaulted us as soon as we walked in. Pete was more direct.

"Smells like ass in here," he whispered to me behind a hand. "Ass splashed with eau de toilette."

Around the walls were posters of past and upcoming tournaments and framed signed headshots of Golden Gloves winners and welterweight champions. I recognized one guy by his headshot; he was our local boxing champ, Sergey Aminev.

The gym was packed with determined, focused faces. In the

ring, a trainer held up oversized mitts while a girl, solid muscle and shimmering in sweat, threw split-second punches at them as he waved his arms up and down, side to side, their motions choreographed, as if their minds were melded together. A couple of guys were hitting the heavy bag and speed bag tirelessly. In the corner, one brick wall of a dude was jumping rope so fast, the blurred rope was nothing more than an illusion whistling and whipping through the air.

A bell buzzed and all the noise and action stopped.

An older guy in a gray tracksuit that matched his gray hair and goatee was leaning against a wall with folded arms, one leg crossed over the other. He had the kind of smirk that seemed permanently tattooed on his face.

"You looking for someone?"

Intimidated by everything about this guy and this place, I turned to Pete for help.

"Um . . ." I rubbed at my mouth, then my jaw. "I was looking into maybe taking up boxing?"

The guy's smirk deepened; dimples appeared on either side of his carefully manscaped goatee.

"Taking up boxing?" He threw my words back at me. I could feel my cheeks go thermonuclear. "This isn't Zumba, kid."

I grabbed Pete's arm. "Come on, let's just go." But Pete stared this guy down, then gestured skyward to my height.

"Look at him. Do you seriously think he's cut out for Zumba?"

The guy ran his fingers down his beard. "I hear Zumba's for everyone. At least that's what my mother-in-law tells me. Helps with her rheumatoid arthritis." He was messing with me, I could tell by the crinkle around his eyes.

"Look," I said. "I came here because . . . I heard it could help me, that's all."

"Help you with what?"

"Forget it." I stopped myself from explaining. Every word I'd uttered since I walked in made me feel like a total idiot.

The bell buzzed and everyone was back in motion, the *thwunk thwunk* of the jump rope, the thudding smacks of gloves hitting the heavy bag, the dribbling of the speed bag.

Pete huffed a stream of exasperated air. "He was at the Balcony, okay? He's dealing with stuff. I'm the one who talked him into trying this out."

The smirk wasn't as permanent as I thought; it wiped clean off the guy's face. His skin, already pretty pale, practically turned as gray as his goatee. He rubbed the back of his neck, then looked up at me. "Sorry about that." In an about-face, he jutted his hand out. "Leo. Leo Springer. This is my gym. And you're?"

I took his hand and we shook. "Lucas."

"Lucas? Lucas what?"

"Rossi."

He looked me up and down, and I could practically hear the information click into place.

Guys like Leo, they knew all about the Rossi family, especially Jason, what he should have been, the hope so many people in the Rockaways had for him to go on and make it big, make a name for all of them. Like Sergey Aminev did.

But then it was over and Leo moved on.

"You run, Lucas?"

"Not really," I said.

"You're gonna start." He waved me to follow him. "Work up to five miles."

"Five miles?"

Leo stopped and glared at me. "You already giving me lip?"

I shook my head. "No . . . uh . . . how often?"

"Every day, if you're serious about this. Got it?" I nodded. I was serious, I thought. Was I? I wasn't sure anymore. I mean . . . five miles!

Leo handed me a jump rope. "Just give me a couple of minutes of this so I can see where we're starting." I tripped over the rope, my own feet, before it ever had a fighting chance to whistle and whip through the air.

Leo grabbed the rope from me. "Square one. That's where we're starting. That's fine. You'll get it. Orthodox or southpaw?"

I tried to remember which was which. "Uhhh . . . ?"

He explained, slowly, like I was having a hard time keeping up . . . which I was. "Do you punch with your *right* hand or your *left* hand?" He lifted one fist, then the other, illustrating.

I don't punch, I wanted to say, but that wasn't the answer that would get me in. "Right." I held up my right hand up.

He folded his arms. "Show me your orthodox stance."

I lifted both fists up in front of my face; he shook his head.

"You're a righty. So put your left foot forward and left fist up." He demonstrated for me. "You're gonna jab with your left, then come out hard with your right." I got into what I thought would be the proper stance. Leo shook his head again.

"Move your shoulder so it faces your opponent. Legs wider, shoulder width apart. Not so stiff, bend your knees a little, left foot toward your opponent. Loose fists, not so tight. Hold your right hand up here, by your chin. Left hand down in front of your face. Chin down. Eyes up. Okay, hold that."

I felt stupid, but I held my stance as he stepped back, narrowed his eyes. When my elbows started to slip, Leo's hand came up, fast, stopping just short of hitting me. I flinched. "Hands down, man down. Always keep your hands up."

While I was still in stance, he smacked me in the gut with the back of his hand. I wasn't quite ready for this attack either but I managed not to flinch this time. "Not bad. But we want them to be as hard as a stack of cinder blocks."

He folded his arms again. "You're obviously a strong kid, but to be a boxer you're gonna have to bleed for me." He nodded his head once. "Million-dollar question: Why are you here?"

I knew what he meant, but it didn't stop that swampy pit in my stomach from swirling. I'd been asking myself that same question since that night. Why *am* I here? Why me and not Jason?

"I told you . . ." I stumbled.

"Nah. For real. What's gonna make you get up at five in the morning to run?" He tapped his head. "What's going to keep you going when you think you got nothing left?"

I didn't have an answer.

"You ask anyone here and they'll all have something different to tell you." He ticked off his fingers. "Money, fame, *fitness*." He jutted his hand out to me, as if that might be my answer, and I could borrow it if I liked.

"Ladies!" the guy at the speed bag with the shaved head called out with a big grin.

"Ha, you wish," Leo hollered back. He thumbed over his shoulder. "Honor's stepfather told him he'd never amount to nothing. So every time he gets in the ring he's proving something to himself. 'I'm *somebody*.'" Leo jabbed his thumb into his chest.

I took a deep breath, sucking in all the pungent air, waiting for him to kick me out for not having a real purpose yet.

"Follow me." Apparently not. Then he turned and pointed to Pete. "What about you?"

Pete shook his head with a panicked expression.

Leo held his palm up. "Fine. Stay here, then."

I followed Leo to his cramped office. Sitting down behind his desk, he pulled out a piece of paper and started writing. "I'll write you down a bunch of exercises you should start doing right away, okay? How old are you?"

"Seventeen," I said. "Eighteen in January," I added.

Still scribbling, he said, "Good age to start."

He reached in a file and pulled out another sheet of paper. "Get this signed."

"What's this?" I looked at the form.

"Parental consent."

"Aw fuck."

Leo looked up at me. "Problem?"

I sighed. "Do I really need this?"

"Yep. Until you turn eighteen." He handed me my list of exercises. "Come back with that form signed and a credit card on Saturday morning and we'll get you started."

I met Pete waiting for me by the door. Before we left, my eyes panned around one last time. My fists clenched in some muscle memory, as if I'd done this before or was always meant to. I watched the guy jabbing at the speed bag, the fluid rhythm of his fists, his intense focus. My arms itched for a turn. I wanted this.

When my father came home that night, I talked him into signing the parental consent form. He ran interference and convinced Mom. I think they were both counting on me giving up on it after a couple of weeks, like I did with football, and before that soccer, and before that T-ball. I also agreed that I would only train, not compete.

That Saturday morning, I went down to the gym for my first session. Leo showed me how to wrap my hands to protect them. I borrowed some loaner gloves that were still moist with someone else's sweat inside. Leo ran me through basic punches . . . jabs, crosses, hooks, and uppercuts. He watched my moves with eagle eyes, serious, calculating.

Then he clapped his hands. "A'right. Let's do this."

I spent an hour working out: fifteen minutes of jumping rope and shadowboxing—sparring with an imaginary partner—eight three-minute rounds on the heavy bag, fifteen minutes of ab and core exercises, with one minute of rest in between.

Leo wacked me in the gut when we were done. This time I clenched my abs, ready for him. "Hands hurt?" he asked. I nodded. "Shoulders sore?" I nodded again, trying not to throw up in front of everyone. "Abs on fire?" More nodding. "Feel like you're gonna puke? Good. Go home now. Come back Monday. We'll do the whole thing over again."

The loaner gloves left a residual stink on my fingers as if I had shoved them under my pits for hours. I bought my own gloves. I could already tell I was going to use them a lot.

Leo took me under his wing. I like to think it's because he saw so much potential in me, but I know it's most likely because I'm one of those poor kids everyone feels sorry for since that night. He didn't mess around though. If I didn't do exactly what he said, he was going to drop me. So I got up early and ran every other morning before school. I practiced my two-, three-, four-, five-punch combinations on the heavy bag at the gym. Sparred with Kenny, one of the trainers, to work on my aim with mitt drills.

Over the past nine months, I've grown to love the sounds of the gym: the predictable ring of the electronic bell—three minutes on, one minute off for rest—the thwacking of the rope, the repetitive dribbling of the speed bag, the deep thuds of the heavy bag. These are the sounds that drown out the screams and gunfire that still echo in my head.

My phone buzzes again.

Where are you? Why aren't you answering?!

I'm coming.

"Gotta go," I say to Pete, turning to head out before my mother really starts to lose it.

Jess

Our chain-link gate groans as I push through it backward, while digging in my backpack for my house key.

The stress headache that started in Reggie's sauna of an office this morning has reached a crescendo, jackhammering behind my eyes.

"Jessica!"

I turn around to find Mrs. Alvarez coming down our front steps.

Mrs. Alvarez has been our neighbor since always and the closest person to a grandmother to me. She babysat Ethan first then both of us when my mother went back to work after her maternity leaves. Now she's Mom's de facto babysitter. She visits my mother every day. Some days, she helps my mother around the house. On Mom's bad days, they just sit and watch television together.

She walks over to me, her cardigan over her shoulders, buttoned at the neck to hold it in place. Her gray wig is immaculately combed, as always. I can tell she put on a fresh coat of red lipstick just to step outside. Mrs. Alvarez never leaves the house without her wig and her lipstick.

"We were worried about you. The school called this morning. They said you missed first period. Where were you?"

"Looking for a job," I say. "*Someone* has to." A different kind of pressure builds up behind my eyes; I try to force it back down. I don't think I do a great job of hiding my feelings from Mrs. Alvarez though.

"Oh, dear." She wraps her arms around me, patting my back, which feels like she's trying to coax a burp out of me. I breathe in her familiar scent, of powder and old-lady perfume, embedded in my memory from a time when I was well cared for.

"PSEG called also," she says, twisting the collar of her cardigan nervously. "It seems you're a few months behind on the electricity bill."

"Great." I've been trying not to stress out about the growing pile of envelopes on the dining room table.

"There's still money in the account. I *know*; I saw her checkbook. She just needs to sit down and write the checks!"

There's a lot my mom needs to do but doesn't. Like get out of bed, take a shower, make dinner . . . all of these would be great starters.

"Whatever money's left won't last much longer," I say, and Mrs. Alvarez nods, her face grim.

"I wish I could help more." She rubs her swollen knuckles. "You know, with Mr. Alvarez's pension and my Social Security checks, I'm only just getting by myself."

"I know." I hug her, just for being awesome. "I got a job, at Enzo's, so that should help. At least a little, right?"

"I'm sure it will." She puts a hand on my back and nudges me forward. "I made too much soup today. Chicken noodle. Go eat something. You're thin as a whisper."

"Okay." I nod, grateful for Mrs. Alvarez. She's always making too much food, which is how she takes care of us. Home-cooked meals won't fix what's broken, but they don't hurt either.

Once inside, I kick the door closed behind me. The house is a mess and smells like sauerkraut, which I fear may be coming from my unwashed mother.

Mom's in her usual place, on the worn-out brown recliner in front of the television. Her blond hair is limp and unwashed. Her dull brown eyes are glued to a cooking show.

I walk up and place a gentle hand on her shoulder.

"What are they making?"

"Coq au vin," she answers, her voice flat.

"What's in it?" I ask, trying to engage her.

"Chicken legs," she offers.

"Hm. Sounds good. Speaking of which . . . Mrs. Alvarez said she brought over some chicken noodle soup. Did you eat yet?"

She shakes her head and glances over at me. "I'm not hungry."

It's hard to look her in the eyes these days. I've seen a lot of sad eyes this past year, but my mother's are the saddest.

"Mrs. Alvarez said we're late with the electric bill," I tell her. Mom runs a hand down her face like this is already overwhelming her. "Maybe I can help you pay some bills? I can write the checks and you can just sign them?" I offer, glancing behind me at the mail on the table, feeling my stomach knot with another twist of misery.

"I can't right now, Jess. Maybe later." She turns her attention back to the television as the onions sizzle.

I miss my mother as much as I miss Ethan, if not more.

At Mrs. Alvarez's insistence (*What you need is to get out of this house and get some exercise, Nicole! Some fresh air will do you a world of good!*"), Mom tried to take a walk around the block a few weeks ago. A neighbor a few houses down found her sitting on a chair on her front stoop, sobbing. Apparently, she saw a boy skateboarding that looked like Ethan. I have the opposite problem. It's the not seeing him, not hearing him, that haunts me. At school, at home. I can't escape the silence.

I walk down the hallway, stopping for a minute outside of Ethan's room, door shut to embalm his last day with us. I don't understand the appeal of cemeteries. His bedroom is where I would visit him, if I could. But Mom begged me not to go in there.

"Jess! No!" She grabbed my arm to stop me, soon after he died. She made it sound like I was about to dance on my brother's grave when all I was doing was trying to find a way to be closer to him. To feel him near me again.

I pivot and go to the bathroom in search of some Tylenol, Advil, baby aspirin, anything to dull this pounding headache. Inside the medicine cabinet I find a diorama of the Nolan Family: Before and After. Dad's razor, the one he forgot to pack when he ditched us two years ago, the first blow to the Nolan family. There's a tube of benzoyl peroxide that Ethan and I shared. Some old Neosporin. Ethan's retainer that we had to replace twice at five hundred dollars a pop because he used to lose *everything*. And the newest addition: Mom's prescription of Zoloft.

Mom took them for about four months after Ethan died, after she left her job, and then she stopped taking her pills, stopped going to therapy. She said they weren't helping; the pain was still with her every waking moment. And then she got worse. She didn't want to get out of bed or take a shower or eat or anything. I found the psychiatrist's card in my mother's purse and called to ask her what to do.

"Your mother is noncompliant," the doctor said in a tone sanitized of compassion, as if I was going to sue her for malpractice and she was refusing to accept any blame.

"No, she's *sad*. And you're not helping her!" I hung up.

"She's not very nice," I told Mom later that day as she lay in bed. "Maybe we can find someone else, though? Maybe you just need to try another medicine?"

"What's the point?" Mom said. "It won't change anything."

No medicine would bring Ethan back is what she meant. But it could possibly bring my mother back, so I mention it every so often; I get the same answer every time.

With a slam, I shut the cabinet as if I can shut out the memories attached to everything inside, and make my way to the kitchen. There's a large cottage cheese container on the counter, Mrs. Alvarez's calling card. She always recycles her yogurt or cottage cheese tubs to store her leftovers. I pour some chicken soup into a bowl and bring it over to Mom, setting it on the round end table next to her. Her wedding band and engagement ring are on the table. Two years later, she finally took them off.

"Want me to put these somewhere safe?" I ask, scooping them up.

"Just leave them here where I can see them." Her eyes catch mine and she nods, as if her logic is perfectly clear. She taps the table with her finger.

Okay, so maybe she hasn't entirely accepted he's gone for good.

I put them back where I found them. "You should eat."

"I'm just not hungry, Jess," she says, sounding so defeated by a bowl of soup.

I take the chair next to her and offer her a spoonful.

"Jess." My name is a complaint on her chapped lips.

Your mother is noncompliant.

I move the spoon closer to her mouth. I'll hold it here all day if I have to.

"All right," she says, too tired to argue. She takes the bowl from me and eats. For a fleeting, beautiful second, her eyes sparkle like they used to and she smiles at me. "Thank you." We hold each other's gaze, gently. Then her eyes turn sad again. "I'm sorry, Jess."

I look away, nodding. She doesn't make me any promises she can't keep, like *I'm trying*, or *It will get better*, even if right now I really could use some hollow platitudes.

So I change the subject to tackle the topic I've put off for too long.

"Mom? You really need to take a shower. Your hair is . . . well, to be honest . . . it's starting to smell. Do you need help or something?"

She runs a hand softly down her hair, barely grazing it. "It's fine."

I shake my head. "It's really not. Will you try? For me?"

It gets her up out of her chair and she walks to the bathroom. If I was afraid she was going to take too short of a shower, the opposite happens. She's in there forever, or at least until she must've run out of hot water. Then she comes out in her robe, her cheeks flushed from the steam and heat. She looks almost like her old self.

"I'm going to go lie down for a bit," she says, then turns toward her bedroom. I won't see her for the rest of the night. The bills will have to wait, again.

Or not.

I search for the most recent electric bill on the dining room table and open it.

Yikes. We owe four hundred and twenty-five dollars.

I find Mom's checkbook and write out a check to PSEG, finally putting to use those life skills we learned in eighth-grade Family and Consumer Science. The only thing left is Mom's signature. I stare at her closed bedroom door down the hall then forge her signature, just like I've done all year, on every form that came home from school, on every note I wrote to excuse me for being late, for leaving early.

When I'm done, I stick the check in the envelope, slap a stamp on it, and put it aside to drop in the mailbox tomorrow.

There are more bills I could pay, but I'm afraid to. Afraid

to see how quickly we tear through what's left in the checking account. So I leave them and go to the kitchen to sit down at the kitchen table to eat what's left of the soup straight out of the cottage cheese tub.

The refrigerator still has pictures Ethan and I made as kids, held up with magnets. "Happy Mother's Day" flowers made out of construction paper. A Valentine's Day heart, with a crooked "I Love You" written in crayon. Ethan had better fine motor skills than I did. His hearts were always perfect. Mine always came out kidney-shaped.

Ethan got the better end of the DNA pool—he got Mom's blond hair; I got Dad's red hair, pale skin, and freckles—but he wasn't obnoxious about his good looks. About other things, sure. He was my older brother by eleven months. When we weren't teasing each other or fighting, we would crack up with just a sideways glance or a twisted expression, the kind of giggles I only shared with him, not even with Marissa.

There were so many nights when Ethan's friends and Marissa would come over for dinner. We would drag chairs in from the dining room to squeeze everyone around the kitchen table. But all of that is in the past. Now I'm surrounded by empty chairs.

Lucas

If being pulled out of school to go to the doctor when I'm not sick isn't bad enough, being the only eighteen-year-old sitting in the pediatrician's waiting room is humiliating.

Dr. Patel's kaleidoscopic waiting room looks like a box of crayons ate a bag of jelly beans and then vomited all over the room. No color was spared in the decorating, from the cheery apple-green and bright blue walls to the orange and purple plastic chairs. Over in the corner is a table where I used to color or play with the Legos, next to the PlayStation game on the wall Jason and I used to fight over. We even went into the exam room together. It was easier for Mom to schedule both of our annuals at the same time. Not like I ever let Jason out of my sight anyway.

Jason and I were off the charts in the height department, but he had a two-year running start on me. It was Dr. Patel's annual gag to tell me to keep eating my veggies if I ever wanted to catch up to my big brother. It became obvious by the time I was twelve that Jason was just always going to be taller than me and I was never going to catch up.

Dr. Patel comes out holding my file, his once wiry gray hair now a puffy cloud of white.

"Lucas." Dr. Patel's smile emerges from his craggy face. "My favorite patient."

A little girl sitting with her mother frowns at him. "You're *all* my favorite," he assures her with a wink.

He looks down at my folder a moment as I walk up to meet him. Mom grabs her purse and follows. I turn around to stop her. "Ma, I'm going to go in by myself. Okay?"

Mom stops in her tracks. Adjusting the straps of her purse on her shoulder, she says, "Sure. Of course," even though her shocked expression is that of someone who was just blindsided. "Just make sure to tell him you were coughing all night."

"I will," I say, but think, *You just did.*

Crayoned drawings of sick kids visiting the doctor are taped on the walls of the exam room. Steering away from the paper-covered exam table, I sit in the chair reserved for parents. Dr. Patel leans back against the table and folds his arms, my folder stuffed under his armpit.

"What's going on, Lucas?"

"I'm not sick," I begin. "I coughed a couple of times because I choked on my spit while I was snoring!"

His bushy eyebrows levitate above the round steel frames of his glasses, but he doesn't say anything.

"She's scared, I get it. I'm scared too. But it doesn't help that she's always hovering. And my car keys are missing and I think she did something with them, because she thinks *everything* is too dangerous," I keep going. "She wants me to go to Queensborough next year because she's afraid I'm not ready to go away yet. I mean, maybe I'm not . . . but I think *she's* not ready. Do you know what I mean?"

He *hmmm*s as he flips open his folder and reviews my chart. Then he pats the table. "Humor me. Since you're here."

Dr. Patel puts the stethoscope in his ears as I sit on the table that used to seem so high when I was a kid. He chuckles and aims the chest piece at the ceiling. With a squeak on the linoleum floor, he goes up on the tippy-toes of his rubber-soled shoes, craning his neck to exaggerate our already drastic height difference.

"Helllooo up there!" He laughs, then waves me down. "You know what? Hop back down. You're too tall for me now," he says, with a smile of pride on his face.

A memory of that same smile, those same words, just about knocks me over. Instead of me, it was Jason. The last visit to Dr. Patel before Jason told Mom his next doctor's visit was going to be down the hall at the family practice.

The stethoscope is on my back under my shirt. "Take a deep breath, Lucas," Dr. Patel instructs me. But I can't. My lungs clamp shut.

"Deep breath, Lucas," he says again. I try, but my breath stutters. I'm smothered by the grief and pain that keep hitting me when I least expect. The feeling of Jason's body on top of mine, squeezing the air out of me. The moment I realized the panicked heartbeat pounding through my body was mine alone.

At some point the stethoscope on my back is replaced by Dr. Patel's hand as I work through this latest setback.

A while later, Dr. Patel walks behind me back to the waiting room. My mother stands up from her chair abruptly, pulling the straps of her purse up to her shoulder.

"Healthy as a horse," Dr. Patel says. "Bet he has the appetite of one too."

Mom nods and smiles, but it's weak. "He was coughing *so* much though."

"His lungs are clear."

"Oh . . . okay. Well . . . *good*," she says, relief easing the worry lines from her face. She used to be stressed about work. Now I'm the cause of those little lines that are deepening around her mouth, her forehead.

Dr. Patel looks at me and then at my mother. "Lucas, why don't you have a seat. Mom and I are going to talk in my office for a bit."

The alarm is back in my mother's eyes, as if Dr. Patel is going to tell her in private that I'm suffering from some incurable disease.

I hope finding out from Dr. Patel that I'm not seriously ill is enough to relax that permanent look of pain from her eyes. But she's not going to like what he *is* going to tell her.

She's silent on the way home. Every so often she opens her mouth as if she's about to say something. Then she exhales and closes her mouth again. I should ask her what she and Dr. Patel talked about. But I really don't want to know.

Finally she turns to me and says, "Are you feeling better now?"

I nod and point ahead at the intersection. "Can you drop me off at the gym?"

She stops at the red light and tilts her head. "Really? After what happened in Dr. Patel's office?"

"It helps," I tell her.

"You're sure?" she presses.

"Positive."

"All right," she says, giving in.

Maybe the doctor's visit wasn't a complete waste of time after all.

I train with Kenny and Leo for two hours, then come back home to do homework. The doorbell rings a little while later.

"Hey, Mrs. Rossi." From my bed, I listen to Pete work his way through the house, making the obligatory stop in the kitchen so my mother can ply him with food. He's in my room a few minutes later holding a plate of tacos, one lifted to his mouth, kicking the door shut behind him.

"Damn, your mom can cook. What the hell does she put in here?" The lettuce hanging out of his mouth makes him look like a human paper shredder.

"Preservatives," I answer.

Pete plops down on Jason's bed with his plate. That's the kind of thing that would set my mother back several months if she saw it. My mom still changes Jason's sheets every week, when she's dusting his shelves and trophies. There's a picture of Reggie and

Jason up there. The same one Reggie has on her desk at work.

Jason and I shared a room since we were kids. I thought I'd get the room to myself after he graduated, but he didn't go away to college like we all expected. I can still hear my father hollering, "You're throwing your life away!" Little did we know going to the movies with me would be his real undoing.

Jason didn't even want to see the movie. But Mom was in LA for work, Dad was working late, and I was going to go to a party. Jason was sitting at the kitchen table eating, as always, while I was getting the details from Pete.

"Where's the party?" Jason asked after I got off the phone.

"The old warehouse, on Brunswick." I was kind of excited to tell him about it; I thought of Jason as more of a friend than a big brother. I mean, two years is not that big of an age difference.

"You're not going." Jason stood up to put his plate in the sink.

"Who died and made you boss?" I said. (An expression I've stopped saying since that night. That and "Drop dead," "I'll kill you," "You're dead to me," "I died laughing," etc.)

He walked over to me, slowly, menacingly, staring down the bridge of his enormous nose.

"I made me boss. Mom and Dad are going to blame *me* if anything happens to you on my watch."

So, he went online and got us tickets to the latest superhero disaster movie at the Balcony.

Mom quit her job right after that night. She was pretty high up at an ad agency. A VP or SVP CD or ECD, some combination of letters that said she was very important and very good at making commercials. I'm pretty much her only job now. That puts a lot of pressure on me.

After Pete inhales his food, he grabs Jason's football off the shelf and lies back on the bed, tossing the ball in the air. Pete is oblivious; he has no boundaries. He doesn't respect the shrine because he doesn't recognize it as a shrine. I'm grateful for his blinders because I'm kind of tired of all the invisible lines we keep trying not to trip over.

"Want me to pick you up again tomorrow?" he asks.

"Yeah."

"Jason had to have another set of keys to his car somewhere," Pete says, spinning the ball around in his hands.

"Not like I can ask him." It doesn't even bother me when Pete says stupid shit; the way people tiptoe around mentioning Jason bugs me more. "How was work?"

"Fine." He tosses the football up in the air. "So I have news. Reggie hired someone today."

"Oh, that's good. Who?" I told a couple of guys at school about the opening, but no one was really interested. Besides, we need someone who's not going away to college in a few months. Come August, we'll need to fill Pete's position too. But I really can't allow my brain to travel that far ahead. One day at a time is about all I can manage.

"Want to guess?" Pete lifts the ball and lobs it across the room to me. I catch it.

He's got a goofy look on that tells me it's not going to be anyone I ever expected.

"Mr. Riccardi." I toss the football back.

Pete and I keep coming across flyers stapled to utility poles on every block for our old tech teacher's band, the Dead Freds, a Grateful Dead cover band. There are two Freds in their band. They have a regular gig at the Salty Dog every Wednesday night. I wouldn't be surprised if Mr. Riccardi showed up at Enzo's one day looking to nail down a third job, since everyone knows teachers, especially tech teachers, get paid shit.

Pete catches the ball.

"Younger."

"Peachy." Peachy's name is actually Pete Chee, but his first and last name just naturally run into each other—and eventually, Petechee became Peachy. Peachy's father is an electrician. He's always at our store buying stuff he needs for his jobs. I could see how our employee discount could work out for them.

Pete scrunches up his face and shakes his head. "You're not even trying." He tosses the ball back.

I catch it, shuffling it from hand to hand while I give it some thought. Someone who will shock me, obviously. But can still physically do the job.

"Charmaine." I toss the ball. Charmaine was the first girl ever to join the high school football team. She's pretty awesome. And strong as hell.

Pete catches the ball and grins. "Warmer!"

"Warmer?" I catch it next. "A girl?"

Pete shrugs, but he's still smiling, which tells me I'm right.

A girl. I need to think of another girl as strong as Charmaine.

I rattle off a bunch of names, the two of us tossing the ball back and forth with each one.

Erin.

Jasmine.

Natalie.

Mina.

Pete holds the ball ready to toss it again. "You're never going to guess."

I pick up my phone. "This is stupid. I'll just text Reggie."

"After all this, you'd actually consider robbing me of my reveal? Fine! It's Jess Nolan."

He tosses the ball at me. I'm still holding my phone, stunned. The ball hits the wall by my head and rolls onto my bed.

"Jess *Nolan*? She's . . ."

"Small," Pete answers for me.

Actually, that wasn't what I was going to say. I was thinking she was at the Balcony that night too.

Now her smile and wave earlier today make a little bit more sense. Did she know then that we were going to be working together?

This is not good.

Boxing and work are my escape. Away from the prying eyes of my mother, my teachers. I think of Jess's expression earlier today. The not-so-secret society-of-survivors look that says we shared something really messed up.

I have to wonder if other people find some measure of comfort in being around survivors of a shared tragedy. Because I sure as hell don't. It's bad enough Reggie and I work together. But she's like family. I don't want another person in my life who is tragically and irreparably damaged by the same disease that's running rampant through our neighborhood. Waking up every morning to Jason's empty bed is reminder enough. I may not believe in ghosts, but I see them all the time.

"Grief is uncomfortable," Dr. Engel said once. "People try to run away from it rather than confront it."

"I confront it every fucking day," I told him, in one of our less productive sessions.

"That's just ridiculous. I'm calling Reggie right now." Her voice mail picks up. "Reggie . . . seriously, Jess Nolan? What'd you get soft or something? Call me back!"

When I hang up Pete's frowning at me, his disapproval radiating off of him in sonic waves.

"What?"

His frown intensifies. "'*What?*' Dude, are you seriously trying to get Jess fired before she even starts?"

"No!" I argue, even though I am. "I mean . . ."

He holds his hands up in the air, indicating he wants me to pass him back the ball. I pick it up from where it landed on my bed and toss it.

"Here's how I see it." He catches the ball. "If Jess is applying for a job at *Enzo's* . . . fucking Enzo's, dude . . . maybe Jess kinda really *needs* this shitty job."

I flop back on my pillows in defeat.

Jesus.

I close my eyes and rub them with the heels of my hands.

Grief is uncomfortable.

Seriously, Dr. Engel. If I knew how to run away from it, I would've done it by now.

Jess

I throw my backpack and jacket in my new employee locker and shut it with a loud clang.

"Ah, I should've told you—you'll need to bring a lock. Anything valuable in there you don't want stolen? I can hold it for you today," Reggie offers.

"Not really." The only thing worth anything to me is my ancient phone, the one my parents got for me for my thirteenth birthday. Mom and Dad were both working then; the phone to them was a practical investment, in case of emergency. Four years is pretty old for a phone. I doubt anyone other than the Smithsonian would ever want it, but I keep it in my pocket all the time anyway. It's my lifeline in ways my parents never anticipated.

She smiles. "Okay, so let's get you started."

Reggie leads the way through a dimly lit corridor that opens to a warehouse, a labyrinth of metal shelves stocked with inventory. Heavy metal doors open up, letting in bright sunshine. A beeping freight truck backs up to the loading dock.

"Perfect timing," Reggie says. "You get to help unload the truck."

Two guys—one tall and pale, the other dark and stocky—walk into the warehouse, laughing. I recognize the pale one from school, Pete Brickner. The other I don't know. Lucas comes up a few feet behind them. He's cracking up too. I must've just missed a helluva joke.

"Guys, Jess is here," Reggie announces.

Lucas stops laughing at the sight of me. He leaves the other guys and walks over to us, clapping his hands once in front of him. "Right. Orientation."

"Just have her shadow you guys today," Reggie tells him, and walks away.

Lucas stares over at the loading dock as the delivery driver opens his rear door. "Are you sure about this?"

At first, I think he's asking the truck driver; then I realize, no, he's talking to me. Before I can answer, he says, "Last chance to change your mind. I promise none of us will judge you if you tear out of here." He sort of chuckles like he's joking, but it doesn't really seem like he is. Besides, it's just not that funny.

I shake my head. "No . . . I'm good." Lucas looks around the warehouse scratching his head.

"So, should I help unload the truck?" I offer, straightening my spine, trying to fill the gaps between each vertebra to give the appearance of being a few inches taller and a few pounds heavier.

He exhales again and then hands me a clipboard. "Maybe for your first day you should just start off with inventory. Pete, get the bill of lading for Jess."

"Okay." I nod so he'll see just how cooperative and great I'll be at this job. Any excitement I felt about landing a new job is completely overshadowed by his obvious doubt in me. I hate that he's already managed to shake my confidence.

Pete walks over and smiles. Lucas is hard to miss at school because of his size; Pete's hard to miss because he radiates happiness wherever he goes.

He hands me a bunch of papers. "Bill of lading. Basically just a list of everything that *should* be on that truck. You don't want to sign off on something that didn't come in," he explains. I nod and clip it to my board, following him.

As we walk away from Lucas, Pete leans closer like he's about to share a secret. "So *that* was a particularly underwhelming welcome, huh? We're not known for our warmth and hospitality back here." He sticks his hand out and I shake it. "I'm Pete."

"I know. Jess."

"I know." He smiles. "Just figured we should make it official. That's Joe." He points at the other guy, who smiles and waves.

"Pete! Grab a pallet jack and get started." Lucas speeds past us pushing some kind of handcart with two long prongs in the front. A pallet jack, I guess.

Pete cups a hand to his mouth and shouts after him. "Back off, brah! I'm helping the rookie acclimate to her surroundings!"

Lucas turns around and bows with one hand holding the pallet jack. "I bequeath to you my duties, Sir Loin of Beef!"

"You keep trying to bequeath me your shitty job, dude. Nobody wants it!"

Pete turns to me and grins. "Reggie put him in charge of all of us for some stupid reason. It made his big head even bigger." He grabs a pallet jack. "Okay, let's do this."

I'm determined to at least look like I know what I'm doing, even if my insides are curdling. I square my shoulders and get to work, making sure every SKU number on every box is on the bill of lading Pete gave me. It takes them a half hour to unload the truck. When I'm done counting and crossing off, I hand the clipboard to Lucas.

"It's all here," I say.

"Okay, thanks." He takes the clipboard from me without making eye contact.

"I double-checked," I offer, looking for some kind of approval.

With the worst attempt ever at a smile, he walks away.

I follow behind him. "What should I work on next?"

He stops and runs a hand through his mop of hair.

"Ummm . . ." He searches around the warehouse for something for me to do. "Why don't you just break down those boxes over there. That's easy," he says.

Easy? Does he even *hear* how insulting he is?

I fold my arms. "I'm not looking for *easy*. What do you *need* me to do?"

Joe calls out from the corner. "I could use some help with these crates."

I perk up. "I'll do it."

Lucas looks uncertain. "I don't know. That may be too hard for you."

My hands ball up by my sides. Rage at being undervalued, underestimated, dismissed surges up inside of me. I don't want to get fired for telling him off. Let them get to know me first before I start freely expressing myself. So I take a breath to douse the angry flames burning inside of me. Calmly, I ask, "How would you even know what's too hard for me?"

He blows a stream of air out his mouth and nods. "Okay. You're right. Go help Joe," he says, then walks away.

Joe watches me approach. He holds up a metal crowbar and wedges it in between the cracks of the crate.

"Just lean into it and push the lid open. Then unload the boxes onto a hand cart"—he gestures against the wall where there are several—"and once a cart is full, I'll show you where to stock all the stuff in the store."

Sounds simple enough. He hands me a crowbar and I find an unopened crate. I put it exactly where he placed his and push with all my might. It doesn't budge.

Out of the corner of my eye, I see Lucas watching me from across the warehouse, his arms folded. Waiting for me to fail is my guess.

I have to crack this open. I *have* to.

"Maybe lean all of your weight into it," Joe offers quietly. At least he's on my side. Then he looks at me and rolls his eyes.

I lean against the bar until my feet lift off the ground. The lid pops open abruptly, throwing me off balance. I land on my feet but I can't stop the forward momentum. The crowbar clatters on the ground as I stumble, my hands reaching out for anything to stop my fall as I crash into a cardboard box. The box and I go down and I hear a crack as I fall on top of it.

Joe rushes over and gives me a hand up. His eyes dart between me and the box stamped "FRAGILE, THIS SIDE UP."

"I heard something break. Looks like it didn't come from you."

My heart thrums in my ears. I feel three pairs of eyes staring at me.

Joe takes a box cutter out from his back pocket and slices the box open. He looks in and shakes his head. Pete joins him.

"Our first casualty," Joe says, and side-eyes me.

Pete looks in the box next and grimaces. My cheeks are radioactive. I steeple my hands over my nose and mouth to hide my embarrassment. "I'm so sorry."

Pete pretends it's no big deal, but I saw the look on his face. Pity! The worst!

"It's okay, Jess. It happens," Pete says, then looks over my shoulder.

I feel Lucas's presence behind me, but I can't make myself turn around and face him. He walks around us and bends over to inspect the damage.

"Oh yeah, it's a goner." He looks at me and winces. "You okay though? Did you get hurt?"

I shake my head. "No . . . I'm fine. I'm so sorry. I'll pay for it. Take it out of my salary." I bumble the apology through my fingers.

I'm waiting for him to say, *I told you so.* And he'd be right.

But he doesn't. He laughs, not at all what I was expecting. "Shit happens, Jess. It just happened sooner for you than anyone else."

Pete and Joe both laugh at that.

Lucas points at Pete. "What are *you* laughing at?" He turns back to me. "Just last month, this guy backed the forklift into a shelf and knocked down all the household cleaners."

"Oh man." Pete squeezes his eyes shut and winces. "They had to evacuate the building. The ammonia and the bleach mixed together. A hazmat crew had to come in to clean it up."

"Cleanup in aisle six," Joe says, giggling.

"What about you?" Pete shoots back at Joe.

Joe sobers immediately. "Don't," he growls.

But Pete does: a fertilizer spill that took them all night to clean up.

Pete turns to me. "We can't make it a week without some kind of accident. I have no idea why Enzo hasn't fired us all yet. Remember the time . . ."

As Pete tells another story, Lucas catches my eye. He shrugs and smiles. I accept it. At least I still have a job.

I spend the rest of the afternoon and evening shadowing Joe or Pete, stocking shelves with hammers, paintbrushes, ceramic tile, even carpeting. I hardly see Lucas for the rest of my shift.

At seven o'clock, Enzo turns the sign on the door to "CLOSED."

"You survived!" Joe says over his shoulder as I follow him to the back.

Barely, I think, but I force a smile. A heroic smile. A triumphant smile. A smile to try and convince him I'm really not a walking liability.

"Quitting time!" Pete skids around the corner and races past us.

At our lockers, I slip my heavy arms through the sleeves of my coat, and I know I'm going to be in agony tomorrow. My arms tremble from today's workout; my lower back aches with every step. But I don't let it show on my face, even when they snicker as I slowly slip my backpack over my sore shoulders.

"Need a little help?" Pete teases.

I smile back, pretending to be in on the joke, not the butt of it. Then I pass by Lucas, who's flipping through some paper-work.

"Good night," I say tentatively.

"You coming back tomorrow?" he asks. He looks up with a smile, a big one, the first real smile all night, and . . . whoa. It's like opening the window on a perfect spring day.

"Wild horses couldn't keep me away," I say, shuffling past him on tired legs.

He makes a snorting sound not unlike that of a wild horse.

Every muscle in my body mocks me on my walk home.

I stop and pull my phone out, staring at it. I don't want to go through old texts. I *need* someone to talk to. A little voice of reason begs me to put the phone away and just go home. But I can't. Tears pulse behind my eyes rehashing the day.

I find my and Marissa's old thread, the one I keep rereading.

I know it's pointless. I know she won't get this text, not for months at least. But that doesn't stop me.

> So hey . . . Colorado, huh? What's that like? I checked out the school's website. Therapeutic horseback riding. That's cool.

I hit send.

A part of me unravels just a little bit more when instead of the chirp of her reply I get silence. But I keep texting.

> Yeah, okay, enough with the small talk. By the time you get this, this will be old news. I started a new job. Remember Lucas Rossi and Pete Brickner? A year older than us? I work with both of them now.

Send.

> So THIS happened: I was only there for about 15 minutes when I knocked over a sink and broke it. Like the one you have in your downstairs bathroom. Expensive, right? No, don't tell me! I don't want to know! I thought I'd set the world record for getting fired!

Send.

> They all tried to make me feel better about it. But . . . ugh . . . PITY! *shudder*

Send.

> Pete's super nice. So's this other guy who works there, Joe. He's older. Graduated a couple of years ago. Lucas, though . . .

Send.

I wrangle up the thoughts racing around in my head about Lucas.

> He's harder to crack.

Send.

> But he's cute. And speaking of crack, he's got one of those butt-crack chins.

Send.

> Cleft! Ha, looked it up.

I glance around to make sure I'm still alone.

> Here's the thing. He can barely look at me. It's WEIRD!
> It's like if he looks at me for longer than two seconds he'll turn to stone or something. And I really don't think he wants me to be working there.

Send.

> Actually, I KNOW he doesn't want me there. He pretty much said as much.
> But I need this job.

Send.

> **Why do I even give a crap what he thinks?!!!**

I lean back against a brick wall and watch a plane roar over the Rockaways, so close I can see the blue-and-red Delta tail.

Swirls of emotions tangle up inside of me. Gratitude for the job, and for Pete's and Joe's kindness. Humiliation over the sink incident. But it's Lucas's first and last impressions . . . and that *smile* . . . that rattle me the most.

Out of nowhere, my brain comes up with a line from *Young Frankenstein*, aka *the* best movie ever made. Gene Wilder shouts, "Alive! It's aliiive!"

Quietly, I maniacal-laugh to myself, just a little. It's something Marissa and I would've done under the circumstances if she were here to listen to my tale of woe. Because this is a laugh-or-cry moment if there ever was one.

Lucas

I beat the crap out of the heavy bag, trying to build up my south-paw to keep my body in balance. I'm way past ten rounds by the time Leo checks in on me.

He taps his forehead. "What's going on up there?"

"Nothing."

"Ha! You said it, not me!" He laughs. I keep punching. "*Something's* going on up there. I've never seen this much fight in you."

I dance around to keep the adrenaline going. "Had a bad day. Just trying to work it off."

"Bad day" is an understatement. Bad day is stepping in dog shit. Cracking the screen on your phone. Forgetting to hit save on the English paper you worked hours on. No, this was a rotten day. And the worst part is it's all on me.

That accident with the sink wasn't Jess's fault; it was mine. When Reggie trained Pete and me, she gave us plenty of time to ease into the job. Jess felt she had to prove something on her first day because I made her feel like she couldn't handle it.

She proved me wrong.

Why'd I have to make that stupid crack about her tearing out of there on her first day? I can't stop replaying how fast her face went from open and friendly to a tightly clenched fist.

I rip off my gloves and grab the rope. Today, for the first time, none of this seems like enough. I could wear myself down to a puddle of sweat and I'd still feel like I had more to give.

Leo starts to walk away.

"Hey, Leo?" He turns back. "I think I'm ready."

"Ready for what?"

I nod over at Honor, who's training on the speed bag for a match this weekend. "A match. I want to do it. I think I'm ready."

Thwack thwack thwack.

Leo walks back over as I whip the rope around. "Yeah, but are you *ready* ready?" He taps the side of his head again.

Thwack thwack thwack.

I nod and pant. "Yeah. I think so."

"*Know* so. Then we'll talk."

Thwack thwack thwack.

"I know it. I'm ready."

Leo claps his hands. "Okay, then. Get your gear on. You're gonna spar with Honor."

I swallow back the nervous bile that creeps up at just the thought of sparring with the undefeated Honor "Big Mac" McAllister.

Kenny helps me lace up my gloves. Honor climbs into the ring with a huge shit-eating grin like he knows he's about to mop the floor with my sorry white ass. Leo shakes my shoulder to draw my attention back to him. He holds up three fingers in front of my face.

"Three rounds. Then, if you still want to fight, come to my office and we'll get started with the paperwork." He turns to Honor. "Challenge him. But dial back the charm a bit. Got it?"

Kenny pops my mouthpiece in and Honor grins at me. "I'll try not to mess up his pretty-boy face *too* much."

Three rounds.

The bell buzzes. "Here we go," Leo says.

"Keep the ice on it to keep the swelling down," Leo instructs me as I'm leaving the gym. Honor and I bump knuckles as I pass him on my way out. Funny how that works, how there's no hard feelings outside the ring. There's a time and a place for all that anger, and I've finally found it.

Tonight I learned that I don't mind getting hit. Every punch Honor got in, I shot back with three more. The pain fueled me; it lanced all that poison inside of me that's been festering. I finally figured out what to do with it.

On the walk home, I stop outside the meat store and look at my reflection in the glass. I grin, and then immediately regret it because it splits my fat lip open.

Leo said he would get the paperwork started for my boxing license. Once that's in, I can fight my first match. I'm ready.

From my bedroom window, Mrs. Graham's open garage door stares back at me. Her maroon Buick Century, as old as I am, is parked inside. It was open when I got home from the gym, over an hour ago. She never leaves her garage door open.

She probably just forgot to close it. *Focus,* I tell my racing thoughts, the ones that seem to leap to the worst-case scenarios lately. I try to shake the disturbing images popping into my head: Mrs. Graham's frail, broken body crumpled at the bottom of her stairs, calling out for help in a feeble voice. Mrs. Graham bound, bruised, and battered by some guy pretending he needed to come in to read the gas meter.

I've been trying to make some headway on my term paper. It's on Simon Wiesenthal's book *The Sunflower,* about how as a young Jewish concentration camp prisoner he was summoned to a wounded Nazi's bedside. The Nazi (his name is Karl, but I prefer to call a Nazi a Nazi) begs Simon to absolve him for his part in the burning alive of an entire village of Jews. He says he can't die without Simon's forgiveness. Simon says nothing. Unfortunately, this plagues Simon for the rest of his life, wondering if he should have forgiven the Nazi soldier.

My assignment is to write a paper supporting the power in extending forgiveness. I wanted to do it on the power of *withholding* forgiveness. That makes more sense to me. So much more sense. But that's not what Mr. Wong assigned.

The paper's not due until May, but I've been having a hard time getting anywhere with it. I think it's pretty obvious why.

My blinking cursor seems to ask what I want to do: work on this paper or quiet the chorus of worried voices in my head over Mrs. Graham's well-being.

I already know the answer.

I race down the carpeted stairs that do nothing to buffer my pounding feet.

Sitting on the couch in the den, Mom looks up from her book. "What's wrong?" It doesn't take much to trigger a five-alarm panic from her either.

I open the junk drawer.

"Mrs. Graham's garage door is open. I want to go check on her. Where's her key?"

Mrs. Graham gave us a spare key when she got locked out a few years ago. She hasn't needed it since, but we always have it in case of emergency. Like now.

Mom jumps up off the couch and comes to the kitchen, shutting the drawer. "You can't just barge in there like that. I'll call her first."

She picks up the phone, waiting while Mrs. Graham's line rings. Mom looks up at the kitchen clock. Nine twenty. "It's late. I hope I don't wake her. You're sure her car is there?" Mom looks over at me with the receiver still pressed to her ear.

"Yeah. It's in the garage."

The phone rings seven times and then the voice mail picks up.

"Hi, Marie. It's Jill. We noticed your garage door has been open for a while and wanted to make sure you were okay. I'm sending Lucas over now to check on you."

She hangs up and takes the key out of the junk drawer and hands it to me.

"Ring the bell a few times first. She doesn't hear well these days." I can see the change of heart in her face. "You know what? I'll come with you."

I hold my hands up in the air to stop her. "I got it. You stay here. I'll call you if it's . . . something," I say, hoping, praying it's nothing, not something. Because I don't know if I can handle another something.

As I jog across the street, I turn on the flashlight on my phone to check Mrs. Graham's garage first to make sure she didn't fall down and . . . God, that would be so awful to find her here. But no, the coast is clear. No sign of Mrs. Graham.

On her porch, I ring the bell, holding it for a beat longer than I would for any other home because of Mrs. Graham's hearing issues. I open the screen door and press my ear against the wood door for any sound, preferably her footsteps.

Nothing.

I ring again.

Then I pound.

I step back onto the walkway and crane my neck up. The lights are on. A bedroom window is open.

I cup a hand to my mouth. "MRS. GRAHAM! CAN YOU HEAR ME? HELLO?"

Then I pound on the door again and hold my finger against the bell until Mrs. Graham throws the door open, a phone pressed to her ear.

"Hold on, Louise . . . *Lucas!* For God's sake, what wrong? Are you all right?"

My body sags in relief. "Oh thank God . . ." I mumble. Then in a louder voice so she can hear me, I say, "We tried calling!"

"Was that you?" She holds her phone away from her ear to look at the receiver. "I don't know how to use that call answering yet. Every time I push a button, I hang up on someone."

"Your garage is open. I got worried."

She steps farther out to look.

"Oh . . . will you look at that!" She presses a veiny hand to her forehead. Then she says into the phone, "I blame you, Louise! You got me so exhausted today running all over the place taking you to all your damn doctor appointments, I left my garage door open. The boy across the street thought I died or something!" She cups a loose hand over the mouthpiece and whispers loudly, "She's a *hypochondriac.*" Then she reaches her hand out and squeezes mine. "Thank you, Lucas. You're a sweet boy. Do you mind shutting it for me while you're here?"

"Sure." I nod. She turns away but not before I hear her arguing with Louise again.

"Well, you weren't supposed to hear that. But you *are* a hypochondriac and you know it!"

Mrs. Graham shuts the door, even though now I'm wondering what Louise hit back with. I reach into the garage and push the remote to shut the door. Her empty garbage cans are still out on the street. I bring those up and deposit them neatly behind her fence gate.

Back home, there's no sign of my mother in the den.

"Ma!"

She calls down from upstairs, "One sec!"

I open the junk drawer to put the key back. Something familiar peeks out from under the organizer tray. I slide it out with one finger. My boxing-glove key chain.

I shut the drawer just as Mom comes down the stairs.

"Everything okay?" she asks.

I nod. "She's fine. She forgot to shut the garage door when she got home."

Mom walks past me to the sink to wash the frying pan. With her back to me, she says, "I worry about her living alone. I hope her kids are checking in on her from time to time."

I watch as she cleans up the mess from dinner. Tacos, again. We're more like a Taco Monday family. The Old El Paso taco shells are still on the table, waiting for Dad to come home from another late night, next to a bowl of shredded lettuce, a bowl of diced tomatoes, and a jar of mild salsa. It's how my family does Mexican food. We pretend it's the real thing.

Like how I try to pretend I didn't just discover my mother hid my keys from me so she'd have one less thing to worry about—me dying in a car accident—because then we might actually have to talk about our feelings.

I'll need my dad's help on this one. I don't want to embarrass her by telling her I found the keys, and I definitely don't want to talk about how she's been too overprotective because that will lead to *why* and I just can't deal right now. Maybe Dad can talk to her without me actually being involved.

Up in my room, I'm no closer to filling in the blank document open on my screen. The cursor still blinks at me, judging.

I go to my desktop and open RAK.xlsx instead. I reread the last entry and add a new one.

April 1 Covered Joe's shift when he called in sick

April 2 Found a dog that got loose from his yard, brought him home

April 3 Checked in on Mrs. Graham. Brought her garbage cans in.

I scroll through each entry. Two hundred and thirty-three random acts of kindness to date since I started counting, when I was desperate for something to make me feel my being here wasn't a mistake. Some are no-brainers, things people should just do anyway, like give someone a seat on the subway if they obviously need it more than you do. But some days it's a struggle to find a way to make a difference.

If the randomness of my continued existence is still a huge, giant existential crisis, I hope these small acts count at least a little toward earning my continued room and board on this planet.

I close my eyes, redirecting my thoughts, like Dr. Engel taught me. When the graphic images overpower the present, trying to pull me back into that dark place. When I can remember every ounce of my brother's dead weight pressing down, suffocating me, after he threw himself on top of me like two-hundred-and-forty-pound body armor to save me.

I don't ever want to take my existence for granted. Especially when Jason's Corner reminds me every day that I'm in the universe's debt because it took the wrong Rossi brother.

Jess

> This will crack you up: I got caught staring at Lucas's butt today.

> Joe saw me. He just said, "Uh-huh," and kept walking. But I could hear him laughing. Busted.

> So even though I didn't get fired for breaking an expensive sink on my first day, I'm definitely going to get canned for ogling my boss!

> And yes, it was a very cute butt.

I've been working at Enzo's for a week and I've managed not to damage any more merchandise. I can't say the same for the rest of the guys. Joe backed the forklift over a fireplace screen, mangling it. Everyone covers for each other here, so sometimes even Reggie doesn't know what kind of messes these guys make.

There are no deliveries today, so I've been restocking shelves up front. I try to hide the grimace of pain every time I stretch my arm or squat down to reach a lower shelf. But it's okay. Physical pain is so much better than the other kind of pain.

It rained most of the day but it stops right before my break. Outside is damp but the air is fresh and sweet compared to being inside the warehouse all afternoon, so I take a white resin chair out by the loading dock to eat the sandwich I packed from home. Pete takes a break too, and drives around the lot on the forklift making donuts and figure eights at a whopping three miles an hour while I eat.

When he's done playing, he takes another chair and drags it out next to mine. He turns it around and straddles it, folding his arms along the back of it.

"How's Marissa doing?" he blurts, out of nowhere.

"Uhhh . . ." I pause. "I don't know."

"Why not?" he asks. Overhead, a patch of blue appears in the parting clouds.

"She's not allowed to have her phone," I answer, watching the blue sky stretch, trying to squeeze out the clouds.

"That's gotta be hard. I used to see you two together everywhere," he says.

"Yeah."

"Still . . . it's good that her parents got her into that school, right?"

Marissa wasn't okay after that night. I mean, no one was. My brother died, but she was covered in his blood. Going to the private school in Boulder was a healthy move. I just wish I could've gone with her.

I stretch out and tap my toe in a tiny puddle on the blacktop. Pete reaches his foot into the puddle next to mine and gently taps his work boot in the water.

"You must miss her though, right?"

I clear my throat. "Yeah." Darting my eyes between the sky and the puddle, I add, "I miss *both* of them."

I groan to myself, *at* myself. I blew way past just missing them last week when I started texting my basically imaginary best friend. If Pete notices, he doesn't say anything. We eat in silence for the rest of our break.

LUCAS

"You *asked* her?"

Pete's driving again because Dad and I still haven't figured out how to tell Mom I found where she hid my keys from me.

"Yeah. What's the big deal?" Pete shrugs his thumbs up in the air off the steering wheel.

"You can't just ask her about Marissa! God . . . that could have backfired so badly!"

Pete doesn't get it, and maybe I should just be happy for him that he doesn't. That he wasn't there and isn't prone to being set off by the smallest thing.

His ears turn pink. "Don't make me feel bad. This is who I am."

Now I feel bad for making him feel bad.

I flip through Spotify for music and find a song on his driving playlist, a really sappy Top 40 one he likes that he knows I can't stand. I crank up the volume. He turns to face me with a huge grin. "Apology accepted."

Pete makes it way too easy to be his friend.

He bops his head to the music, singing along under his breath. Then he adds, "Besides, she was fine about it."

"Fine?"

He pulls up to Five Guys, a major hike but so worth it. There are other burger joints closer to home, but not like Five Guys. I grab the store door and pull it open.

"Yeah. I mean, she was *sad*. Obviously," Pete says. "She said she misses both of them. I felt bad, you know? Like I think she doesn't have anyone close left."

Inside the store, I let go of the door and it starts to shut behind me as if shoved by a strong gust of wind. I grab it before it slams.

The guy behind the register looks up. "Yeah, sorry. Door's busted."

"I noticed," I say, easing it shut.

Pete and I order our usual, bacon cheeseburgers and fries.

I fill our cups with Coke while Pete pumps ketchup into several paper dispensers.

"What else did she say?"

"Who? Jess?"

"No, the ketchup. Yes, Jess." I take a long sip.

He shakes his head and scoops up all the ketchup, carrying it over to a table. "That was it."

Following behind, I tug on the straw with my teeth. "Okay."

"You should try it sometime."

"Try what?" I ask.

"Talking to people about their feelings," he says.

"Ha!" I laugh as we grab seats facing each other and sit.

"And maybe stop projecting all your feelings onto everyone else while you're at it," he says, shoving a straw in his drink. He takes a sip and scrunches up his face. "Buyer's remorse. We shoulda gotten the milk shakes."

"You sound like Dr. Engel."

A big guy walks by outside. He stops and eyes me through the window.

"Does he like milk shakes too?" Pete asks.

"Who?" I ask, staring back at the guy, watching as his eyes narrow, like he wants to start something with me.

"Dr. Engel. Dude, our signals are off today."

The guy is still glaring at me. Then he walks away.

"How would I know if Dr. Engel likes milk shakes?"

A bunch of things happen all at once.

The guy out on the sidewalk returns, this time with backup. Two of his friends flank him. They throw the door open, and a cold breeze follows them. Every muscle in my body tenses.

"Number fifty-two!" The woman behind the counter calls our order.

Pete, who has his back to the door, doesn't see them come in. He pushes away from the table. "I got it." He stands up and there are two loud explosions, one after the other. Boom! BOOM!

A woman screams.

The three guys walk up to the counter. It's a holdup, I think, but I can't move. The muscles and bones in my legs liquefy.

My eyes search for the guns, for the cause of the gunshots that just rang out through the store. I wait for the chaos to erupt, for people to run away. But the chaos is internal.

The guys are still at the counter, pointing up at the menu. There are no guns. My brain scrambles to keep up, but my body has other plans.

Black spots appear before my eyes; everything in my peripheral vision goes gray.

I can't hear anything over my heart pounding in my ears.

I'm sitting down but I feel like I'm falling sideways.

Pete's face is in front of mine. His eyes are huge, round with worry. A woman in blue scrubs comes over and shoves my head down between my knees.

I'm bent over for a while, until my hearing comes back and I stop feeling like I'm about to pass out. Someone puts a cup of ice on the table. Red fingernails dip into the ice and rub it along the back of my neck. It's the same woman in scrubs; I stare down at an orphaned slice of bacon on the floor next to her Crocs. I'm embarrassed, but the ice helps and I'm still too dizzy to ask her to stop, and besides, at least she's a medical professional.

"Are you feeling a little better?" she asks. I can't lift my head to look at her yet. I might still tip over. Instead, I nod.

"Pete?" I croak. "Can you get me home?"

All I can think of is the safety of my house, the finish line, my bedroom. I need to get out of here, right now.

I stand up, holding the table. The red fingernails wrap around my forearms, holding on to me.

"Take it slow." Then she's talking to Pete. "Where's your car?"

"Right up front," Pete says. He pulls the door open for us and holds it until we're out.

They ease me in the car, and Pete reclines the seat back so I'm practically lying down.

"Date night." I manage to squeeze a joke out. Pete laughs in relief. He thanks the woman and starts the engine.

Perspiration soaks through my shirt. I'm boiling from the inside out.

"Crank the air," I say, my voice hoarse. Pete pushes a button and adjusts the vents so they're hitting me in the face.

We drive in silence for a few minutes. I start to feel better. Enough that I can really savor the embarrassment of nearly passing out at Five Guys.

"Sorry," I say, adjusting my seat up a few inches.

Pete makes a *psshhhh* sound, like it's no big thing. But then he asks, "What happened?"

I draw a deep breath and take it all the way to the bottom of my lungs before releasing it. "I heard a loud noise and it . . . did something to me."

"The door slammed," Pete says. "And my chair fell over at the same time. It was definitely loud. A woman screamed. Did you hear her?"

I nod.

His silence requires me to give him more information. "I think I might be even more fucked-up than I thought," I say, trying to pull off a self-deprecating joke. But Pete doesn't laugh.

He puts a hand on my shoulder. He looks at me like . . . no, not Pete. He's the last person left who hasn't looked at me *that* way.

"I'm fine." I laugh weakly, trying to erase the worry from his eyes. "Hey, at least I'll have something to talk to Dr. Engel about on Wednesday!"

I reach over and turn the music up to drown out the pitiful voice inside of me telling me I'll never be okay again.

Jess

> Remember that funk my mom was in when my dad took off? I thought it couldn't get any worse than that. I was wrong. It's so much worse this time.

> The other day I made us scrambled eggs for dinner. You know what she said? "Ethan used to love brinner, remember?" No, that was ME! I loved brinner! Not Ethan!

> It's like I don't exist anymore. I've been erased.

I stop at my locker on the way to Spanish.

"Jess!" Pete shouts my name as if I've been hiding from him all day. I look up and find Pete and Lucas approaching down the hallway. Pete's face is glistening with sweat.

"Did you just get out of gym?" His face is as white and waxy as a ball of fresh mozzarella.

"No. I'm gonna hurl. I think I got food poisoning at lunch."

Lucas rolls his eyes. "You didn't get food poisoning. I ate the same thing as you, and I'm fine."

"Wait for it, my friend," Pete says, clutching his gut.

Pete turns back to me, ignoring Lucas's eye roll. "Can you cover my shift today?"

"Yeah, not a problem," I say. Pete sighs in relief.

"Thank you." He pats my shoulder and walks away, cutting through the thick stream of students. "I'm gonna hurl!" he calls out, much louder this time. A path clears as everyone gives him all the space he needs to get to the nurse's office. I hope he makes it in time. There's nothing worse than the smell of puke in the hallways all day.

When I turn from watching Pete leave, Lucas is still here.

"What?" I ask suspiciously. He shrugs and folds his arms. This is already the longest he's ever stood next to me that wasn't work related.

Lucas leans against my neighbor's locker and smiles. He has the kind of smile that brightens his entire face. A tiny voice inside of me thinks whatever I'm doing that is amusing him is worth it for that smile. But I tell that voice to shut up.

I lift up on my toes and push all the papers, binders, and textbooks around, trying to ignore him.

"Your locker's a mess."

"No shit."

"What're you looking for?"

"My Spanish book."

He peeks in my locker.

"Oh . . . I see it."

I move my jacket and reams of paper out of the way.

"If it were a snake, it would've reached out and bit you by now," Lucas says with a laugh.

I look, *really* look, and I still don't see it. I move my APUSH and precalc texts to the side.

"Warmer," Lucas says, chuckling under his breath.

The hallway thins out. The bell is going to ring any second, and I still have to haul ass upstairs to class. I'm running out of time.

Lucas makes a peace sign in front of my face.

"How many fingers am I holding up?"

"Two," I answer. He shrugs again.

"Well, it's not your eyesight then. I mean, you're looking *right* at it." I reach in my locker again and start over.

Lucas sighs in defeat. "Just say the magic words."

"Abracadabra," I answer.

"Not that one."

"Hocus pocus."

He looks like he's trying not to laugh.

"Kalamazoo."

A snort escapes from his mouth, but he folds his arms in a renewed effort to be serious. We are the last two people standing in the hallway.

"Baton Rouge." He shakes his head in disapproval over that one. I shrug. Then he unfolds his arms and reaches in.

"You win. Here." He hands me my book. It was right in front of me, just like he said.

"Thank you."

"See? Maaaaagic!" He wiggles his fingers by his ears in some kind of jazz hands. The bell rings. "Ugh . . . we're late. Better hurry up." He turns and jogs off down the hall.

"You're out of your jurisdiction. You're not my boss here," I call after him. As he's running, he throws his head back and laughs, a sound of pure joy that fills the empty hallway.

LUCAS

Jess is alone in the break room, a can of Coke in one hand, phone in the other, her thumb tapping furiously on the screen. Her feet are up on a seat. When she sees me, she lowers them as if she were caught doing something that was against Enzo's ever-so-strict rules.

I drop my takeout from Gino's on the table and pull a seat out. "Aren't you eating?" I ask, stacking two slices together.

She lifts her can up.

"That's it?" I ask.

"I'll eat when I get home." She scrolls through her phone.

"I'd be starving if I waited that long. This is just a snack." Then I remember she's covering for Pete. She wasn't supposed to work tonight. "Crap. You usually bring something from home, right?"

She nods. "Yeah."

"You want to borrow a couple of bucks to buy a slice?" I offer.

Her face clenches. "No. I'm fine," she insists.

I push the box in front of her. "I got three. Take one."

She looks at the slice, really looks at it, contemplating. "No. Thanks though."

Sensing her hesitation, I push the box closer in front of her. "I'm not going to eat all of it."

"Then why'd you buy it?" She pushes the box back.

I point to my eyes. "Always bigger than my appetite."

She shakes her head and sips her soda. "You haven't even started eating yet. You might want it."

I take a bite, just to humor her. "Ohmygod, I'm so full already," I say, chewing on my first bite. When I swallow, I say, "It's an occupational hazard to lift seventy pounds on an empty stomach."

"Right." She snorts.

"Says so right in the employee handbook."

"We don't have one of those."

"If we did, it'd be on page one." I slide the box back and forth in front of her.

Stuffing my face with three slices of pizza while she's stuck here with no food doesn't feel right. Even that one bite I ate for her benefit takes the bumpiest, most guilt-ridden route to my gut.

Plan B. "Okay. Let's play a game. Odds Are."

She glances up from her phone. "Huh?"

"Odds Are. Guess a number between one and thirty. If it's the one I'm thinking of, you have to eat this slice."

"And if it's not?" she asks, smiling.

"I'll get Reggie to give you the week off."

Her smile deepens. "Paid?"

"Sure, why not," I say.

"You're being a complete and utter pain in the ass about this stupid slice of pizza, but fine: twenty-seven."

I pick up a pen from the table and use it to ding against her Coke can. "We have a winner!"

"Totally rigged." She laughs, but she finally accepts the slice. "Happy?" she asks after her first bite.

"Thrilled. Now I can eat."

Jess takes her phone out again while we chew. I watch her hands, how small and delicate they seem yet how deceptively strong they are. She has not backed down from any job since she started. It's almost a problem. The rest of us ask for help from each other all the time. Jess, though, she thinks she needs to prove something. And I know it's because of how I acted on her first day.

"You're doing a great job here by the way," I tell her, as if that will undo the damage.

"Thanks." She stares at my lip and points. "Am I being nosy if I ask what's going on with your lip? It doesn't seem to be getting better."

I grimace. "Sparring." I've been sparring with Honor to get ready for the match for a week now. He seems to always get in a few clear shots at my mouth. Leo says it's my own damn fault. *You wouldn't have a fat lip if you didn't leave yourself wide open.*

"Right. *Boxing*," she says with so much distaste, she may as well have said, "Right. *Sewage*."

"What's *that* supposed to mean?" I ask.

Pink blotches bloom on her cheeks. She backpedals. "No,

nothing. Sorry. I mean, I heard people talking about it, how you're a boxer. That's all."

"I train. But I've never competed."

"Makes sense," she says.

"Why's that?"

She lays her phone on the table, screen down. "I don't really get boxing. It's so brutal."

I try not to let it bug me. But it does.

"You ever hear of Sugar Ray Leonard?"

"Yes. I've *heard* of him," she says defensively.

I ignore the bite in her voice. "He said boxing is the ultimate challenge. Nothing tests you the way you test yourself in the ring."

She glances over her soda can at me. "Why do you need to test yourself?"

I take a bite of my pizza. "Because it sucks to go through life feeling helpless."

She hesitates a moment then nods. "Okay, I get that. Sorry for all the questions."

Hunching over my food, I shrug it off. "It's okay. I just hear it a lot. There are guys at my gym that were in gangs. Leo—he's the owner of the gym—he tells every guy that comes in to choose: streets or ring. You can't have both."

She pauses. "Doesn't it hurt though?" Her hand reaches out, pointing to my mouth. My mind wanders, picturing her hand making contact with my lip, grazing it gently.

"You get used to it," I say, my voice a little huskier. "Knowing you can handle the pain is part of why I do it. If I can handle that, I can handle anything."

She's quiet for a second before answering. I like that she's giving my words room to breathe, to settle in, that she's not quick to judge like everyone else. "I guess that makes sense."

She takes a last bite of her slice and throws the crust back in the box. "I'm still bummed I guessed twenty-seven. A paid week off would've been nice."

"You monster!" I point to the crust in the box. "The bones are the best part!"

"Says who?" she asks, laughing.

"Says everyone!" I retrieve her crust and fold it in half before shoving it in my mouth.

She watches me chew, shaking her head slowly. "All right, then. From now on I'll have to keep all my crusts—"

"Bones," I correct her.

"*Bones* for you. It'll be the biggest bone collection you've ever seen."

Most days, Jess seems guarded, like she's hiding behind a steel storefront gate wrapped in barbed wire. She's friendly enough, but pretty much keeps to herself. But right now, her guard slips and she smiles. Really smiles. A blinding, solar flare of a smile. And all I can think about is what it would be like to kiss her.

Jess

> Didn't Lucas used to go out with Krista G? The cheerleader. Not Krista V, the stoner. Asking for a friend. HA! As if.

> I HAVE no friends, except you and you're 1,822 miles away! (I checked.)

> Wondering if he has a type. Because if it's Krista G, his type is so not me. I'd have more luck if his type was Krista V!

On the way home from work, I stop at an ATM to withdraw twenty dollars, then I head to Key Food.

Starting around the perimeter of the store, I add eggs, bread, and cold cuts to my basket, checking for sales so I don't go over what's in my pocket. Soon, the weight of the basket digs into the flesh of my forearm.

It's been a while since I had a salad. I pick up a head of lettuce, a cucumber, and a tomato. When I pass the towering rows of apples, my mouth waters. On a whim, I pick up the biggest, reddest one I can find. I'm definitely going to eat it on the walk home.

As I turn the corner of an aisle, I almost walk right into Lucas.

"What are you doing here?"

He looks down at me in amusement and lifts his basket.

"Speed dating."

"Ha-ha." I walk around him and he follows. "But you were talking to Reggie when I left. How'd you get here so fast?"

"It's not that I'm fast; you're just slow. You were taking your time analyzing every item on every shelf." He mimes holding something up close to his face to scrutinize it, then puts it back on its imaginary shelf.

"Were you *watching* me?"

"You weren't hard to miss." He points to my red hair. Mom used to call me her beacon for the same reason; she could always pick me out of a crowd of children. "Salad?" He glances in my basket. "And one lone apple. Are you going home to feed your rabbit?"

"I can see why you'd deduce that, Sherlock," I say. "But . . . no. No rabbit." I glance in his basket: a box of pasta, a bag of frozen meatballs, and a jar of sauce. A loaf of Italian bread juts out. Dammit, now I want spaghetti and meatballs! "Shawarma?"

He lifts a jar of sauce from his basket. "Reggie's making dinner to thank me for helping her move into her new place. Except somehow I'm buying all the food." He puts the jar back in his basket. "You should come."

His invitation comes out of nowhere. I shift my basket to my left arm. "Oh . . . no . . . that's okay. Thanks anyway." I let him off the hook since he's obviously just being polite, even if my stomach is growling now just imagining a plate of spaghetti.

"Why not?" He looks down at my basket. "You could throw that stuff in her fridge."

"Still stuffed from the pizza," I lie, holding my stomach before it grumbles.

"Come hang out at least." He starts walking toward the checkout and I find myself moving alongside him.

"It's kind of obnoxious to show up at someone's house uninvited, don't you think?" I resist, just barely. I'm not fully invested in this protest.

"I'll text Reggie now to make sure it's cool. Which it will be."

We get to the express ten-items-or-less checkout. I recognize the cashier, Sherri, from when Ethan worked here.

"You go first," I tell him, buying myself a few more minutes to add up everything in my basket a second time.

Lucas puts all his items on the conveyor belt. When he's done, I put my groceries on the belt. Lucas waits next to me, texting. "Reg says great. She's glad you're coming."

A smile emerges. I'm actually going to hang out with people who might be friends tonight. I haven't let myself miss being around people. I've been so busy with Mom and babysitting. But now . . . now I let myself get swept up in the excitement.

I hand Sherri a twenty without even looking at the total, still grinning like an idiot at Lucas.

"You're short," Sherri announces in a booming voice, looking around to make sure everyone heard her.

"What? No. I can't be. I added everything up."

She nods to the amount on her screen. Twenty dollars and seventy-eight cents.

"Don't you have seventy-eight cents?" she says in the same loud voice. Heads turn to look at me.

"No," I mumble under my breath, refusing to make eye contact with anyone. I take the apple out of the bag. "Take this off."

As Sherri goes to take the apple from me, Lucas shoves a dollar in her hand instead. "Here."

I mutter a weak protest. "It's okay. It's just an apple." Just the one thing I wanted for myself. A crisp, sweet, juicy apple.

"Stop. For a dollar? Let's go." He grabs my bag and turns to leave. Sherri finishes ringing me up. With an apple in one hand and the twenty-two cents in change she shoved in my other, I rush to catch up to Lucas.

"Thank you. I'll pay you back tomorrow, okay?"

"It's just a dollar, Jess." He looks over at me, then says, "Fine, buy me a soda at work if you want."

With his bag in one hand, mine in the other, he leads the way out of the parking lot and I fall in step with him.

"So she was a piece of work, huh?" Lucas jerks his head behind him.

"Sherri the Shamer." I wipe the apple on the front of my shirt and start munching on it. "Ethan worked with her. She's a sadist. He told me she got her kicks yelling 'DECLINED!' whenever someone's credit card was maxed out. Humiliating people is her happy."

"I forgot Ethan worked here. I think he was one of the first ones in our grade to get a job."

"Yeah. As soon as he turned sixteen. Right after my dad moved out." I choose my words carefully, making it sound like Dad moving out was something that we all mutually agreed upon in a family meeting, instead of my father deciding we were a gangrened limb in his life that he needed to amputate if he was ever going to stop drinking.

"Which way is Reggie's?" I ask as we reach the intersection.

He turns left in the direction of my house.

"Not far from you, actually. She has a basement apartment on Gipson."

I side-eye him. "And how do *you* know where I live?"

He snorts. "Paranoid much?"

I don't let him off the hook. "It's not paranoid if you're stalking me around the store while I shop then tracking down where I live." I smile just enough to let him know I'm teasing. Kind of. I take another bite of my apple.

"Yeah, well, *Sherlock*, you're the one who filled out employment papers at Enzo's with your address on it. Remember?"

"Oh right," I say, feeling a little silly, and maybe a teensy bit disappointed. I kind of liked the idea of him trying to find out more about me.

On the corner of Mott and Redfern, Shu steps out of his fish store holding a large white bucket. Lucas stretches an arm out to block me from taking another step just as Shu dumps the water on the sidewalk. We both hop back as the stench of day-old fish fills the air.

"Whoa. That was close," I say. I turn to Lucas. "What was that? A sixth sense?"

He shakes his head ruefully. "Nah. Just learned my lesson the hard way once. And once was more than enough."

The main road narrows as we walk, nail salons, "We Buy Gold" stores, and street vendors giving way to my neighborhood. A few families adorned their front yards with kitschy lawn ornaments, lawn gnomes, and Blessed Mother garden statues (or, as Ethan called them, Marys on the Half Shell), or the perennial favorite, all-season Christmas lights.

"So, are we okay now?" I ask. The orange globe of the sun is setting behind him. Angling my head to see him without suffering permanent damage to my retinas, his face becomes backlit. He notices me battling the sun and scoots around me to walk on my right side. I glance up at him, really noticing his eyes for the first time. Enzo's lighting doesn't do them justice. They're not brown. They're slate, somewhere between blue and brown. A little hard to figure out. Just like him.

"Now?" he asks.

"I mean . . . at work . . . I could tell you weren't all that excited about me being there."

He grimaces. "Sorry. I hope you didn't take that personally."

"Oh, no, of course not. How could I ever take 'last chance to change your mind' *personally*?"

A car alarm starts whooping next to us at the curb. Lucas shouts over it, which is kind of funny because it makes it seem like he's trying *really* hard to convince me it wasn't hate at first sight. "It wasn't about you, I swear! More about stuff I'm still dealing with!"

Maybe to avoid straining his vocal cords, he goes silent, even after we're far enough away from the car alarm to talk normally again. I figure that's the end of that conversation. Then he says, "I've been having a hard time being around other people who were there that night."

I throw my apple core in the nearest garbage can and wipe the juice off my hands on my jeans. "I get it. For me, the worst part is when people say, 'That's Ethan's sister.' It used to mean something totally different than it does now. I didn't mind it, then. Now . . . when people say it, I know what they're really saying. When they look at me, I know what they're really seeing. I wish I could go back to just being Jess."

Lucas's throat bobs and he nods. He doesn't answer me right away. Maybe I shouldn't have been so honest.

His voice is hoarse when he finally speaks. "Being Jason's younger brother was great most of the time. Everyone loved him and looked up to him. And because I was his younger brother, I kinda got to bask in his glory, you know?" He laughs softly, almost embarrassed. "I was always in his shadow, but it wasn't bad. Now, though . . . it's like I'm always standing in the shadow of his ghost."

He stares at the sidewalk. "So, after . . . you know . . . I made a deal with myself . . . to try to put out as much good into the universe as I can. Like, maybe my purpose for still being here is to give back?" He scratches the back of his head with the grocery bag still in his hand. His bicep and tricep flex under his T-shirt sleeve. I tear my eyes away.

"Like, pay it forward?" I ask.

He chews on the inside of his lip. "Kinda? I try to do at least one good thing a day, even if it's small. It makes me feel less . . . useless."

I nod.

"I should shut up now," he says, laughing nervously.

"Why?"

He taps his ear. "'Cause I hear myself and it sounds stupid."

I smile. "No, it doesn't sound stupid. It . . ." I stop to try and find the words. "It's trying to make sense out of what happened."

"Yeah. Exactly." He smiles at me, almost looking relieved.

Sometimes when I'm trying to open my locker in a hurry, it won't budge. I have to ease into all the numbers of the combination carefully. When all the numbers line up, I hear it, feel it fall into place with a satisfying *click*.

Right now, with that smile, I can hear the sound of Lucas Rossi opening up to me.

Click.

LUCAS

There was no pity in her eyes. No X-ray look, like she was scanning me for leaks or hairline fractures.

Jess just got it.

The random-acts-of-kindness thing was something I hadn't told anyone. Not even Pete. But Jess seemed to understand how it helped me, every day.

Okay, so maybe there is some benefit to hanging around other people who shared the same experience. We don't have to always explain ourselves, that's for sure. We're both trying to figure out how to piece our broken selves back into the world.

But what if we're just that, two broken pieces that end up jabbing and hurting each other and everyone around us?

Jess

"Here, give me that." I go to take my bag out of his hand; he lifts it out of my reach.

"I got it," he says, twisting his entire body away from me.

I lean around him to grab it and he dodges me, bobbing around on the sidewalk like we're in a boxing ring.

"Too slow," he teases, weaving back and forth.

I give up. "Fine. Knock yourself out."

"I actually did once." He lifts his bangs and bends down to show me a scar on his forehead. "Jason and I were playing football in the house. I was five. I was running to catch it, focusing on the ball when I should have been keeping an eye on the wall coming at me. Knocked myself out. Woke up to my mom running with me in her arms to the car to take me to the hospital."

What compels me, I don't even know, but I trace the bumpy scar with my fingers. His eyes widen in surprise, just enough that I jerk my hand back. God, Jess . . . boundaries!

"How about you?" he blurts out, but it comes out like one word. *"Howboutyou?"*

I raise one hand in a scout's honor salute. "No, never knocked myself out trying to catch a football. Honest."

He laughs. "Scars?"

I lift my chin and point. He has to duck again to see it. "I'd like to say I was doing something really cool when I got this, but no. I tripped on the sidewalk outside of White Castle."

This time he reaches his finger out to trace it. I brace myself so I don't pull away or, worse, lean into his hand.

"Impressive," he says, his finger running along my scar. "We can always embellish."

"Embellish?" I try to laugh but it comes out more like a nervous shriek. He removes his finger but I can still feel the warmth of his touch lingering there. "How?"

"You used to play softball, right?" he asks.

I nod. How'd he know that?

"I used to see your team play at the park," he answers as if reading my mind, but then he adds, "Did you know your eyes squint when you're suspicious?" He pitches his head forward and narrows his eyes, pinching up his face to imitate me.

Am I that obvious? Does he also know that I check him out all the time when I think he's not looking?

Lucas holds both hands up in the air, painting a picture, the grocery bags dangling off his thumbs. "So replace White Castle with Little League. Bases were loaded . . . two outs . . . bottom of the ninth. You were at bat. You hit a line drive way into left field. You ran to first, then second . . . oh my God, you headed for third! The outfielder picked up the ball, but no, wait! She fumbled! The crowd went wild! You ran for home! The shortstop scooped up the ball, threw it to the pitcher, who then threw a wild pitch home. You dove headfirst for the plate. The umpire called it. Safe! Game over! Your team won! But your chin had a little run-in with the catcher's cleats."

I'm silent for a moment. Then I laugh, ticking off on my fingers everything he got wrong. "You obviously know nothing about softball. First, there are only seven innings. Second, a pitcher would never throw the ball in midplay to the catcher. Third, the shortstop—"

He interrupts me. "Hey, I'm just trying to help you save face. Go ahead, feel free to tell everyone you tripped over your own two feet outside of White Castle."

I giggle. "Okay, you're right. I'm awesome. I earned this scar."

Lucas bounces up and down on the balls of his feet like he's just warming up. "Okay, so what else. We covered scars. Let's move on to the bonus round. Each answer is worth ten points. Say the first thing that comes to mind. What's your favorite color?"

"Blue. No, orange. No, wait, blue."

"You're already terrible at this," Lucas says. "Favorite season?"

"Summer."

"Favorite band?"

"Uhhhh . . ."

He makes a buzzer sound in the back of his throat. "Time's up."

"But I have more than one!"

"Keep going. Favorite food?"

"Pizza."

"Come on. Give me *one* original answer. You sound like you should be saying, 'I'm not a *real* teenager, but I play one on television.'" He drops his voice several octaves, and holds his chin in one hand, mugging for the invisible camera.

I burst out laughing. "Okay. My favorite food is actually kind of gross."

"Now you *have* to tell me," he insists.

"Okay, if I tell you, then you have to tell me something equally gross."

"Deal. Go."

"Rice and ketchup."

He stops walking and slowly pivots to face me, the soles of his sneakers scraping against the sand on the sidewalk. His face is blank. "I was not prepared."

"Gross, right?"

"So gross. Like, I'm seriously trying not to gag right now."

"I warned you." I laugh. "Now your turn."

He raises a finger. "No, we are *not* done discussing this fancy cuisine of yours. I am now highly suspicious of all of your life choices. HOW did you stumble upon this questionable delicacy?"

"I was seven!" I laugh. "My rice got mixed in with the ketchup on my chicken nuggets and it tasted so much better than just the plain rice. And it just became a thing."

"Really? Rice and ketchup has been elevated to a *thing* in your life?"

I clutch my stomach, ready to bust a gut from laughing.

"You promised you had something gross to share!" I point at him.

"I'm afraid nothing I'll say can ever compare to that."

"Pleaaaassse?"

He fights a smile, but barely. "Okay. Here's one of my Lucas specialties. Bananas and mayonnaise sandwiches," he confesses.

"Bananas and mayonnaise?" He nods. "That's so much grosser, and you know it."

He points a finger at me, like he's letting me in on a trade secret. "It's a Southern delicacy."

"But we're not from the South."

"My family took a trip to Nashville one summer. We ate Kool-ickles too . . . Kool-Aid pickles. They were good. Refreshing!"

"Ew!"

My stomach lurches thinking about pickles and Kool-Aid, but he's not done. "You know what else is good with pickles? Peanut butter. But it has to be crunchy peanut butter, on wheat bread. Sometimes I'll even slap some peanut butter on my banana and mayo sandwich. Honestly, I think peanut butter goes great with anything."

"Stop talking!" I cover my ears. "Seriously. I have a very vivid imagination. I'm going to be sick. I can't believe you gave me grief over rice and ketchup!"

We reach the corner of Mott and McBride.

"Do you mind if I stop by my house really quick? Just to drop off the groceries." I point up McBride.

"Sure." He pivots and follows me.

Mrs. Alvarez is outside her house watering her handkerchief-sized lawn, a garden hose nozzle in one blue-veined hand, the other waving at me slowly.

"Hello, Jessica!"

"Hi, Mrs. Alvarez." She stops watering. Her mouth opens wide in a smile as she walks toward us. Oh God . . . she wants an introduction.

"Mrs. Alvarez, this is Lucas. We work together at Enzo's," I say, trying not to make it sound like we're all that close. It would be embarrassing if I introduced him as my friend when this is literally the first time we've hung out outside of work. I could just imagine his head darting over to correct me in front of her. *"Friends?"* I mean, he probably wouldn't actually say it, but he'd *think* it.

"Hello, Lucas." She looks between the two of us and her smile spreads even wider. Her eyes twinkle. I'm pretty sure I know what she's thinking and my cheeks burn. She's shipping us.

I turn to Lucas. "Wait here." Then I reach for my grocery bag and he hands it over. "I'll be right back. It'll only take a second."

I pull my key out from my pocket and open the front door a crack, just enough so Lucas can't see inside as I slide through and shut the door behind me.

I drop the bag of groceries on the dining room table next to the mail and walk to Mom's bedroom. The door is slightly ajar. I push it open, expecting to find her asleep.

Worse. Still in her bathrobe—because, why bother anymore?—she's perched on the edge of the bed with a shoebox filled with photographs. Pictures spill across her lap onto her unmade bed.

"Mom?"

She looks up at me, her eyes raw, tired . . . done. She's holding a picture of Ethan in her hands. As I step closer, I see that they're *all* pictures of Ethan.

She shakes her head. Her mouth opens, but even she seems uncertain about what will come out.

"I don't know how—" Overcome by tears, she covers her face.

"Mom." I sit next to her on the bed to wrap my arms around her, squeezing, so she'll feel me, so she'll find her way back to me.

Her skin smells metallic and sour against my nose, like pennies clutched in a sweaty palm all day. I inhale, trying to find my mother's scent, something familiar lingering underneath. I hold her for a while, waiting for her to say something, so we can talk about it. So we can share our grief together instead of compartmentalizing, her grief over here, and mine over there.

And then there's a knock on the front door.

Lucas

Jess has been in there for a while. I thought she was just dropping off the groceries. Maybe she had to go to the bathroom.

My phone buzzes in my pocket.

> **Where are you guys? Hurry up! I'm starving!**

I text Reggie back.

> **We stopped at Jess's house so she could drop off her stuff.**
>
> **Tell her to hurry her ass up! The water's boiling!**

I wave to get Mrs. Alvarez's attention, who's been watering the same patch of lawn in her fenced-in yard since Jess went inside.

"Do you think I should knock?" I call over to her, looking for validation.

She smiles at me. I don't think she heard what I said.

I walk up the stoop and press my ear to the door to listen for any kind of sounds that would tell me Jess is coming. Nothing.

So I knock.

And wait.

After a minute, I knock again.

The door opens a crack, and Jess slides through it, not opening it any wider than she needs to squeeze out.

Once she's out on the stoop with me she folds her arms across her chest.

"Ready?" I ask.

Something changed since she went inside. Her eyes are glassy and pink around the rims.

"Are you okay?"

"Yeah, I'm fine." She nods briskly, folding her arms tighter against herself. "Turns out I can't go. I forgot I had to do something."

"What?" I ask, taking a step back so I'm straddling two steps. I sense she needs the space.

She stares somewhere off over my shoulder. "I just have stuff to do here."

"Oh," I say. I wish I had some clue what caused the change in her. "No problem. I'll tell Reggie. Next time though, you're coming!"

She struggles to smile but doesn't make a move to go inside.

Waving me off, she says, "Have fun."

When I reach the sidewalk, I turn and look one last time. She's standing on the doorstep, waiting for me to leave.

My steps feel a little heavier as I walk away.

Jess

Once I'm back inside, I rest my forehead against the door, listening to the house sounds. The old fridge humming in the kitchen. The ticking of the clock. My mother crying in her bedroom.

I should have known better than to think I could just walk away from this and spend a night like a normal teenager.

My mother's words ring in my ears. *"I don't know how—"*

I can only imagine how she was going to finish her thought.

I don't know how to make this awfulness go away.

I don't know how to keep on living.

I don't know how to love you without him.

I walk back to Mom's bedroom to sit with her. When she's too exhausted to cry anymore, she climbs under the covers. Pictures of Ethan fall off the bed onto the floor.

"Mom? I think I should call the doctor. Don't you?"

She sniffs under her covers. "A doctor can't make me stop missing him, Jess."

I sit by her bedside rubbing her arm over the covers. It used to help me fall asleep when she did that when I was a kid.

Once I hear her steady breathing, I collect all the pictures of Ethan and put them back in the shoebox. Then I tuck the box in the corner of her closet floor and bury it under all the shoes and purses she never wears anymore because she never leaves the house. I don't know that it's the right thing to do. I'm just trying not to lose her too.

I retreat to my bedroom and plug my earbuds in, listening to music while I search through my videos for distractions.

A warning pops up on my phone: Storage Almost Full.

I don't know how it's almost full; it's not like I've taken any new videos or photos lately.

"All right, ol' Bessie. Let's take a load off of you," I say, to my phone, as one does when they have no one else to talk to.

I plug my phone into my laptop to try and free up some space. Instead, I get another error message: Your startup disc is almost full.

Cursing under my breath, I drag as many homework-related files as I can to the trash. It frees up enough space that I can view videos, but I can't load anything else. And I'm not willing to get rid of any of my old videos. Some days, they're the only things worth smiling about.

I click on a video from a year and a half ago, taken in Marissa's backyard the week before our sophomore year started. Thirty people showed up for her back-to-school party. She had a movie screen up in the yard and hooked up the Wii *Just Dance*. What the video doesn't capture is how the grass felt under our bare feet, damp and cool. How the air held the first crisp bite of fall. And how I sensed even then that it was the end of something. At the time, I thought I was just bummed about going back to school. But now I wonder if it was some premonition that it would be my last summer with my brother and my best friend.

What I did capture on my phone that night was ninety-two seconds of pure gold: Ethan and Marissa dancing to the Spice Girls, both of them flopping around like tangled marionettes to the music. It's so obvious now that he liked her by the way he smiled as he watched her dance when she wasn't looking. A smile unfamiliar to me, because whatever it was he was feeling for Marissa was something new even for him.

The video isn't enough. My brother's memory can't be reduced to megabytes of data.

I cross the hallway and rest my palm, then my cheek, on his door. Once this door vibrated with his music, Ethan practicing guitar. Now it's as silent and lifeless as he is. It's the silence that makes my throat constrict, that makes my entire face ache with the pressure of unshed tears.

The house is dark but there's a stream of light shining under the bottom of his door.

My hand reaches for the knob. This feels wrong. Like I should knock first. Only because Mom made me feel that way. But if the light's on, I'm not the first person to breach the sealed crypt of my brother's bedroom.

I enter slowly, looking around at all the things that are so Ethan: shelves of albums, his guitar, a stack of graphic novels on the floor in the corner. On his desk is his name tag from Key Food.

I pivot around in his room, taking it all in, signs of him everywhere and nowhere. The room is bursting with his stuff, his personality. But it may as well be an empty box without his energy.

As I turn around to leave, I look at his bed. There's a shallow impression of a body dipped into the center of his blue comforter. A strand of long blond hair is on the pillow. My mother's.

So this is what she does when I'm at school or at work. Hangs out in here, where she can be alone with him. Shutting me out from being close to my own brother. It looks like her rule about not coming in here only applies to me.

I grab Ethan's laptop from his desk and go back to my room. Sitting down at my desk, I plug in the charger and flip it open. I can't do anything without his password. But I also know my brother would lose his left hand if it wasn't attached to his wrist, so I try the first sequence of numbers that he could never forget: his birthday. 0103.

And I'm in.

Just as I suspected, there's way more storage on his laptop than mine. I plug my phone into the port and dump at least half my videos onto his computer.

With music playing, I click on one video after another. Marissa balancing a spoon on her nose while rolling a Hula-Hoop around her hips. Ethan and Marissa jumping off the swings at the beach at the same time, and Ethan hitting the ground so hard he crashed and rolled in the sand.

The song playing on my phone and footage on my screen start

to meld together, giving me an idea. I launch iMovie and start cropping and editing old footage, carefully arranging each scene around the music. If I can't have them in real life, I'll keep their memories alive the only way I can.

LUCAS

"Hi, Lucas. Come on in."

Dr. Engel holds his office door open, wearing a rust-colored cardigan that matches his striped tie, which is pinned to his immaculately pressed shirt with a tiepin. My nonna would've said Dr. Engel was a snazzy dresser, up there with her beloved Frank Sinatra and Dean Martin.

I walk past him into his "As Seen on TV" psychiatrist's office: two chairs, the obligatory couch, the well-kept fern, shelves bowing under the weight of academic books and journals, all neatly arranged in a small wood-paneled office. And there's always something humming in the background: the radiator, the air conditioner, the humidifier, the dehumidifier—whatever's seasonally appropriate.

Dr. Engel sits down in his chair and crosses his legs. His khakis have inched up over his thin ankles, exposing winter white skin and showy argyle socks that match his tie and sweater.

Every week it's the same thing: I do the majority of the talking.

Occasionally, we hit gold and he's kind enough to sum up every-thing I said in a neat and tidy package to take home to think about later, like a psychotherapy doggy bag.

Dr. Engel didn't beat around the bush; we got straight to work our very first session. He told me if I was honest about my answers and put in the work, I'd see results.

We established a few things early on in our first meetings:

I feel guilty that I'm alive and Jason isn't.

Jason threw himself on top of me because he loved me.

It was a gift, one that I am having a hard time accepting.

He didn't give me a choice, and sometimes that makes me angry.

Anger is easier to deal with than grief.

So our sessions are often about how to feel the love not the guilt. Dr. Engel always points to his heart (love) first, then his head (guilt) whenever he says this.

"Same with grief," Dr. Engel said. "Grief is something we avoid because it's too painful. So we stay up here"—points to his snowy, neatly parted hair—"not here"—points to his chest.

"Ouch," I said in my best E.T. voice. He smiled. Honestly, I can get away with anything in Dr. Engel's office. It's all part of the experience.

"When does it stop hurting?" I asked after one particularly messy session.

He leaned forward and handed me the box of tissues. "Grief doesn't go away, Lucas. It just gets less hard over time. The trick is learning how to reach in, confront it, deal with it." He swept his hand down like a bird and then soared it back up again. "Swoop down, touch it, then come out of it again."

As I take my seat today, he asks, "So . . . how've you been?"

"Okay?" I answer with just enough uncertainty that he raises an eyebrow, the "go on" nonverbal cue I'm used to by now.

I tell him about the most recent panic attack at Five Guys.

"I just thought . . . I thought I was done with those," I say, wiping my hands down my jeans. "Like how you said the medication and therapy together would reset my thermostat?"

He clicks his pen a few times. "This is the first one you've had in months."

I don't tell him about the near attack in Dr. Patel's office. Maybe being in the doctor's office helped me fight that one off.

"Well, I do think the dosage of Lexapro you're on is working, but I can prescribe Xanax for those times when you have an attack. If they continue though, we'll need to reassess. I don't want you to rely too much on the Xanax. Understood?" I nod. "Are you still boxing at the gym? Getting plenty of exercise?"

"Yeah." I nod. "Even more actually. I'm going to compete in a match in May."

He nods and smiles. "Are you nervous?"

"Well, *yeah*! But I chose to do it, you know? No one's making me."

"Of course," Dr. Engel says. "But we're looking for changes in your life that may be adding to your anxiety. Patterns or events that we can pinpoint. The match could be one."

"So, what? I can't try anything new without my body going berserk on me?"

I close my eyes and rub the side of my face. Sometimes talking to Dr. Engel makes me want to cry. Talking shouldn't make you cry. But it does with me.

He shifts in his seat, crosses his other leg now. "I can only imagine how horrible you must have felt. Many patients describe panic attacks to me as debilitating. One patient told me even though she knew exactly what it was, she still dialed 911. Was there anything you are aware of that happened to maybe trigger this recent attack?"

I tell him about the door slamming, the chair falling at the same time. The woman screaming.

He nods in understanding. "Okay. So there were sounds that seemed like gunshots."

I nod. "It came on really fast though. Like I didn't even have time to process. And I felt like I couldn't move. I train sixteen hours a week, but it didn't matter. I couldn't get my legs to stand up. Pete and some lady had to help get me to the car. And then Pete looked at me . . . like . . ."

"Like what?"

I rub my eyes and sigh. "He was freaked out."

"Your friend loves you and was worried about you. Why is that a bad thing?"

"It is when it's the way everyone around you looks at you as a default setting. Imagine someone shoving a thermometer in your mouth every time they look at you."

Dr. Engel nods, if not in agreement, in a concession. "I see."

"It's just . . . he was the last person who didn't treat me like that."

"Like what?"

"Like I was weak. Damaged."

Dr. Engel's benign smiles holds mine. "Obviously, Pete isn't a trained therapist or medical professional. So what Pete saw was alarming. And he expressed his concern by taking care of you until you stabilized, then took you home. And he couldn't hide his concern. That's not a trespass, Lucas. That's a—"

"Please don't say 'gift.'"

"Why? Is someone caring about you a gift you don't feel you deserve?"

I crack my knuckles in my lap. That question hit home, more than I care to admit. Which is why I'm still in therapy, I guess.

"Think about it, Lucas."

I nod and clear my throat. Then I change the subject. "Sooo . . ." I pull my left index finger to unlock the knuckle that won't give. It pops quietly but is satisfying nonetheless. "A new girl started at work."

He leans back in his chair, waiting for me to continue.

"I mean . . . I *knew* her before she started. We go to school together. And she and her brother . . . they were at the movies that night."

"Hmmm . . ." Dr. Engel nods. *Go on.*

"Her brother died that night too."

Dr. Engel waits patiently, I guess for me to get to the point.

"Considering everything I knew"—I drag it out and exhale—"I was kind of a jerk about it. I tried to get Reggie to fire her."

"Really . . . why?"

113

I shake my head and stare down at my clean white shoelaces. Mom replaced them while I was sleeping, like the shoemaker's elves in that old fairy tale. She's afraid some germ might sneak into the house on a dirty shoelace and kill me in my sleep.

"I've been avoiding being around other people who were there."

"Reminders," he says, and I nod.

"But . . . it was weird . . . we were hanging out yesterday and started talking. I told her about my list. I don't even know why I told her, honestly."

I glance up at Dr. Engel. He has that satisfied look like he knows why I did it, but he's not going to tell me. I'm going to have to figure it out myself. "Well, anyway . . . she got it. Like, I didn't even need to explain what that list meant to me."

He leans a little forward. "Your shared experience validates you."

Now my head nods up and down like a bobblehead toy. "Yeah. Exactly."

I lean back in my chair to consider this "aha" moment. *Validates*.

"Connecting with others who shared a traumatic experience can help alleviate those feelings of helplessness you struggle with, Lucas," he tells me. "It's why support groups are formed, why they have rituals and ceremonies to honor those lives that were lost."

I pull at my fingers until I hear the pop in each knuckle. "Yeah, but . . . what if we're similar enough to be bad for each other? Like ammonia and bleach."

Cleanup in aisle six, I think. I'm ready to explain, but Dr. Engel doesn't ask.

His lips tug down. "There's the risk that a circular pattern can hurt the relationship. Close relationships for trauma survivors may be difficult in general. It requires you to let your guard down." He raises his eyebrow at me. "Interesting boxing metaphor, wouldn't you say?"

I scoff. "Yeah."

Dr. Engel lifts his fists up in front of his face. "You've been working on keeping your guard up for the past year to make sure bad things don't happen to you again. Training your body to respond so you feel less *helpless* . . . I believe that was your word?" He drops his fists. "So letting your guard down to allow people into your life can be stressful. Do you mind if I ask: Are you attracted to this girl? Do you have feelings for her?"

"Uh . . . I guess. Kinda." More than I'm willing to admit to my therapist right now.

He raises one hand. "I only ask because I wonder if this is also something that's contributing to your anxiety."

I flop back in my chair and rub my forehead. "Great."

Dr. Engel isn't fazed though. "Anxiety and excitement are the same physiological response. An adrenaline rush can push a panic-prone person to have an attack."

"None of this is good news, Dr. Engel," I inform him.

"It *is* good news, Lucas. Letting new people into your life, thinking about relationships is wonderful. We will work through this."

"Yeah but don't you think it's a problem that our situations are too similar?"

"Do *you*?" he asks, and I nod, slowly, reluctantly.

His expression is unshakable. "If you're careful, mindful, communicate, trust each other, work on problem solving together, it can work. And work beautifully. You can deeply understand each other in ways non-sufferers cannot."

I take a deep breath and scratch the back of my head. "So what you're saying is it's a crapshoot," I say, trying, and failing, to turn it into a joke.

I stare at the modern geometric patterns of his rug under his feet. His silence is a cue for me to look up.

"I don't bet, Lucas." He shrugs but his eyes don't. They hold on to mine. "But if you like her, and she likes you, and you both put the work in . . ."

By the end of the session, I have a lot to chew on. I also realize I spent most of the hour talking about a possible relationship with Jess, a girl I'm only just getting to know.

Jess

It's Wednesday. Lucas and I both have off from work today. I only saw him briefly in the hallway at school; he waved and kept going. I don't blame him after the way I ditched him abruptly last night. The guy's got his own stuff to deal with; he doesn't need my baggage too.

Pete stops by my locker at the end of the day. He's looking healthy again.

"All better?" I ask him.

He puts a hand over his stomach. "Yeah. I puked once and was done. You working tonight?"

"Nope."

"Lucky." He sulks. "It's more fun when you guys are there." He flops against my neighbor's locker. "You know what I think?"

"What?" I humor him.

"I'm thinking it's bonfire season. It's been nice out. I'm going to see if I can rally the troops to plan something."

His head turns to follow Gwen Welch's trek down the hall.

Pete elbows me, but his eyes are glued to Gwen's back. "Hey, do you know if Gwen's going with anyone to the prom?"

"You're asking *me*?" I point to myself. "How would I know?"

"Gotta go," he says, and chases her down the hall. "Gotcha!" he yells, tickling her. She turns around and squeals, collapsing into his arms laughing.

Why is it so easy to tell when other people are falling for each other and so much harder to figure out when it's about you? Last night was great with Lucas, until I made it weird. What would've happened if I went to Reggie's? Did I blow it between us? Was there ever even a chance of there being an "us"?

The house is brightly lit when I come home from school. Inside, my mother sits at the dining room table opening mail. It's not quite like coming home to something baking in the oven or bubbling on the stovetop, but seeing her up and tackling the bills is a huge leap for her, for us. Now that they're opened though, the bills seem to have multiplied, taking over the entire dining room table.

She looks up at me from her checkbook. "Hi."

"Hi," I say, taking a seat next to her. She's organized bills into piles. Next to her is a running tally of numbers on a lined notepad.

I don't know much about our finances.

I know when my parents both worked they were careful about money, making sure to save.

I know Mom inherited the house. My parents were always relieved that they didn't have a mortgage to pay off.

I know Dad hasn't sent a dime since he left us.

I know unemployment checks stopped coming when Mom didn't make a few of her appointments at the social security office.

And looking at the running tally next to her, I know we owe a lot of money.

Discarded envelopes are strewn all over the floor by my mom's feet under the table. There's a recent bank statement in front of her that shows our dwindling account. Her checkbook is open next to her. Glancing over her shoulder, I can tell from the checkbook ledger that she stopped paying bills around mid-February. She's added a few entries today, under the one I entered to pay the electric bill. She doesn't ask me about it, and I don't offer any information.

"How bad is it?" I ask, glancing at the piles around the table.

"Not great. Now would be a really good time for your father to send some of that money he promised us."

Last time I saw Dad was before Ethan died; he took a job driving a van full of watermelons up from Georgia. He happened to be driving through Queens, so he stopped by to say hello; he left after fifteen minutes. As a parting gift or maybe a consolation prize, he gave us each a watermelon. We couldn't even get in touch with him to tell him Ethan died; he found out two months later, when he called to check in using someone else's phone. How can she possibly think he's going to help us now?

Mom opens another envelope and groans, throwing both hands over her face. It doesn't take 20/20 vision to see the big "OVERDUE" stamp on the bill inside the envelope.

"I can't handle this," she mutters between her fingers.

I act quickly, to fix this, to make this better, because I can't even imagine what it would be like if our lives get any worse. "Maybe I can pick up a few extra shifts at Enzo's."

Sadness settles in the downward tug of her lips. She nods in reluctant approval. "I'm sorry, Jess. We'll get back on our feet, I promise."

It's the empty platitude I've been hoping for and just as hollow as I imagined. I swallow and glance back down at the stack of bills in front of me so she doesn't see terror pounding behind my eyes. These bills are now my bills.

I start making my own piles. There are a few notices from the walk-in clinic from when I got strep in November. There's a last notice for payment from the psychiatrist who called Mom non-compliant. I think she owes *us* money, to be honest.

Mom writes a check and sticks it in an envelope. "I should pay the cable bill, right? So they don't cut us off."

"That would suck," I add, trying to brighten the mood.

Licking the envelope, she looks over at me and smiles. "Language, young lady," she says in a Southern drawl.

After Superstorm Sandy, we lost power for weeks. School was closed, so was Mom's office, but Dad still had to get to work. To pass the time, Ethan, Mom, and I played a lot of Uno. In our extreme boredom, the game evolved into us taking on these odd Southern belle personas—even Ethan. Every play, every discard, we'd announce in long, slow cartoony voices of what we imagined Southern belles sounded like. It became the soundtrack of our home during happy, playful moments.

Even just a glimpse of her old self perks me up. "You forgot to say 'Ooh-nnoooo!'" I say in my best drawl. Mom giggles, and I can't help but laugh too. It's been too long since we had any kind of laugh together.

We continue opening and sorting the bills. Every time either one of us plops a bill down, we yell, "U-noooo," turning our misery into a punch line.

Mom reaches for her mug and takes a sip. In our little corner of the dining room, I smell shampoo and tea. She's showered. She's laughing. She's trying.

Hope bubbles in my belly, making me giddy.

LUCAS

Lim sits with Enzo behind the counter when I show up for work, Lim still in his white apron. Whenever Lim needs a break from the grocery store next door, he comes here to visit Enzo.

They both look up and acknowledge me, Lim with a smile, Enzo with a grunt.

"Lucas." Enzo waves me over with a meaty hand. "How's the girl working out?"

"She's actually really good. A hard worker," I say.

He exhales a dissatisfied burst of air. Not the reaction I would expect.

"Why? Is something wrong?"

Enzo waves his hand in the air dismissively, sweeping me away. "Nothing, nothing."

I find Reggie in her office, massaging her forehead.

"You okay?"

She looks up at me and sighs, shoulders slumping. "Shut the door."

Leaning up against the closed door, I cross my arms. "What's going on?"

She holds up a bunch of papers on her desk and rattles them. "The accountant screwed us over."

"Huh?"

"We got hit with a huge tax bill because Enzo's accountant made a mistake!"

"Oh shit." I scratch the back of my head. "But . . . we're always so busy, right? We'll be okay."

"Not busy enough. We never should've expanded. We might've been able to pull it together if our nut was smaller. Now we have more overhead." Reggie takes the gum out of her mouth and wraps it in a used napkin. Then she folds her arms on her desk and rests her head.

I pull up a chair. "So why was Enzo asking me about Jess just now?"

She props her head up in her hands like it might just roll off without the added support beams. "He's thinking of letting someone go. Last one in, first one out."

"But he *just* hired her!" I argue.

"I know that!" she shouts back.

"She hardly makes enough money to even make a dent!"

Reggie takes a deep breath. "He's looking to cut back everywhere. I've been on the phone for hours trying to cancel orders that haven't shipped yet." She lowers her head back into her folded arms. "I never would've hired her if I knew this was going to happen."

"She's doing a good job, Reg. We need her here."

She reaches her hand out across the desk. "Hi, nice to meet you, I'm Reggie. Clearly we've never met before, because the Lucas Rossi I know didn't even want Jess to work here in the first place!"

"Yeah, but . . . that's changed," I say.

She opens her desk drawer and grabs a tub of ibuprofen. Popping the cap, she pours two in her hand, looks at it, then tips a third one in. "Look, nothing's definite. Let's see if I can dump some of this inventory." She tosses the pills back and chugs them with her mug of coffee that's probably cold from this morning.

Then she points to the door, kicking me out. "A new shipment of grills are coming in today. Make room on the floor."

Jess shows up a little later. She's in a good mood. A weirdly good mood. Like, none of us even know what to do with this happy ball of energy.

"You on drugs or something?" Joe asks her, narrowing his eyes as she bounces around the warehouse with the handcart.

"Nope." She wheels the cart through the swinging doors, her ponytail dancing happily behind her. She's even humming a song under her breath.

A shipment is delayed because the truck broke down on the thruway. By the time he gets here, we all have to stay past closing to unload the truck. It's after eight by the time we're done. We meet by the lockers to get our things.

"Jess, you need a ride?" Pete shakes his keys in the air.

She smiles. "Thanks. I'm not heading out just yet." She makes her way to Reggie's office and pokes her head in. I watch with dread as the door shuts behind her.

Pete turns to me. "Ready?"

"You go," I tell him, my eyes fixed on Reggie's door. I search around for a prop that will serve as an excuse to stay. I grab the broom. "I'm going to hang back a little bit, clean up."

Pete looks between Reggie's closed door and me. Then he smirks. "Knew it." He heads out without grilling me any further, which I appreciate.

I pretend to sweep the floor, inching closer to Reggie's door. Finally, the door opens. I fall back, just around the corner.

"Night." Jess waves over her shoulder to Reggie, closing the door behind her, still in a good mood.

That is, until she takes a few steps. She stops midway between Reggie's office and the bay of lockers, then hunches over, grabbing her knees. She looks like she might throw up. She takes a few deep breaths and straightens, shakes her head a couple of times. I hate spying on her, so I clear my throat. She turns to find me standing there, holding the broom.

"Hi," I blurt out, because I can't think of anything better, smarter, more comforting to say.

She nods at me, then turns to leave.

I throw the broom against the wall. "Jess, wait up. I'll walk out with you."

She stops but doesn't turn around.

Grabbing my hoodie off its hook, I ask, "Are you okay?"

"Yeah?" Her voice breaks.

"Come on," I say. Resting a hand gently on her shoulder, I guide her through the doors and outside. I look around for a place to sit down, desperate to help. Parking meter, fire hydrant, garbage can, mailbox . . . a barren raised flowerbed outside the bank. "Let's go sit over there." I point and she follows.

Jess doesn't as much sit as collapse onto the ledge, folding into herself like a pretzel, arms crossed over her knees, face buried into forearms. She doesn't say anything, and I don't know what to say to someone who is literally hiding from me.

Finally, she breaks the silence. "I was an idiot to think anything could ever get better!" With her head buried in her arms, her voice is muffled. She probably doesn't want me or anyone walking by to see her crying.

"What happened?" I ask, even though I'm pretty sure I know.

She sits up and fists her sweatshirt sleeves to wipe her face. "I went in to ask Reggie if she had any extra hours I could pick up."

"Shit." Her head finally turns to look at me, and her eyes narrow into her "I'm suspicious" face. I'm not a very good liar, so I decide to confess just enough. "She told me that Enzo may have to let one of us go."

"Yeah. Me." She points to her chest. "She wasn't going to tell me until she knew for certain, but since I was looking for more hours, she felt she should let me know that it might be coming. In case I wanted to start looking for something else now. Ugh . . . I *hate* this." She sniffles.

I'm not sure if she means she hates crying, or hates the awful feeling that comes with crying. That's what I hate. People say it's cathartic, that it relieves that buildup inside of you, but for me it's not. It just redirects all that pressure into my sinuses.

"It's not a done deal. Reggie told you that, right?"

She sniffs and looks ahead. "I have to find a job with more hours though. Now."

"What's the rush? You're a junior. You should be focusing on SATs and going to look at colleges. You know, having fun!" I pep it up for comedic effect, but it's clear I've failed epically.

"Yeah, *fun*," she repeats testily.

"Sarcasm noted," I say, still trying to keep it light.

The A train rumbles by in the distance. Across the street, a guy walks out of the deli, smacking a pack of cigarettes against the back of his hand. He tears the pack open and lights a cigarette outside the Blarney Stone Pub.

She shakes her head. "Sorry. I'm just . . . sometimes I think I don't even remember how to have fun."

"Not even a little?" I pinch my index and thumb together.

She laughs to herself, but it's more like a sad exhale. "And college? I can't even *think* about college right now." She bites her lip, and looks away. "Maybe I'll take one of those 'gap years.'" She air quotes.

"Maybe," I say, nodding. "My brother took one."

She rests her hands on the edge of the ledge and sits up a little straighter. "Really? Why?"

I thumb behind me, back toward Enzo's. "Reggie."

"Ohhh." Her eyes widen in understanding.

"High school sweethearts. She was a year behind him. He turned down a pretty decent scholarship. My folks were not happy."

She bites her lip and winces. "I can imagine."

"Jason proposed to her. They had a plan, to go to school together a year later after she graduated. Things didn't work out that way though."

Jess looks down at her sneakers. "I don't think anything turned out the way we thought it would." She glances up at me. "What about you? Where are you going next year?"

"Queensborough," I say. "It was *decided* that I should stay close to home for a year or two."

"What do you mean, 'decided'? By who?"

"My parents, me . . . just, you know . . . to make sure I can handle it. Things haven't been entirely smooth sailing since Jason died."

Her lips press together in a grim line, but she nods like she gets it. I should've known she would.

"You have time, you know," I add. "About college. It's not like that window closes just because you're not ready for it now. A year, two years. It'll still be there."

She picks at the skin around her thumbnail. "I tend to get caught in the day-to-day. Time feels stuck, you know?" she admits. "A year or two from now sounds like a life sentence."

"Sometimes a day feels like a life sentence," I say, and she nods.

"Exactly." Then she lets out a sad groan-sigh. "God, I want to get out of here so bad."

I inch closer to her. "Then make a plan. Even if it's to get out of here in two years, it's something. It helps unstick time."

We're silent for a few minutes. The bus comes and stops in

front of us, its hydraulics hissing as it lowers to let passengers off. The driver looks at us, waiting to see if we're planning on boarding. When we don't budge, she shrugs, shuts the doors, and pulls away again, leaving us in the dark. Dim streetlamps cast shadows under Jess's eyes, her cheekbones, making her sadness even more prominent.

Under the scaffolding across the street, the red, green, and white neon sign for Gino's flickers like an electric bug zapper. Naturally, this makes me hungry.

"What's the grossest pizza topping you've ever eaten?"

"Pineapple," she says with a shudder.

"Really? Grosser than anchovies?"

"I *like* anchovies," she says, a smile rising to the surface.

I shake my head. "This is almost weirder than ketchup with rice."

She laughs a little, nothing like her laugh from the other night. Still, it's so much better than seeing her cry. "When I was a kid, my dad and I would sit down with a loaf of Italian bread and a tin of anchovies and . . . oh my God . . . sooooo good." She closes her eyes and holds her stomach just remembering.

"Are you hungry?"

"Starving."

I nod my head across the street. "Let's get a slice."

She stands up and digs through her jean pockets, pulling out a ball of crumbled dollars. She flattens them and counts, three, before answering. "Okay."

She leads the way and I follow her.

Jess

I almost said no.

But when I reached in my pocket, I discovered a clump of bills that must've gone through the wash. They appeared out of nowhere, unexpected, like a magic trick. They're just what I need to give me a little boost of hope and optimism.

I didn't get fired. Reggie actually did me a favor by giving me that heads-up. Hopefully I can stick it out at Enzo's until I find something with more hours. Or pick up a second job somewhere.

I turn to Lucas with a huge grin. "Don't you love finding money in your pocket?"

His face lights up, brighter than all the flickering street signs combined. My stomach flutters with butterflies in response to his smile. I put a hand over them to still them, but now that they're awake, there's no quieting them.

This is more than just checking out his cute butt at work. I'm starting to *feel* things with Lucas. *For* Lucas.

We cross the street and walk inside Gino's, straight to the counter.

"How can I help you?" the guy working asks.

"One slice for me," I say.

He points a stubby finger at Lucas. "What about you, big guy?"

Lucas bends over to appraise the vast selections behind glass. "Uh . . . give me two slices of that . . . yeah, the one with the barbecue chicken . . . and one regular with cold mozz."

My eyes widen. "Barbecue chicken?"

"Don't knock it until you try it," he says, straightening up.

"I'll try it when you try anchovies."

Lucas scouts the restaurant for an empty booth. "It's pretty crowded."

I lean around Lucas to see if maybe someone's close to finishing their meal and getting up. That's when I see Marissa's mother and little brother, Liam.

"Jess!" Mrs. Connell calls my name. She stands up, arms open, big smile on her face. I walk over to her table.

"How *are* you?" she asks, squeezing extra hard as if to make up for the amount of time it's been since I last saw her.

"Okay," I say. I glance at Liam. He stares down at his DS, ignoring me, his lower jaw jutting out the way it does when he is supremely pissed off. "Hey, Nugget." I reach over to ruffle his hair and he pulls away.

I look over at Mrs. Connell and she grimaces. "He misses you," she mouths.

My heart shatters. Seeing Mrs. Connell and Liam reminds me

of what else I've lost this year. Marissa slept over my house the night Mrs. Connell was in labor with Liam eleven years ago.

"How's Marissa?" I ask.

Mrs. Connell's nod is enthusiastic. "She's doing well, Jess. The school is wonderful. She's made friends. As part of the therapy, she's working with shelter dogs. Isn't that amazing?" She flips her hands outward, like, *Oh that crazy universe, so full of surprises!*

But the words that claw at my heart are "She's made friends." Because I haven't found anyone to replace Marissa.

"I just . . . I haven't heard from her." I can't hide the hurt in my voice.

"Oh, Jess," she says, as if she's just understood the root of my pain. "None of the students are allowed to have access to emails or phones."

"Still?" I whine. I can't help it. I thought this school was voluntary. Why are they treating her like she's a prisoner?

"Eventually, as she progresses through the program."

I feel a presence behind me. Turning around, I find Lucas holding all our food.

Mrs. Connell makes a big show of pushing the plates and cups across the table to make room. She gestures across the booth to the empty seat next to Liam. "Sit! There's plenty of room."

Sit down and eat pizza together, like we've done a million times before? I can't. Because those million other times, Marissa was here. But now she's not.

"Oh, thanks, but . . . we were actually getting ours to go."

Lucas looks down at the three paper plates in his arms. "Oh, right." He jerks his head toward the counter. "I'll ask them for a box." He leaves me alone to deal with this awkwardness.

"Are you sure?" Mrs. Connell presses.

A ball of sadness the size of a garlic knot lodges in my throat. I love Mrs. Connell. I miss her and Liam. But I can't do this.

"She doesn't want to sit with us, Mom," Liam snaps, not even looking up from his game.

"No, that's not it." I try to deny it, but there's no point. "Uh . . . I better go. It was nice seeing you. You too, Liam."

I walk to the counter and tap Lucas on the shoulder. The guy behind the counter boxes our pizza and we walk outside together. The air is crisp and bracing against my hot cheeks. We stop at the corner.

"You okay?" Lucas asks.

"Yeah?" Then I shake my head. "Actually, no. That was awful."

"Is it okay if I ask why you didn't want to sit with them?"

I steeple my hands over my nose and shake my head. "Honestly? I don't even know. She started talking about how great Marissa was doing and it bugged me. Most days, I'm happy for her. But right then, I was jealous. That she was able to get away from this. And angry at her, and *everyone*, for leaving me here alone." I wave my hand around Mott Avenue. Then I groan and glance back behind me. "That sure as hell isn't going down as my proudest moment."

Holding the pizza in his hands, he asks, "Want to find someplace else to eat this?"

I stare at him in disbelief. "I just admitted I'm an awful human being. Why aren't you running away? I wouldn't blame you."

His smile is soft, gentle. "You're being honest. My therapist would call that a breakthrough. I say we should celebrate." He lifts the box. "With pizza."

A horn blares. A guy leans out his car window and hollers at the driver double-parked in front of him. Tires screech as he peels out around the parked car.

"I'm not hungry anymore. You can have my slice."

He nods and bites the inside of his lip. "So, do you walk home every night from work?"

"Yeah."

"Okay if I walk you home?"

"You don't have to. And your pizza will get cold," I say, in case he's only offering to be nice.

"No, I know," he says, and shrugs. "I want to though. And I can always reheat it."

And just like that, this shitty night does a complete about-face. This cute, kind boy who I'm pretty sure stayed late at work to make sure I was okay wants to walk me home.

I can practically hear what Marissa would say if she were here. Her shove from behind. *Get it, girl!*

I take a step forward. "Okay."

We walk side by side toward my house.

"Favorite fruit?"

"You like to talk about food a lot, don't you?" I note.

"You've seen me eat. This shouldn't come as a surprise. Answer the question."

"Mango."

"Mango? Can you believe I've never had a mango?"

"We should do something about that."

"Definitely. Okay, favorite holiday."

"Halloween."

"Have you been practicing? You've gotten much better at this."

"Maybe you're just finally asking interesting questions," I say.

"Ouch!" He pretends to reel back from my zinger. "Okay, now you're asking for it. I'm done taking it easy on you. Bonus round: questions are worth fifty points each."

"What do I win?"

"All-expenses-paid trip to Enzo's Hardware. The category is Philosophy. First question: Which is more useful, knowledge or wisdom?"

"Huh. Wow, these really are harder."

"Time's up."

"No chance. Bonus round questions get extra time." We wait at the intersection for the WALK sign while I come up with my final answer. "It's a trick question. You need both."

"Is that your wisdom speaking?"

"Probably." I laugh. "I think wisdom comes from an emotional place and knowledge comes from the brain. The two balance each other."

We walk in step, our arms brushing every so often. Time feels unstuck with Lucas. Like I'm moving forward finally. I like where I'm heading.

LUCAS

We stop outside Jess's house. She doesn't make a move to go inside yet.

"Okay, no more bonus round questions. My brain hurts. Favorite movie?" I ask.

Her face lights up like this is her favorite question so far. "*Young Frankenstein.*"

"Oh my God. The *best*!" I holler. "Ovaltine!"

She holds on to her gate and swings it back and forth. "Roll, roll, roll in the hay!" she sings in a German accent.

The gate swings with more momentum than Jess was prepared for. Her feet stumble under her to catch herself. I grab her elbow.

Jess rights herself and laughs. "Well, that was embarrassing! No more rolling in the hay for me!" She clamps a hand over her mouth. "Oh my God, I didn't mean it like that!" She drops her hand and throws her head back laughing. Under the streetlamp, her eyes and teeth sparkle.

My hand that was holding her elbow lingers, then sneaks up her arm.

God, I want to kiss her. The thought hits me fast and hard. And Jess is right there with me, tilting her head up to meet me.

Then Mrs. Alvarez turns on her porch light and peeks at us through her window. Jess takes a step back, away from me.

"Crap," she mutters under her breath. "Well . . . I guess I better go," Jess says, still grinning at me.

"Okay." I watch her until her front door shuts behind her.

It's not until she's inside that an uneasy feeling elbows my good mood out of the way. My knees are shaky, my ears start to hum.

Fucking adrenaline.

I reach in my pocket for the "in case of emergency, break glass" prescription that I filled after my session with Dr. Engel yesterday. I wrap my fingers around the bottle and shake it. Just feeling it in my hand helps stem the surge from accelerating.

Maybe the universe sent Mrs. Alvarez to interrupt us for a good reason. Like maybe I'm not really ready for this yet after all.

Jess

Next time you talk to your mom, tell her I'm sorry. She'll know why.

In infinitely more interesting news, Lucas walked me home tonight. I kept hearing the song from The Little Mermaid playing in my head. You know the one, "Kiss the Girl"! Sha la la la la la, my oh my!

Pete stops at my locker just as I'm reading over the texts I sent Marissa when I got home last night, still feeling crappy about not sitting with Mrs. Connell and Liam combined with a new buzzy excitement over that near kiss with Lucas.

"Who you texting?" He peers over at my phone.

"Nosy much?" I stare him down, but Pete just grins, unfazed. I pocket my phone and feel around in my locker for my APUSH textbook.

"You're coming tonight, right?"

"To where?"

"The *bonfire*," he says, like we've discussed it a gazillion times.

An alarm rings in my head. Something tells me I should proceed with extreme caution because the answer to my next question is going to hurt.

"Who's going?"

"All of us." He ticks off names on his fingers, people from school, seniors mostly, some people who graduated last year, including Reggie. Even Joe, who graduated a few years ago. And Lucas. "I *told* you I was rallying the troops, remember?"

"I remember," I say. "But I didn't hear anything definite until now."

"Fine, whatever. I'm telling you now. You're coming."

"Maybe."

His head retreats back into his neck like a turtle's. "Maybe? What's this 'maybe' shit? You're coming."

I want to go. I should go. They're my friends now, right? So why am I stuck wondering why Lucas didn't mention it to me?

There were so many opportunities to mention the bonfire . . . at school, at work, outside the bank, walking home after Gino's. And then there was that moment under the streetlamp as his hand inched up my arm . . .

"So?" Pete asks.

"I said maybe," I snap at Pete, and immediately regret it. "Sorry."

His lips flatline. He leans closer, looking around to make sure no one's listening. "Is this about Lucas?"

"No," I lie, trying to save at least a little face.

"You sure? 'Cause I figured he would've told you last night."

I shake my head. "He didn't. But it's fine. Just text me where you guys will be. I'll try to come, okay?"

"Okay. What's your number?" He takes his phone out and enters my contact then texts me: **Beach 32nd Street**. "There. If you need a ride, let me know. I'll come get you."

I don't see Lucas the rest of the day. And I'm not on the work schedule tonight. So I guess I won't be finding out anytime soon why he didn't ask me himself.

Lucas

Pete drives us both to work after school. It's a short shift today since there are no shipments coming in. Just Pete and me; Joe and Jess aren't on the schedule tonight.

"I asked Gwen to prom," he says, smiling.

"Yeah? You guys . . ." I twist my fingers together just because it's fun to make Pete's ears blush.

"Just as friends," he says, though I don't buy it for a minute. "So what's going on with you and Jess?"

"What do you mean?" I ask, clutching the overhead strap.

He drums his fingers on the steering wheel. "I asked her if she was going to the bonfire tonight."

"Oh." I stare out the window. "Is she coming?"

"Dude!" He gestures to me with his hand, like I'm Exhibit A. "You should've been the one asking her!"

"I forgot," I lie.

We hit a red light with a head-snapping stop. Something in my neck pops.

"Look, I feel like I hurt her feelings today. I kinda blame you for that. When I saw you waiting for her last night, I thought you were finally making a move."

"She was upset about work. Reggie told her she might have to let her go. We got to talking about other stuff. The bonfire didn't come up," I say. "So . . . is she coming?" Maybe this will all be okay because Pete salvaged it, as Pete always does.

"Probably not. She said maybe. I sent her a text of where we'd be and told her I'd drive her if she needed a ride."

The light turns green and he accelerates. I clutch the strap in a tighter grip in preparation for warp speed. "And by the way, if you hung back to cheer her up, maybe telling her about the bonfire would've been helpful."

"I know. You're right," I admit, and squeeze my eyes shut. Lying about what's really going on is just making me sound like a complete douche. "I like her, okay? But I don't know if I can do this. My anxiety is ratcheting up lately."

When I think about where I was a year ago, I know I've come a long way. But I'm not entirely okay yet. The predictable schedule of school, boxing, and work keeps me on safe ground. It's the unknown I'm avoiding. And Jess is a big unknown because everything I feel around her is amplified, mostly in a great way. But that shaky feeling last night tells me that the slightest emotional jostle can send me crashing.

"I get it. But maybe you could tell her that too. You could take it as slow as you want or need to, you know?"

Outside my window, our neighborhood blurs by in a streak of

store awnings and cement.

"Look, my two cents; do with it what you want," Pete continues. "I already knew you liked her. I've seen your moves. Your whole face gets all 'huh?' when she walks in the room." He mimes this dopey wide-eyed look that makes me look like a doofus. "I figured last night when you hung back you were going to ask her. I gave you way too much credit."

"Amateur mistake," I mumble under my breath.

"Big-time. But the thing is, I think she likes you too. Joe said he caught her checking you out. So as the great philosopher Plato once said, shit or get off the pot."

"Plato, huh?"

"Yeah. Either him or Socrates."

"Which one drank the hemlock?" I ask.

Pete gives it some thought. "Not sure. But whichever one did, he's our guy."

After work I went to the gym. Even after two hours of working it out on the bags and sparring with Honor in the ring I'm still as wound up as I was in Pete's car. Honor got a bunch of good shots in too; my ribs are aching. Leo was not happy.

He hooked his fingers in the air to reel me closer. "Lemme ask you something," he said. "You up to five miles yet? 'Cause you're getting gassed too fast." He pointed to the ring.

I nodded, panting.

He pitched his head forward, his nose far into my personal space. "Every day?"

My silence was his answer. He raised his hand, stopping short of smacking me in the head.

"What'd I tell you? Five miles . . . *every day*! And control the center of the ring. You need to be the one setting the pace."

"Okay, Leo." I walked away.

But he wasn't done with me. "And another thing!" he yelled. I turned back. He pointed to the ring again. "I don't care what's bugging you. Girls, school, your parents . . . you do not bring it into the ring with you. Got it?"

Leo was a freaking mind reader.

Now showered and back in my room, I flip open my laptop and update my Random Acts of Kindness grid.

April 14 Relocated a spider outside for Mom

I'm sure the spider is grateful I didn't squash it, but it's kind of sad that this is the greatest act of kindness I could come up with today. I save the Excel file and stare at my paper on *The Sunflower*, which is still in the blank-canvas state, other than my name, class period, and title: "*The Sunflower:* The Power in Extending Forgiveness."

Forgiveness.

Simon Wiesenthal asks: "*You, who have just read this sad and tragic episode in my life, can mentally change places with me and ask yourself the crucial question, 'What would I have done?'*"

Easy! Under those circumstances, I would have done exactly what Simon Wiesenthal did. How can you forgive a monster? You can't.

But today, the question resonates differently. Today, I hurt someone. Someone I like. Because I'm scared.

Remorse gnaws at my stomach. I have to try and fix this. I text Pete.

> **Hey. What's Jess's number?**

He sends me her digits and I send Jess a text next.

> **Hey, you there? It's Lucas.**

No answer.

> **Pete said you were a maybe tonight. We're heading over to the beach around 8. You should come! It'll be fun!**

Still no answer. Jess always has her phone with her. Always. There's no way she's not getting my texts.

But it's her silence that makes me realize that being with Jess isn't what I should be worrying about. Messing this up and not being with her—even after such a short time—is a much scarier scenario.

I shoot Pete another text.

> **Don't need a ride. Meet you there.**

I run downstairs, grab my keys from the junk drawer, and head for the front door.

"Mom, I'm going out. I'm driving."

Footsteps race up the basement stairs.

"What about your keys?" she says, out of breath.

I hold them up between my fingers to show her. "Found them."

She stares back at them with a guilty expression.

"I won't be late," I say, shutting the door behind me. This is Dad's mess to clean up later. I'm not playing this game anymore.

Jess

Want to hear something pathetic? Every one of my friends is sitting around a bonfire while I'm in my room texting YOU. Pretty sad, right?

Lucas sent me a pity invite. Pete probably told him what happened.

I thought maybe things were going somewhere with him. He either chickened out or I'm super bad at picking up on romantic overtures.

I should go. I shouldn't let Lucas be the reason I don't see my friends. Right?

Why aren't you here to tell me what to do?!

Mom's in bed. At least she hasn't been sleeping all day. She's been okay since we went through the bills together on Wednesday.

To distract myself, I rewatch old videos on my laptop to find more footage for the video I'm editing. I find one of Marissa from Halloween last year. Marissa on a sugar high is even more hysterical than usual, like when a puppy has the zoomies, chasing his tail around in circles until he collapses in exhaustion. Sitting on her bed, candy wrappers all around her, she bounces up and down excitedly, her blond hair flouncing around with her. In between licks of a lollipop, she tells me every last detail of that night's episode of *Scandalous Liaisons*.

"So then Hunter came home and found Rachel on the couch, cheating on him with his best friend, Sawyer. Just as he's telling her to pack her bags and get out there's a huge explosion in the apartment complex. The redhead, who everyone thought had moved to Australia but obviously didn't, blew the place up! Okay, so then they cut to the hospital where Rebecca is having her baby. Bobby's by her side, right? Holding her hand, ready to cut the umbilical cord. The baby comes out . . . they only show Bobby's face . . . And, oh my God, best scene ever! The look of shock on his face says, 'That's not MY baby!' He should win an Oscar. . . . No, wait, what's the award for TV? . . . Whatever . . . So he storms out of the delivery room and runs right into Vivienne, his old girlfriend, who's a nurse at the hospital. And they do that awkward running-into-an-ex thing except you can tell they both want to do each other right there. But then all the people from the apartment complex explosion are being wheeled in and Dr. Wheeler is running with Rachel on a stretcher, yelling, 'CODE BLUE!' Seriously, Jess, how can you not love this show?"

"Because it sucks," I say to myself. But my hating it never

stopped Marissa from giving me a blow-by-blow account of every episode, every week, always sending me a middle-of-the-night video of her recap. Watching her cheers me up, makes me feel like she's right here with me instead of someplace across the country where I can't reach her.

My phone buzzes next to my leg on the bed. It's Lucas again.

> Hey, are you home? I'm parked outside your house.

> What the . . . ?

> WHY???

> Can I come in to talk?

> Fine. Come around the side of the house to my window.

My heart pounds in my throat waiting. A few seconds later, he's outside my window, waving as if this is not super weird. I lift the window up and he folds his arms on the sill. Before I can say anything, he says, "I tried texting you before I came over."

"Yeah, and I didn't reply."

"I know," he admits with a half smile, half wince. A very cute one at that. "I've been parked outside your house for fifteen minutes. The porch light is off. But I really wanted to talk to you." He sucks air in through his teeth. "That sounded really creepy. You want me to go?" he asks, leaving it up to me.

I scratch my arm and huff as if the decision is harder than it actually is. "No. It's okay. But come in before Mrs. Alvarez sees you and thinks you're a peeper."

"Okay, I'll meet you at the front—"

"No! Come through the window. My mom's asleep," I say quietly so he knows to keep his voice down. "She goes to bed early."

"Okay. Pop the screen."

I unlock the screen and he removes it, resting it against the house. Then he pulls himself up through the window, his forearm muscles flexing from the effort, pulling in one foot then the other. I give him wide berth as he stumbles into my bedroom.

He falls back on my twin bed, leaning back against his elbows, his long legs hanging over the edge. He looks around my room with open curiosity. I try to see it through his eyes. A tapestry Marissa brought back for me from Mexico hangs over my bed. A corkboard over my desk is covered in dozens of pictures of Marissa, Ethan, and me over the years. There's one of the whole family too, when I'm about ten, before we all fell apart.

"So . . . why aren't you at the beach?" His eyes land on me.

"I'm still debating," I say.

"Why?"

"Why?" I fold my arms and lean my weight on one foot. If he really wants to do this, we'll do this. "Maybe because I've been trying to figure out why *you* didn't tell me last night when we were hanging out."

He sits up straighter. "I just forgot."

"Forgot?" I snap. "You know who found me to tell me? Pete. Not you. So maybe you didn't tell me because you didn't want me to come."

He bows his head and dangles his hands between his knees. With a deep sigh, he says, "You're right. I'm sorry."

My heart flattens. Maybe I liked it better when I just *thought* he didn't want me to come.

He looks up at me. "I've been dealing with some stuff. Well, anxiety issues, to be honest. For the past year. And lately I've had a few more flare-ups."

"Lately?" I ask.

He nods. Lately as in since he met me? Am I anxiety-inducing?

"I haven't been great with changes. Like, my body just can't handle them. Not yet, at least. That's why I'm staying home next year too. My therapist said even good stress is still stress. And I guess I've been feeling a lot of good stress around you."

"What's that even mean? Good stress?" I shake my head, not following.

"Good stress, meaning I like you."

"Oh." I sit down in my desk chair.

Lucas scratches the back of his head with a perplexed look on his face almost as if the words coming out of his mouth are so unscripted they surprise him as much as they do me. "I'm trying to figure it out," he continues. "Being around you is way better than not being around you, so I really don't know what my problem is. I mean, I do and I don't. Besides the anxiety . . . I have a new prescription for that though." His laugh is more of a confused "huh." But then he adds, "It just feels like . . . I don't know . . . like it's too soon for good things to be happening to me. Does that make sense?" He looks up at me now, with a bewildered expression that squeezes my heart, makes me want to rush over and hug him.

I nod. I know exactly what he means. Life continuing happily ever after without them feels like the greatest betrayal.

Then he cracks his knuckles.

"Now I'm thinking maybe I should've checked to see if you liked me too, *before* I dumped all this on you." His smile is so sweet, so vulnerable. It reminds me a little of Ethan's smile watching Marissa dance. My heart swells to the brink of bursting.

"The feeling is moochual." I imitate Teri Garr in *Young Frankenstein*. I know he'll get it and he does. His grin is uncontainable. It spilleth over.

"So." He cracks one knuckle after another. "I get that I screwed this up. But it's Friday night and according to my therapist, I'm supposed to work on trying to partake in healthy teenage activities. Which probably means you should too." This time his smile is more hesitant. "Come on," he presses. "It'll be fun."

I look at my window. An open invitation, reentry into the world.

"Reg and Pete are already there," he says as if that will sweeten the deal.

"Oh, well, okay, then. Why didn't you say so earlier?"

He stands up. "Wiseass. Come on."

He hops back out the window and holds out a hand to help me out. I stare at it for just a moment, but I already know I'm going to take it.

Sneaking out of my house is too easy, which is depressing because it reminds me that there's no one really keeping tabs on me.

But with each second I'm away from home, a heaviness lifts.

My heart starts to hum with excitement, looking at the open road ahead of us. With the car windows open, the fresh ocean air flows cool and sweet through my lungs.

We park on Beach 32nd and walk the rest of the way to the beach. I can see the orange flames from the boardwalk. Voices drift over to us in between the crashing of the waves. As we walk closer, I make out Reggie's and Pete's laughter.

"We're here!" Lucas calls, our footsteps muffled by the sand.

Pete and Reggie hoot and clap.

"About time!" Reggie says, raising her beer to toast us. She appears to have fallen in a ditch, only her head and white Converse break the surface of the sand line. Lucas stops at a cooler and grabs two beers, handing me one. We find a spot around the fire to sit down, cross-legged. His knee brushes up against mine as he settles in. I could move over an inch and give him more room . . . but I don't.

Pete crawls across the sand to reach us.

"Hey, rookie!" He lifts his beer. "Glad you made it. Sorry about this morning. I blame him." He points to Lucas.

Lucas leans around me to answer Pete. "I blame Socrates."

"We still buds?" he asks me. I nod and he slams his beer bottle into mine.

Pete leans around me again to address Lucas. "Car problem resolved?"

"Sorta." Lucas shrugs.

"What happened?" Pete asks.

"Tell you later." Lucas shakes his head and Pete nods in

understanding. They have the cryptic coded body language of best friends like Marissa and I used to. Eyebrows lift, shoulders shrug, all fillers for unspoken words. An entire conversation just took place between them.

A senior named Dominic throws a piece of driftwood on the bonfire; the flames undulate blue and lavender from the salt. People applaud like it's a magic trick. From across the bonfire, Reggie waves me over. "Jess! Come here!"

I get up and walk around the circle to her side and she slides over in her ditch, patting the empty space next to her.

"Beats lugging a chair, right? Try it out."

I ease in next to her. The sand hugs my body like I'm sitting in the palm of a giant's hand.

"Nice, right?"

"Very." I lean back against the sculpted incline. My feet are up at an ergonomically designed angle. "I never thought of digging out a recliner chair in the sand."

"Patent pending." She takes a sip of her beer, then leans closer. "I have good news."

I perk up. "I could use some of that."

"Enzo's accountant got us an extension. We're okay for now," she says. Then she nods across the fire at Joe, who has his arms wrapped around a girl sitting between his legs. She whispers in my ear. "Joe gave his two weeks' notice today. We can't fill his position yet, but I could give you a few more hours. Would that help?"

I nod. "A little more would be great. But why is Joe quitting?"

"Nikki's pregnant," she says. "I should've known something

was going on. He's been taking a lot of days off all of a sudden for doctor's appointments. Then the other day he was on his phone out back. Sounded like he was setting up an interview. He found something else, full-time with health insurance."

I look back over at the couple canoodling like they're the only people here. "They're so young though."

"Twenty," Reggie says. "Not like *16 and Pregnant* young, at least. They've been together for a while. This just pushes Joe to get his shit together, you know? He can't work at Enzo's forever. Not like me." She stares ahead at the black ocean. Whitecaps rushing the shore froth in the moonlight.

I laugh under my breath, in case she's joking. But I don't think she is. "You don't *have* to work at Enzo's, do you?" I ask.

She lifts a shoulder. "No." Gazing down at her left hand, she twirls the engagement ring on her finger with her thumb. Maybe the act of removing it off her finger is something she's not ready to do yet. Like my mom. "This was all supposed to be temporary. Just a little inconvenience. Then we were going to have our whole lives together."

Her eyes remain fixed on her ring, the whisper of a diamond swirling around and around.

"Want to hear the saddest story?" Without giving me a chance to answer, she imitates me, "Sure, Reggie! I *love* sad stories!" She looks down at her lap, laughing bitterly to herself.

"I'm listening," I tell her.

She tips the beer to her lips. "We were at a party, celebrating. Jason got into University of Alabama, with a really good scholarship. I mean, it doesn't get any better than Crimson Tide, right? A fucking dream come true."

I nod, even though I have no clue what Crimson Tide means. I know Jason played football, so I guess it has something to do with that.

"And theeeeen . . ." She smiles, the saddest smile yet. "I started thinking about him leaving me and the beer tears started flowing. How *ever* would I live without him?" She wiggles her fingers in the air dramatically. "I told him I didn't want him to go. And Jason, being Jason . . ." She takes a shaky breath.

Chatter and laughs mix together with the ocean's roar, but in our little ditch in the sand, all I can hear is Reggie's heartbreak.

She leans her head back and stares up at the stars. "The next day I told him I didn't mean it. But . . . he'd made up his mind."

"Probably because he really didn't want to leave you either," I offer.

"I should've made him. You know? I could've. But I was being selfish. I couldn't imagine living a year without him. And now . . ." She shakes her head against the sand and tips her beer back to her mouth.

We sit together in silence. I stare up at the inky blackness of the sky, puncture holes in the tapestry allowing pinpricks of light to shine through. I read somewhere that when you look at the stars, you're looking at the past. What we see with the naked eye is light from up to three thousand years ago. Even the stars that seem like fixed objects in the sky are illusions.

A distant memory comes back to me. Fourth of July, when

I was seven. My parents loaded Ethan and me in the car to see the fireworks at Coney Island. Dad bought us treats from the ice cream truck, Ethan a Good Humor Strawberry Shortcake bar, and a Bomb Pop for me because I wanted to taste the fireworks. Imagine my surprise when my ice pop tasted nothing like fireworks or red, white, and/or blue. It tasted like sugar water. Ethan reluctantly traded his ice cream for my Bomb Pop. He wasn't even a whole year older than me, but he was always my big brother.

Across the fire, Lucas turns away from a conversation with Pete at the same time I look across at him. He smiles and makes his way across the fire to join us.

Reggie climbs out of her sand La-Z-Boy. "Just remembered, I have to ask Pete something. Lucas, you can take my seat!"

She meanders around the fire.

"Subtle as a sledgehammer," Lucas mumbles, watching her walk away. Then he points to the seat next to me. "Plus, now I can't ask, 'Is this seat taken?'"

"All yours," I offer. He climbs in next to me, the confined space pressing us much closer together than when Reggie sat here.

"Sorry. Am I crushing you?" he asks, trying to inch away, but there's nowhere for him to go.

I shake my head. "I don't mind."

He looks over at my abandoned beer in the sand next to me.

"Do you need another one?"

"No." I shake my head again. "I don't really drink. I went to an Alateen meeting when my dad was in rehab a few years ago. Alcoholism runs in families. Red hair might not be the only thing I inherited from him, and I really don't want to test it and find out."

He looks embarrassed. "Oh . . . sorry. I wouldn't have shoved a beer at you if I knew."

"I'm okay," I tell him, and he smiles.

"Still better than staying home though, right?" he asks, cracking his knuckles with his thumb. He seems even more nervous than I am and my heart is trying to drill its way out of my chest.

"Way better," I tell him with a grateful smile. If I were home right now, I'd be reliving the past instead of making new memories.

Lucas wipes the sand off his hand on his jeans, then reaches over to carefully take mine in his. His hand is warm, big, strong.

He looks over at me and takes a nervous breath. "So . . . do you want to maybe hang out again, just the two of us?" He holds up our clasped hands.

His hand is so much bigger than mine. This shouldn't work. We shouldn't fit. But my hand slides into place like it belongs there.

I don't need to be alone anymore. I don't *want* to do this alone anymore.

I squeeze his hand. "Definitely."

Someone is shooting off fireworks farther down the beach. It doesn't matter that the Fourth of July is still months away. People love their fireworks, any excuse to set things on fire and watch them go boom. From here, I watch them ascend into the sky and waterfall down, bright and colorful.

As we watch the fireworks, Lucas lets go of my hand and wraps his arm around my shoulders. I nestle in to his warmth. Getting stuck in the now isn't so awful when the now is this good. But I allow my brain to unstick and fast-forward, imagining more times like this with Lucas. Days and nights that are more happy than unhappy.

Reggie's head darts up. She looks past us in alarm. "Guys, the cops are here."

"Shit." Joe bolts into action, throwing beer bottles in the cooler to hide them. He grabs a bucket and heads to the shore to fill it with water to put the fire out. Kevin and Dominic each grab a handle of the cooler and take off into the night with it.

"Party's over," Lucas says to me, reaching a hand to pull me out of the ditch.

Pete sways over, hands in his pockets. His lids hang heavy like store awnings. "I need a ride home," he slurs. "I'll leave my car here tonight."

"Sure," Lucas says.

Everyone scatters like cockroaches. The night may have started crappy and ended too soon, but it was still pretty perfect.

Jess

Maybe my crappy job won't be so crappy anymore now that Lucas and I are a "thing." (Exactly what that thing IS is TBD, but still!)

What base is holding hands? Negative first? Is that even dating?

Kiss the girl already, man!

Everyone at work the next day is weirdly chill, which makes me start to think maybe nothing really happened last night. Maybe it was all in my head.

About an hour into my shift, Joe holds up a bottle of weed killer.

"See if you can find more of these in the back."

When I get to the bay of shelves in the back of the warehouse that has all the lawn and weed supplies, I find Lucas grabbing a box of Roundup.

"Joe asked me to get those," I say, hands on hips.

"He asked me too. I think he's up to something," Lucas answers, lifting the box onto his shoulders.

A little while later as I'm restocking light bulbs, Joe's voice comes over the intercom.

"Jess, Lucas, please report to the break room."

When Lucas and I both show up, there's a tin of Altoids and a tube of ChapStick on the table. Joe's phone is lying between them playing "Let's Get It On," by Marvin Gaye.

Lucas pockets the Altoids. "Someone's suddenly got too much time on his hands now that he gave his notice."

Pete comes in late, closer to noon. The only person who doesn't know it's because of his hangover is Enzo.

I walk over to Pete and Lucas at the paint center. Pete's sitting on the stool staring at the paint shaker like the vibrating can is the most riveting thing he's ever seen.

"This is about all I can handle today," he admits, stopping the machine to take the can out. He takes his bottle of water from under the counter and chugs. Wiping his lips with the back of his hand, he says, "Hey, let's go bowling tonight."

"You sure? You don't look so hot," I point out. He's as white and waxy as the day he had that stomach bug.

He scrunches up his face, dismissing my concern. "I'll be fine by then."

Lucas turns to me. "You want to?"

"Yeah," I say, trying to hide my enthusiasm. "I haven't bowled in a while though. Do they still have gutter guards?"

"Yeah, for *five-year-olds*," Pete answers. Propping his elbow on the counter to hold his head up, he adds, "Someone tell Reg. I'm not ready to move yet." He closes his eyes and moans.

Lucas's hand grazes my back. "I'll tell her," he says. "So I'll pick you up tonight?"

I smile and nod. "Sure."

Lisa Loeb's one hit from the nineties, "Stay," plays through the speakers. A pregnant woman stops to collect paint chips, different shades of pink, murmuring the words to the song while holding a hand over her belly. A lump forms in my throat. I really don't know why that song and those pink paint chips and that pregnant woman are making me choke up like this. It's a mixed bag of sad and happy, all swirling together.

For the first time in a while, I like being a cog in our neighborhood. I like belonging again.

When I get home from work, Mom's not sitting in her chair watching the Food Network. She's not at the table, where there's still a stack of bills. I check in her bedroom; she's not in bed either. Panic threads through my veins. I'm about to run out the door to ask Mrs. Alvarez if she's seen her today when I see a note on the kitchen table.

> Jess,
> I went out to run an errand.
> xo
> Mom

I should be happy, but the thought of my mother out on her own fills me with panic. The last time she went out alone didn't end well.

"Everywhere I go, I see him," she sobbed that day the neighbor brought her home after finding her crying on her front stoop.

I understood what she meant. I see Ethan everywhere too, especially in the hallways at school. But my grief is different from my mother's. Losing Ethan was like losing the best part of my memories, my database, every picture in my mental hard drive . . . gone. Losing a child is an entirely different beast.

I channel my nervous energy into cleaning up while she's out. Opening the windows, I take out the vacuum and run it around the house. Then I take a rag and wipe down the surfaces. When I get to the end table next to her chair, it's what I *don't* see that startles me.

Her rings are gone.

Searching on my hands and knees, I check under the couch. They must have rolled under, somewhere.

Did they get sucked up in the vacuum?

Minutes later, Mom comes home to me sprawled on the floor, my hand shoved deep into the open vacuum bag. The floors and I are covered in grit.

She stares at me, mouth open.

"Hi," I say, forcing a smile.

I can tell by her weary expression that the outing took its toll on her.

"I'm going to lie down for a bit," she says, heading for her bedroom, too exhausted to ask me what I'm doing elbow-deep in hairballs and dust.

Her bedroom door shuts. I dump the bag upside down.

No rings.

It's not until after I replace the vacuum bag and clean up the mess I made that I think maybe Mom just decided to put the rings back on. I could've saved myself a lot of mess by just waiting half an hour.

I stop by Mom's room to see if the rings are back on her finger. She's curled on her side, her shoulders shivering under the blankets. I take a step closer.

"Mom? Are you cold?"

I hear her soft sob, a gasp, the crinkling of something clutched in her fist. I reach over and take the slip from her hand.

It's from a pawnshop, with my mother's name, address, and items she pawned off.

Rose-gold wedding band. Engraved: "My love, my life, my friend."

White-gold engagement ring, 0.40 carat.

I crawl next to her on the bed, hugging her from behind. "It's okay, Mom. It's not like you needed them anymore." I don't even tell her what I really think, that she should have pawned them off as soon as he left us.

She shakes her head, her hair rasping against her pillow. "It's just one thing after another! I can't do this anymore," she cries.

I'm not entirely sure what she means by that, but her words feel like ominous dark clouds. That sinking-in-quicksand feeling is back. It's up to my eyeballs, suffocating me.

Lucas

My jaw works overtime to break down this rubbery steak; even the bottled marinade couldn't save this meal. I'm secretly looking forward to a burger at the bowling alley later.

Dinner as a family is more of a recent thing, especially on a Saturday night, when Jason and I both used to be out with our friends. But now we all try a little harder to find time together.

Tonight, though, no one's talking. It was easier when Jason was here. There was always something interesting going on in his life to talk about. When it gets this quiet, it's as if I can hear my parents' thoughts, hear Jason's name rolling around in their heads. Maybe they don't even notice how bad the food is because all they can think about is how empty our lives are without him.

"So . . . I have news," I say, sawing into my steak. "Ummm . . . so . . . there's this girl . . ."

Dad's head jerks a little, surprised, but he keeps chewing with a smile on his face, waiting for me to go on. Unlike Mom.

"Is that why you snuck out in such a hurry last night?" she asks, refilling her glass of iced tea from the pitcher.

"I didn't sneak out. I *told* you I was going out," I remind her. She smiles at me, but it's a smile that tells me that's not how she chooses to remember it. Dad clears his throat. Clutching his fork tightly in his giant hand, he scoops peas and carrots and raises them to his mouth before they spill back on his plate.

"What's her name?" he asks.

"Jess," I say.

"Jess?" Mom asks. "Jess who?"

"Jess Nolan. You don't know her," I say. "She's a junior."

"Oh." Mom nods. "But . . . Nolan . . . wasn't there a boy—?"

"Yeah." I cut off the unnecessary end of that sentence.

Mom turns to my father, who's busy cutting into his steak and avoiding her eyes.

I pop a piece of meat in my mouth just as she turns to me. "I don't know if this is a good idea, Lucas."

"Why not?" I manage to squeeze out the words around a mouthful of food.

She shrugs and spears her steak. "I don't know. To me, it sounds like it would be too painful, for both of you."

Dad turns to Mom, treading carefully. "I don't think it's a bad thing, hon. They could support each other."

Mom chews. Inhaling through her nostrils, she swallows and says, "Maybe. But I think we should ask Dr. Engel what he thinks."

Now I'm pissed. "Not that it matters one way or another, but I already talked to Dr. Engel about this. I *like* Jess. I'm happy when I'm around her. I mean, that *is* what you guys want for me, right?"

It's silent again for the rest of the meal. Dad and Mom are shooting each other looks that only married couples understand. All I know is, I lost my appetite. This is Jason and Reggie all over again. Well, maybe a little less extreme since Jason and Reggie were engaged when things escalated with Mom and Dad. But still.

"I'm done." I turn to head upstairs, more done than they can imagine. I leave my MSG steak on the table, half-eaten.

In my room, I shut the door. Slamming would be more satisfying, but the high pile of the wall-to-wall carpeting makes us a slam-free home. I grab Jason's football and flop back on my bed, tossing the ball up in the air and catching it as their voices drift upstairs, still discussing me and my life as if I'm not old enough to move out right now if I wanted to.

Their murmuring grows louder. My parents don't have big blowout arguments, but I can hear the tightness in Mom's voice, even if I can't make out what she's saying. My father usually backs down. But tonight, he's flexing a muscle in his voice. Cabinets shut with force, the pots clang a little louder, but the fight is over.

His muffled footsteps lumber upstairs, socks on carpeting. A smaller person might be able to sneak up the stairs. My dad, even without shoes, still rattles every floorboard.

He knocks first, something I always appreciate about him.

"Lucas?" He pops his head in. "Can I come in?" He fills my doorway, waiting for permission, as if he's not the guy paying the mortgage on this house every month.

I wave him in and he walks around the room, still in his wrinkled work pants and shirt, hands on his hips. Jason's Corner is a magnet, and no matter how hard you try, you can't avoid staring at it. Especially Dad.

"So, about Jess. You like her?" he asks, his back not quite to me, pulling an orphaned nail out of the wall with his fingers.

My father is not the touchy-feely-talky type. We talk, but sometimes the only way he can get through a serious conversation is by distracting himself with some DIY project, or the knobs on the grill, or the nozzle of a gas pump. We had the sex talk while he changed the oil filter in the car.

"Yeah," I say, trying to make my voice sound as resolute as possible. "I mean, Dad . . . it's like . . . I don't even know if we're *dating* yet. I was just trying to make conversation at dinner." I gesture with my hand out the door. "I didn't expect to hear that I need my therapist's permission to like a girl."

"I know . . . we don't know everything, Lucas. I'm sure you figured that out by now. We make mistakes. Lots of them." He exhales. It's not a sigh I get to hear often. It's a white-flag kind of sigh. "Look, if you guys *do* start dating . . . whatever that means these days . . . your mom and I would like to meet her. Invite her over for dinner so we can get to know her."

That's it? Jason's arguments about Reggie went on for months.

Dad reaches over and picks up the picture of Jason and Reggie. Now he fully has his back to me.

"We gave your brother too much grief over her," he says, his shoulders collapsing under the weight of pretty much everything.

Once again, my brother had to take a hit for me to keep on living.

The bowling alley is full of sensory overload. Bowling balls spin down waxed alleys, pins crash, the air reeks of greasy food and shoe deodorizer . . . but what oppresses the senses most is the grating pop song blasting over the speakers. Reggie seems to be the only one enjoying the music, singing along, "Oh, baby baby . . . Oh, baby baby . . ."

She admires her shoes as her toes tap against the floor to the beat. "What is it about bowling shoes? They're so comfortable."

Pete holds his ball up to his chest in deep concentration, then storms the foul line in his three-step drop-to-a-knee move his uncle taught him when he was a kid. It's equal parts highly choreographed and embarrassing but Pete swears by it. The ball races down the center of the lane looking like a strike, but at the last second spins off to the left, leaving Pete with a tough spare.

He punches his fist in the air. "Oooh! Snake eyes! The dreaded seven-ten split!" He spins around to face us. "Bet you five bucks I got this."

I pull a five out of my pocket. "On."

Pete rests his hands on his hips and turns to Reggie. She shakes her head.

"Why? Scared you'll lose?" he challenges her.

With a bored expression, she takes a sip of her soda. "Nah. I just don't give a shit."

Pete waits for the ball return to spit out his "lucky" green ball. Then he holds it up to his chest, studying his targets, visualizing the two pins going down (he's told me his technique). He doesn't get the spare—the ball slips into the gutter at the last second.

Pete curses his way back to us. "Game over," Reggie announces glancing up at the scoreboard. "Smells Like Teen Spirit" is blasting, a much better nineties selection. "Anyone want to play another game?" Reggie offers in a voice that begs us to say no.

"Where's our food?" Pete looks around for our waiter. We ordered burgers at the beginning of the game and they never showed up.

I slurp my ice in response, looking around the bowling alley for the umpteenth time, hoping Jess will show up. Reggie's eyes narrow.

"Just call her," Reggie demands.

"I *did*. She said she didn't think she could come but if something changed she'd meet us here."

"Call her *again!*"

"Why? Obviously nothing's changed since the last time I talked to her."

A group in the lane next to ours are bombed. Our burgers may be MIA, but their waiter hasn't missed one opportunity to refill their pitcher of beer. Two of them start going at it. Their voices rise, but only a few words drift over to us.

A tall, skinny guy with a hooked nose and a pronounced overbite stands up from his chair, splaying his arms back and puffing out his chest, more rooster than human. He walks over to another guy, round and pink. Swine to his friend's fowl, friend turned foe. It's *Animal Farm*.

"It was *my* shit, asshole. You had no right!" Rooster Man says.

Pig Face is angry, but cautious. "Phil, you're being stupid. Sit down and shut up."

Next to Phil's empty seat, a woman is for some reason knitting a blue blanket. Only now she's just holding the knitting needles and yelling, "What is *wrong* with you two?"

It's the yelling combined with the surreal out-of-context image of that woman knitting in a bowling alley that starts to mess with me, triggers that out-of-body moment where I don't feel here or there. Like standing outside a window watching my life acted out by someone else.

Watching their heated exchange, my body tenses, my breathing becomes more difficult, my lungs less obliging to do their job.

Phil grabs his jacket and shoves his arms through his sleeves. "Go fuck yourself, Nick." He jabs at Nick's chest; Nick flinches as if the finger is a weapon. Phil's eyes are sticks of dynamite ready to detonate.

After he leaves, Nick shakes his head in disbelief. His group tries to laugh it off, but no one is doing a great job of it. Least of all, me.

Wiping my damp palms down my jeans, I feel the tightening in my chest. I bolt up out of my seat. Reggie looks up at me. "You okay?"

I lie. "Yeah. Fine. Just . . ."

I look at the front of the bowling alley, to the big windows. Outside the entrance, Phil is smoking a cigarette. He didn't leave. He's going to come back in and when he does . . .

"We should go." My voice is too loud, even in the bowling alley. It echoes in my ears.

Pete protests. "We didn't get our food yet."

"I don't care." I slip my arms through the sleeves of my hoodie. "You coming?"

Reggie pats the seat next to her. "I see the waiter coming with our burgers. Just wait. After we eat, we'll all go." She cranes her neck to follow the waiter's trek.

My body won't let me sit. It's spring-loaded to flee, to run and hide, before Phil comes back.

"I can't. I'm sorry," I blurt out before rushing out of the bowl-ing alley. I have to pass Phil and for a quick second the logical side of my brain chimes in, telling me his secondhand smoke is probably presenting more of a hazard to my well-being than any retaliation plan he's hatching right now.

Inside my car, with the doors locked, my anxiety ebbs. I rest my head against the steering wheel, wondering if I'll ever really be okay again.

Then I sit up, turn the key in the ignition, and back out of my spot. I know where I want to be and who I want to be with.

At a red light, I text Jess.

Done with bowling. Can I come by?

Meet me at my window.

When I get to her house, she's waiting for me by her open window, biting the corner of her lip. I reach my arm toward her. "Ready?"

Her face explodes in a grin and any fears I had of her regretting last night evaporate into the warm night breeze. She grabs my hand.

"Is your mom sleeping?" I whisper, my hands on her waist to help her out her window.

Her eyes that were just shining with excitement dim. "Yeah . . . finally," she says. We crouch down low through the narrow alley between her house and Mrs. Alvarez's.

"Where are we going?" she asks inside the car as I pull away from the curb. Her barely there scent fills the car, vanilla and some kind of unpretentious flower. Shampoo, probably, but it's a perfect Jess scent.

My heart thrums to a different beat than it did at the bowling alley. It's an excited, hopeful rhythm.

"I have an idea." I grin.

I drive back to the beach, where we were just yesterday. The boardwalk is still bustling with people strolling, soaking up spring air. As we walk down the steps to the sand, Jess stops to pick up some rocks. We walk over to the lifeguard stand and climb up so if anyone else has the same idea that a night like this needs to be savored at the beach, under the moonlit sky, at least they won't trip over us.

Jess points to my feet dangling over the edge. "I see you take bowling very seriously."

I flex my feet, still in the hideous bowling shoes. "I kinda forgot to return them."

"*How* is that possible?" she asks, a tickle of a giggle in her voice.

I groan, dragging a hand down my face. "Long story. I left

abruptly." Then I turn to her. "So, what happened tonight? Why didn't you come?"

She hops the rocks in her hand, watching them bounce. "Family stuff."

I wait for more. When she doesn't say anything, I shoulder-bump her.

"Hey."

"Hey back." She smiles.

"Is it something you want to talk about?" I ask.

She shakes her head and looks down at the rocks in her hand.

"Okay," I sigh. "It's just . . . is it me?"

Her head darts up at that. "What? No."

"You sure? Not to be paranoid but . . . You were all psyched about going until you weren't."

She shakes her head again, her lips pinched. "Not about you. Promise." She tears her eyes away from her rocks and meets my questioning gaze. "My mom's been having a tough time since Ethan died. Some days are bad. Today was a . . . *really* bad day. I didn't want to leave her."

"Oh. Was it okay you left her tonight then?"

"She was asleep," she answers. "When she doesn't want to deal, she sleeps."

"So . . . are *you* okay?" I ask.

She tilts her head back against the chair and closes her eyes, inhaling. A smile spreads across her face. "So much better now," she says. I get it. The salt air, the beach. It washes everything away.

I lean back against the seat. Her hand dangles next to her leg, inviting me to take it, so I do. She threads her fingers through mine.

The fiery panic from the bowling alley is gone, smothered under the weight of pure bliss. The only thing better than sitting on the beach under the stars is sharing it with Jess. We tilt our heads back up to face the night sky again. I inhale, picturing the therapeutic salt air sweeping through my body, cleansing every vessel.

"I wish I could live on the beach."

"You could get a job as a lifeguard," she offers, gesturing to our chair like a game show model.

I laugh. "What? And give up my sweet gig at Enzo's? You know we get a twenty-percent employee discount there, right?"

She gasps and covers her mouth with her hand. "Twenty percent? I think *someone* must've forgotten to tell me that during my . . . '*orientation*.'" She lets go of my hand so she can make air quotes with her fingers.

I wrap my arm around her shoulders, watching her face, how it lifts when she's happy.

The waves swooshing in the night are soothing, calming. If there was ever a perfect moment for a kiss, it's right now. I turn in my seat, pulling her closer. Anticipating my move, she rushes forward to meet me, lifting her face up to mine.

I want to say in the history of kisses, ours will be the one sonnets will be written about. But that's not what happens. The word you never want to hear when you kiss someone is "Ow!"

Our noses don't just bump into each other, they smash and

grind. A sound like a knuckle cracking emits from deep inside my nose.

We both lean back, cupping our noses. I'm terrified if I pull my hand away I'll see blood. Jess's eyes tear from the sudden impact.

And then . . . she bursts out laughing. Cracking up so hard I grab her sleeve so she doesn't flail herself right off the lifeguard chair and make a humiliating moment even worse.

"Are you okay?" I ask her. Maybe I smashed her nose into her brain and did some damage.

"Oh . . . my . . . God!" She gasps. "I'm so sorry!"

Pinching my nose to straighten it, because I'm pretty sure our collision knocked it out of alignment, I ask, "What are you apologizing for? I'm the one who nearly took you out!" Now we're both laughing.

She wipes the tears before they spill out of her eyes. "I mean," she gasps, "I knew my first kiss would probably be a disaster, but holy crap!" She stops to catch her breath. "I had no idea we'd both end up wounded in action!"

I sober, just slightly. "Your first kiss?" I tilt my head. "Really?"

She shrugs one shoulder and side-eyes me. "Maybe?"

I wrap an arm around her shoulder again and she nestles into me. We're both scrunching our faces up, twisting our lips from side to side to realign our noses with our faces. "Well, if that's the case, there's an old saying that applies to this situation."

Nuzzled up next to me, she asks. "Yeah? What?"

"When you fall off a horse . . ." I let the rest dangle.

She giggles. "Oh *please* . . . go on, Grandpa. I'm intrigued.

Which one of us is the horse in this saying of yours? You, or me?"

I laugh. "I mean if you fall off, you have to get back on again. So . . . just let me know when you're ready to try again, that's all."

We stare up at the stars for a few minutes, quietly. So quietly that it almost knocks me out of my seat when Jess announces, "Ready!"

Her face tilts up to mine, expectantly. I reach my hand up to cup her cheek and a snort/giggle escapes from her lips.

"I'm not kissing you until you stop laughing. I can't handle any more humiliation tonight," I tell her, willing to wait this one out.

She presses her lips together and nods, forcing herself to take this seriously. "Aye, aye, Captain," she says, and giggles again. She shakes her head like she's trying to knock the giggles out, then nods. "Okay, *now* I'm good."

I lean in carefully this time, watching as her eyes sparkle. Our lips touch, softly at first. My hand runs through her hair, soft and smooth. Her hand grabs my jacket in a fierce grip, holding on like she might never let go.

Jess

Sha la la la la la, my oh my!

We've gotten much better at this kissing thing. No more injured septums!

Heading to work now but will write more later.

It's the last day in April and our Lawn and Garden Department is a hub of activity. Pete says it's always like this; the first really warm Sunday brings out all the ambitious gardeners. I can barely keep the shelves stocked. Customers keep stopping me to ask where we keep the lawn seed, the fertilizer, the spreaders. It gives me an idea. Instead of taking my break, I arrange a lawn-care display at the end of the aisle.

A woman comes in, hair in a ponytail, the knees of her jeans covered in mud. She stops to look at my display.

"Oh, good," she says, grabbing a small bag of lawn seed. Then she grabs a handheld seed spreader and a sprinkler. "Need these too."

A man flanked by two older women rushes through the store a little while later, talking almost as briskly as he's walking.

"When we got off the cruise ship, the rain was coming down so hard, lizards were running across the street on their hind legs, like they were holding their skirts up out of the water! I kid you not! Lizards! A parade of them! I'm telling you, it was a deluge, for six days straight. It's like I took a vacation on Noah's ark. Then I come back to *cockroaches* in my kitchen. I don't know which I hate more: lizards or cockroaches!" He turns to me. "Where's the Raid?"

I open my mouth to answer him, but he's distracted by my display. "Oh, while I'm here . . ." He grabs an oscillating sprinkler and a small bag of seed in the other; then he power walks off with his friends to find Raid.

I'm restocking the display after a few more people picked it over, when Reggie walks by. She stares for a moment, her eyes sharp, critical. I think she's about to tear into me for not clearing this with her first. Pointing at the display, she snaps, "This makes so much sense. Why haven't we been doing aisle caps all along?"

I didn't even know this kind of display had a name.

The best part about working at a small independently owned hardware store is Enzo does whatever he wants. On Sundays, he closes early to spend time with his family. At two, Enzo turns the sign over to CLOSED and Lucas drives me home.

"Want to do something later?" he asks, pushing a strand of hair behind my ear.

"Maybe," I say, and nod to the house. I don't go into too much detail about my mother, but he seems to get what I mean by "maybe" without making it about him. I appreciate that more than he probably realizes.

The past two weeks have been great with Lucas. We already have our own secret language, the smile, the head nod. *Meet me in the back.* Timing it so we're not walking to the warehouse at the same time. "We have to stop running into each other like this," Lucas said today as we accidentally ran into each other's lips, repeatedly, then sped off in opposite directions before anyone would notice.

They noticed.

Now that I'm home, I feel my shoulder muscles tightening from the mulch delivery. I open my nightstand drawer to find the ibuprofen I bought a week or so ago. Underneath layers of junk— Kit Kat wrappers, flyers from school, a cell phone bill (did I pay this?)—I find pamphlets.

Not long after the night at the Balcony, Mrs. Walker, the school psychologist, called me down to her office . . . me, and half the student body, each of us allotted an entire period to talk about how we were doing since the shooting. Some kids you couldn't keep out of her office. Other kids had to be practically dragged out of their classrooms for their meetings. I was, obviously, in the latter group.

It wasn't Mrs. Walker's fault that I didn't say much. I couldn't help thinking there was nothing I was going to tell her that a hundred other kids hadn't already said. *I'm sad. I miss Ethan. My best friend isn't coming back to school. I don't understand why this happened.* Plus, every time I looked up, someone new was peeking in at us through the door window, weepy-eyed and desperate for Mrs. Walker to help guide them through their grief. Their big sad eyes on me made me feel like a bug caught under glass. I forfeited the rest of my time; they seemed to need her more than I did.

Mrs. Walker told me to make an appointment to see her whenever I needed or wanted to talk. Then she handed me a bunch of pamphlets: "Helping Children Feel Safe in Unsafe Times," "Coping with Trauma," and "Starting the Healing." I've read them, a bunch of times, and still haven't found useful advice that speaks specifically to my family situation: "What to Do When Your Mother Won't Get Out of Bed."

I fold a brochure into a paper airplane the way my father taught Ethan and me when we were kids and launch it across the room. It sails in a loop before fittingly crashing to the floor.

I dig a little deeper into my drawer for another form of pain relief. A tiny roach Domie let me keep the other morning. I grab the lighter from my drawer and spark it. Three hits. It's just enough to cut the edge.

The buzz starts to settle in when Lucas texts me.

Hey.

> Hey back at you.

What are you doing?

> Staring at the ceiling. You're interrupting.

Ha. So, I have an idea.

> I have a million of those. I plan to tell you every single one.

> Ready?

Okay, you're being weird.

You're just noticing this? Not very observant of you.

I'm having second thoughts about asking you out on a date now.

A date? You buried the lede! What kind of date?

Can I come by and surprise you?

Sure. I'm a fly by the seat of her pants kind of girl . . . said this girl, never. Tell me. I'm not great with surprises.

I get it. Okay. Well, it's kind of cheesy but in a good way I think.

Pizza?

Ha! No. Cheesy like a sunset cruise around the harbor. I thought it sounded kind of fun.

That's actually really sweet. I'm in.

Cool. Pick you up in half an hour?

Sure. Can we get pizza first though? I'm kinda hungry now that you brought it up.

I didn't, YOU did. But sure. See you in a couple.

LUCAS

I race downstairs, in a hurry to pick up Jess.

"Lucas?" Mom comes out of the kitchen wiping her hands on a dish towel. "Did you ask Jess about dinner?" Her smile is too eager-to-please.

"Not yet," I say.

"Really? Why not?"

"Because . . . it's just . . . I don't know. I'll ask her." I throw my hands up in the air.

"How's Tuesday?"

"We both work late Tuesday."

"Well, maybe Wednesday? After Dr. Engel," she presses. I really think she's getting ahead of herself. No one invites the girl they like over to meet the parents for dinner this soon. If Mom is trying to make up for all the grief she and my dad gave Jason about Reggie, then the pendulum swung too far in the opposite direction.

"I'll see." I avoid answering her.

She throws the dish towel over her shoulder and huffs. "Well, you tell me what day works for her, then."

I know how much it sucks to walk around with sandbags of guilt hanging around your neck. As I'm tying my sneakers, I give in.

"I'm actually heading out now to see her. I'll ask her. Okay?"

Mom watches me tie my shoelaces. "Didn't you just see her at work?"

"Yep," I answer. "That was work though."

The TV blasts from the den. Dad calls out, "Lucas! Yankees are playing Cardinals!"

Mom gestures to the den. "The game's on," she says, as if she has any interest in the game.

I kiss her on the forehead and grab the keys off the peg on the wall. "If I stay and watch the game, how will I ever find out what night Jess can come over for dinner?"

She snaps the dish towel at me, whacking me in the butt as I'm leaving. "Wise guy. Where are you two going anyway?"

I shake my keys in my hands, anxious to head out without any further interrogating.

"Sunset cruise around the harbor."

Mom's face goes soft, relaxing all those stressed-out lines that pressed into her skin after Jason died. My mother is dropping her guard right before my eyes.

"Oooh," she coos. "That's really sweet." Then she adds. "Be careful," because if she doesn't say it every time I walk out that door some awful thing might slip through in between the cracks and ruin our lives. I can't blame her for thinking this way. It's already happened to us once.

"How have I lived here all of my life and never done this before? I mean, LOOK! That's the Statue of Liberty!" Jess points over the boat railing, her face awestruck.

I'm really patting myself on the back for this one. Jess is having way more fun than I expected. All around us, everyone's snapping pictures on their phones, then tapping on their screens to post them on Snapchat, Facebook, Twitter, Instagram, whatever. The only two people who haven't taken one picture yet are Jess and me. And it's not because we're jaded New Yorkers who see this shit all the time. It's the exact opposite. It's because we've taken this for granted all of our lives and want to really experience it now.

The cruise took off from the pier at Forty-Second Street. We watched the sun set as we sailed under the Brooklyn Bridge. Jess finally took her sunglasses off when there wasn't a lick of sun left. Now the boat is sailing around Ellis Island, giving us a close-up view of the Statue of Liberty's glowing green robe, her lantern blazing against the night sky, the New York skyline lit up behind her like it's ready to party.

Jess takes a potato chip out of the bag and crunches on it. "Can you believe I have *never* been to the Statue of Liberty? Crazy, right? Look at it! It's right in our backyard!" Her overabundance of enthusiasm blends in with everyone else's, except theirs is booze-infused. Turns out the harbor cruise is a bit of a party boat. Everyone's drinking around us.

"Or the Empire State Building. What kind of bullshit is *that*?" she asks. It seems like a rhetorical question, so I shrug. "People come from all around the world to go to the observation deck." She grabs my hand. "Let's do that next, okay?"

"Okay." I nod, trying to figure out her weird mood.

"We can't take it for granted, you know? It's what everyone does. You think, it's always going to be there, so there's no rush. I don't want to do that anymore." Her attention seems a little gummy tonight, sticking to the oddest things. Then she goes quiet, her eyes still darting along the skyline, soaking it all in.

I think I understand her meandering train of thought. Up until a year ago, my biggest problems with my brother were his farts and his snoring. Never ever would I have imagined him not being in my life. Maybe Jess's right about not taking *anything* for granted. You just never know anymore.

Jess takes her phone out and taps at the screen. I look over her shoulder; she pulled up "12 Fascinating Facts About the Statue of Liberty."

"Did you know Lady Liberty wears a size 879 shoe?" She glances down at my feet. "That's even bigger than yours."

"Marginally," I add.

A man dances by holding up two beers, one in each hand. He wears a wide-brimmed hat that looks better suited for Australia's outback, not a cruise ship sailing around New York Harbor.

"Hey-oh!" He dances back our way. Pointing to Jess's phone in her hand, he asks, "Want me to take a picture of you two?"

I'm about to say no, when Jess shoves her phone at him. "Yes please!"

He hands me a beer and then licks the froth off his thumb before taking Jess's phone. Jess wraps her arms around my waist. "Say CHEESY!" she says, which elicits a shrieky, over-the-top laugh from her. Outback and I swap again, beer for phone, and he dances off to his friends.

Jess looks at the picture of us, grinning.

"Hey. I need to ask you something."

"'Kay." She uses her thumb and forefinger to zoom in on the picture.

"Can you come over for dinner with my parents Wednesday night?"

Her head snaps up, her smile vanished. Now I have her attention.

"Why?" she asks, alarmed.

"They want to meet you," I say, feeling incredibly stupid now.

She blinks a few times and licks her lips.

"Are you okay?" I ask.

"I'm thirsty," she says. She digs in her pockets for money.

"Jess, if you don't want to come, it's okay. I'll come up with something."

"No! I want to come. I'll come," she decides, nodding furiously.

"You're weirded out. I can tell."

She nods. "Yeah, but in a good way. In a really good, really cheesy way. You just surprised me, that's all." Her smiles stretches like elastic across her face.

"I like this extra-cheesy side of you," she adds, and leans up on her toes to peck me on the cheek.

Jess

So I'm thinking skull-and-crossbones tee and Daisy Dukes to meet the BF's parents? Très chic, non? And who the hell meets the parents this soon anyway? That's just weird! What next? Curtain shopping? China patterns?

Shit, I hope they like me. Shit, I hope I don't drop a bunch of $!@!%&-bombs in front of them.

Smoothing my hair down, I stare at my reflection, pinching my cheeks for color. I turn halfway around to inspect my outfit. The jeans don't have any holes in them, and the T-shirt doesn't advertise any kind of drug, crime, foul language, or perverse graphic.

If Marissa were around, she would've been here hours ago to help me get ready. She would be hugely disappointed in my choice of clothes. Even I am, and my standards are pretty low to begin with. Staring at my reflection, I scowl back at my scowl. We could go on like this all night.

The front door opens. Good, Mrs. Alvarez is here. I asked her to come stay with Mom. She hasn't been doing great since the wedding-ring meltdown.

"Jessica! I made too many stuffed peppers! I'm putting them in the refrigerator!"

I rush into the kitchen to get her to stop shouting. I don't want Mom to wake up yet, not until after Lucas comes to get me.

Too late. Mom comes out of the bedroom. Hugging herself, she pads into the kitchen to join us.

As Mom takes a seat at the table, Mrs. Alvarez looks her up and down, taking in Mom's rumpled nightgown, her unbrushed hair. Pinching her lips, Mrs. Alvarez looks at me with angry eyes. She opens her mouth to say something; I shake my head. Not tonight.

She settles for an irritated huff of air through her nostrils. "Nicole. I made stuffed peppers. You're going to eat one. No arguments." Her voice is firm, scolding.

"Fine," Mom says, rubbing her face.

But then Mrs. Alvarez can't hold her tongue a second longer.

"Why are you still in your nightgown?" Mrs. Alvarez presses.

Mom props her elbows on the table and puts her hands on her cheeks to hold herself upright. "I haven't been able to get out of bed. I tried. I really did. It's like my body has a mind of its own."

Mrs. Alvarez marches out of the kitchen. The medicine cabinet squeaks open and closed. She comes back with the Zoloft and puts it on the table in front of Mom.

"You need to start taking these again so you get your energy back," she says.

I know Mrs. Alvarez means well, but Zoloft aren't multivitamins. Before I can say anything though, there's a knock on the door.

Mom looks up at us, confused.

"It's for me," I tell her.

"Who is it?" she asks.

"Lucas," Mrs. Alvarez answers for me, her eyes lighting up at just the mention of his name, the way they did when I first introduced Lucas to her.

"Who's Lucas?" Mom asks, looking between us.

I open my mouth but Mrs. Alvarez cuts me off again. "Jessica's boyfriend," she says with a huge smile, the kind Marissa would have when she was talking about a boy.

Mom turns to me with a betrayed look. "Boyfriend?"

"It's really new," I try to explain.

Lucas knocks on the door again.

"Where are you going?" she asks.

"Dinner at his house. Which is super bizarro because we just started dating. I'll be back later," I call over my shoulder, squeezing out the door sideways to meet Lucas.

On the front porch, I pull the door shut firmly behind me and smile. "Hi."

"Hi." He looks past me. Terrified, I follow his gaze, afraid Mom followed me out like a ghost trying to trap me inside the house with her for eternity. At the living room window, Mrs. Alvarez has pushed aside the curtain to watch us. She waves at both of us now with a big grin. I wave back and take his hand.

"Let's go." I tug him away from my house.

Lucas is my escape. I want to take him as far away from this place as possible so these two parts of my life don't meet. Not yet. Maybe not ever.

He holds the passenger door open for me and I climb in. It's not until we pull away from the curb that I start to relax.

He's quiet for a few minutes, eyes darting over at me with a look I can't quite grasp.

"How's your mom doing?" he asks. It feels like he's tiptoeing around the bigger question, like maybe why I didn't invite him into my house like any normal girlfriend. I can't see a future where Lucas will ever be invited to dinner at my house. But what if *normal* is what Lucas wants, what he expects?

There's no way I was going to let him see my mother that way, in her nightgown at six o'clock on a Wednesday night. Or worse, see how angry and hurt I am because of her, for giving up, for leaving me behind, for thinking she's the only one who lost Ethan. I adjust the strap of my seat belt, avoiding him, this conversation, the honest truth.

"She's okay," I lie, pumping the brakes on the conversation.

When we stop at a red light, he reaches a hand over the console and I take it. It's warm and dry but quickly starts to get clammy. It must take a lot of energy to keep a skyscraper like him in operation.

His words stumble out of his mouth. "Have you ever gone to

see someone or talk to someone about what happened?"

"You mean like a therapist? Besides Mrs. Walker?" He nods. "No. I mean . . . no . . ."

"Why not?"

"Too expensive." I leave it at that.

"Insurance covers it," Lucas says.

He says it like it's obvious, obvious for someone who has privileges he can't even imagine someone else not having. A family that looks out for him, basic needs taken care of every day. "Not ours. Light changed."

He drives, his eyes forward. We're both silent. His comments squirm uncomfortably under my skin. But by the way he huffs through his nostrils, he seems annoyed by something I said too.

"What's your mom making for dinner?" I say to change the subject.

"Some variation of hamburger surprise is my guess." A hint of his smile returns. We park in front of his house a few minutes later. Purple crocuses dot the neatly tended flowerbeds, bulbs planted and carefully arranged months earlier before the cold set in. Flower baskets outside the windows hold purple and yellow pansies. This is the most self-respecting house I've ever seen.

As we approach the front door, Lucas warns me, "Heads up. We have to take our shoes off in the house. My mom saw something on the news about how many germs we track in. She became kind of militant about it after that."

Of course she is. Because that's what a mother who cares does.

He opens the door and announces, "We're here!"

We both kick our shoes off by the door, next to an even larger pair of men's black dress shoes. His father's, I imagine. *Fee, fi, fo, fum.* Welcome to the giant's house.

Mrs. Rossi comes out of the kitchen to meet us, drying her hands on her apron. To say I'm nervous would be a huge understatement. My tongue glues to the roof of my mouth. But Mrs. Rossi's cheery smile looks *too* cheery—I think she's nervous too.

"Hi, Jess."

"Hi, Mrs. Rossi. Thank you for inviting me over."

Loud lumbering comes down the stairs.

I smell the blood of an Englishman!

"Hey, Dad." Lucas turns, still holding my hand. "This is Jess."

Spoiler alert: I now have an idea of what Lucas will look like when he's middle-aged. And it's not horrible. A little thicker around the middle and a full head of gray hair.

"Hi, Mr. Rossi."

"Jess." Once he reaches the bottom of the stairs, he leans over and pecks me on the cheek, more air than lips. "Glad you could make it." He gestures with his hand for us to walk ahead of him, through the living room to the dining room.

Mr. Rossi takes a seat at the head of the dining room table, already set for dinner, and Lucas and I take seats by a huge china closet filled with crystal glasses and gold-rimmed plate settings too delicate for a house of giants.

"So, Lucas tells me you work together?" His eyes twinkle when he smiles.

Lucas smirks. "Don't let Jess's size fool you. She's freakishly strong. The circus is trying to recruit her."

I make a face at Lucas, then turn back to Mr. Rossi. "They all made fun of me when I first started."

"Didn't help that she broke a sink on her first day," Lucas chimes in.

"Yeah, but now I like working at Enzo's. You get used to the sore muscles—it's not that bad."

Mr. Rossi looks over at his son. "Well, that's good to know. Lucas likes to make it sound as if he's breaking rocks down at the quarry."

The oven timer goes off. A few moments later, Mrs. Rossi joins us with a Pyrex casserole dish and places it down on the table with oven mitts. The heady aroma makes my mouth water; I swallow so I don't openly drool in front of everyone. Mrs. Rossi doles out huge servings on every plate, and as soon as Lucas and Mr. Rossi pick up their forks, I dig in.

I try to pace myself, but it's just so delicious. There's beef, cheese, and noodles, and it's salty and tangy and saucy and it's hugging my stomach. They're talking around me, asking questions about school and work, and I nod and answer when I absolutely have to, but this dinner has my full and undivided attention. When I clean my plate, mopping up every drop of sauce with a slice of bread, Mrs. Rossi asks, in a kind voice, "Would you like more, Jess?"

I know I'm supposed to say no to be polite, but . . .

"Yes, please." I hold out my plate.

A real smile blossoms across Mrs. Rossi's face this time, not like the nervous one from before.

"I'm so glad you like it," she gushes as she spoons another huge serving on my plate.

Lucas scoffs. "Careful, Mom. Jess isn't used to all this monosodium glutamate in one sitting. She might balloon like Violet from *Willy Wonka*."

Lucas and his dad both laugh, the sounds rumbling through the room like thunder. Mrs. Rossi smiles like it's something she's used to and puts up with, but this smile is nothing like the one that lit up her face when I handed her my plate for seconds. Like the guys at work with their tired "cleanup in aisle six" gag, it looks like Mrs. Rossi's cooking has been the butt of a joke for too long.

"Hey." I shoot Lucas a quick glare. "Cooking's not easy. You should be really grateful that your mom makes dinner for you every night."

I probably just swung the door wide open into my home life. The laughter comes to a full stop.

Mrs. Rossi seems to choose her next words carefully.

"Do you like to cook, Jess?" It's the most delicate way of sidestepping the landmine I set for myself.

"Like? No. You'd be amazed at how many things I can burn. Did you know if you boil eggs for too long the yolks will turn green? And you can't microwave them either. I learned that the hard way."

Mr. Rossi chokes a little but then he laughs, which relieves some of the tension.

"But I can hold my own. And my neighbor is always bringing us food. Tonight she brought over stuffed peppers," I add.

"Mrs. Alvarez," Lucas adds, and nods. "She's nice."

I smile at him. I like that he likes her, even if he only just met her and he's saying it to be polite. She's old and can tell the same story to me every day as if it's the first time she's ever shared it, but she takes care of me more than anyone else these days.

"Mrs. Alvarez tried to teach me how to cook a couple of times, but everything was 'Add a handful of flour . . . more if it needs it . . . Taste it? Does it need salt?' I mean, how am I supposed to know if it needs more flour or salt if I've never cooked before?"

Mrs. Rossi nods, nibbling on her lower lip in thought.

"Well, I'm sure Mrs. Alvarez is a better cook than I am, but I can give you a few cooking tips. Easy things you can do yourself," she decides, nodding to Lucas. "Pass the bread to Jess."

After dinner, I help bring the plates into the kitchen, where Mrs. Rossi opens the pantry doors and the freezer to show me different dinner options and combinations. She pulls out a large frosty package of frozen ground beef and holds it up like a trophy.

"This right here is a lifesaver. Family size is the most economical; then divide it up into plastic bags and throw it in your freezer."

She turns to the stove, showing me her large frying pan.

"Just brown it in a skillet . . . you know what *brown* means, right? Break it up with a spatula until the pink is gone." Then she pulls out a box. "Then add this and stir it together. Get some buns, and you have sloppy joes. Or . . ." She pulls out a packet from the pantry. "Add this instead for tacos."

She keeps rattling off her favorite recipes and writes some tips down for me. The kind of practical tips I didn't know I needed to get from my mom before she started having more bad days than good.

When Lucas takes the car keys to drive me home later that night, Mrs. Rossi rushes to the front door before I leave.

"Jess, wait!" She pushes a plastic food container into my arms. "Take a little home with you. I made too much."

I know what "I made too much" really means, but I don't argue.

"See you soon, I hope." She kisses me good-bye on the cheek. I nod and turn away before she sees the tears well in my eyes.

Lucas is quiet as we get in the car and buckle up. We pull out of their driveway and turn down his tree-lined street. New spring leaves round out the trees' silhouettes against the dark sky.

He reaches over and grabs my hand, exhaling deeply, as if he's nervous. "So . . . what'd you think?"

"Your parents are so nice," I say. But what I really want to say is they're so nice and normal. Tonight was great, but it was also a painful reminder of how much is missing in my life. Missing and missed.

"I knew they'd be over-the-top nice," he says. "They're trying to take it a little easier on me because they were so hard on Jason."

"About Reggie?"

The green light of the dashboard softens the planes of his face as he makes the turns back to my place.

"Yeah," he says. "My parents just thought they were too young."

"She told me why he really stayed when we were at the bon-fire," I tell him.

He sucks in air through his teeth. "Yeah . . . please don't ever mention it to my parents. They don't know that she asked Jason to stay." He shakes his head. "They'd never forgive her."

"That's not fair," I argue.

"I know," he agrees. "Big difference between 'fair' and 'feelings' though."

My *feelings* for his parents aren't as generous anymore. But I have to remember what the Rossis lost also.

Lucas turns to me. "Are you in a hurry to get home?"

I choke on my laugh. "Uh . . . no!"

"Want to go down to the beach?" He runs a finger over the back of my hand. Just that little touch makes my breath stutter with anticipation. I nod and smile back.

Lucas turns the car around and we drive down a beach road that had been covered in sand, splintered wood, and debris after Sandy. So many of the numbered Beach Streets off the boardwalk looked like a ship had wrecked on a deserted island. We couldn't imagine ever rebuilding, but we did. Most of us did, at least. Some homes are still abandoned, reminders that not everyone is resilient, not everyone can find their way back after being knocked down repeatedly.

The Rockaways were built on a sandbar. We didn't start off with the best foundation to begin with. At a certain point you have to wonder why we keep leaving ourselves vulnerable and wide open.

LUCAS

For Jess

The next morning, I find a Post-it on the kitchen counter with Jess's name. Under it, a stack of coupons clipped together: Hamburger Helper, Old El Paso, Ronzoni. At the bottom of the pile is the golden ticket, the coupon my mother looks forward to every week in the Wednesday circular: five dollars off your grocery order. She's giving this to Jess. That's a huge deal.

Progress. I see it everywhere. Even outside the kitchen window, the trees are exploding with spring, each one of those little buds from just a few weeks ago fanning out into tiny green hands. The calendar on the wall by the phone has a picture of a tulip field and a monthly inspirational quote: *Hope springs eternal*. Maybe so, May. Maybe so.

Dates are circled and appointments scribbled onto the days of the month. Looks like Dad's having a colonoscopy on the tenth. Mom didn't even try to come up with some kind of secret code to save him some embarrassment. Nope. It says, "FRANK,

COLONOSCOPY, 10:30 A.M."

Not circled? Saturday, the twentieth. A little more than two weeks away. The day of my boxing match. The only two people who know about that match are me and Leo. I haven't even told Jess yet. I'm not sure when or how I'll break that news to her.

Mom walks by in her fuzzy white bathrobe, sipping her coffee. She glances at the coupons in my hand. "Oh good, you found them. Make sure to tell Jess Wednesdays are double-coupon day."

I don't even know what to say, so I just grab her in a huge hug.

"Oof!" She holds her coffee mug out so she doesn't spill it on me. When I pull away she reaches up and pats my cheek.

Jess has her back to me at her locker, her hair falling in shiny copper waves. She keeps it down at school, up in a ponytail at work. I sneak my arms around her waist and rest my chin by her ear, her hair tickling against my cheek.

"Hey."

She pockets her phone and turns around in my arms to meet me for a kiss.

This really is one of the many new highlights of my day. Just a few weeks ago, I was freaking out that I couldn't handle this. Maybe all those feel-good oxytocin hormones flooding my body are keeping my anxiety up against the ropes.

"Mr. Rossi, Miss Nolan." Mr. Klein, our principal, holds a warning finger up. One finger. First warning.

As soon as Mr. Klein turns the corner, we sneak in another kiss before heading down the hallway, my arm around her shoulders, her waist pressed into my hip. I pull the coupons out of my back pocket with my free hand and pass them to her.

"This is from my mom."

She flips through them and smiles. "Oh. Thanks."

She doesn't get it.

"It's a big deal. She gave you her five-dollar-off coupon. That's like getting the slice of cake with the flower on it."

Jess laughs and pockets the coupons. "Great, now I want cake."

I don't think Jess grasps the magnitude of the gesture. These coupons are my mother's way of welcoming Jess. Jason would have given his right throwing arm for my family to roll out the welcome mat for Reggie.

I mumble something so pathetic, I wish I could shove the words back in my mouth as soon as they're out.

"Those coupons mean a lot to my mother."

Jess looks confused and upset. "Oh." She takes the coupons back out of her pocket and hands them to me. "Give them back to her. I don't need them," she says, but her cheeks are flaming, because I'm an idiot.

I can hear Dr. Engel in my ear. "If you communicate and problem solve together . . ."

So I collect my thoughts, and take a deep breath. "That came out all wrong. She wants you to have them because she likes you. And I wanted you to know that's a big deal because of everything Jason went through. Like, I wanted you to know that my parents are, um, trying." I scratch the back of my head. "And you would have no way of knowing it's a big deal to me or them, so I'm sorry."

I take my finger and try to erase the worried furrows on her forehead that I caused. "I'm sorry," I say again, and lean to kiss her. And she lets me.

I take her hand and we walk back down the hallway to class. "How about after work tonight we go to my house, watch a movie or something?"

She smiles in relief. Her smile tugs at me, makes my heart jump and do tricks. It's a little scary. And awesome.

It poured while we were at work. Now that the rain has passed, the air is still damp, but sweet-smelling. Clean.

Store awnings trickle rainwater in steady metronomic drips all around us as we head to my car parked a few blocks away. The cars tearing past us whiz over the thin sheen of moisture on the asphalt.

Jess pauses as she comes up to a puddle on the sidewalk by my car. A sly smile sneaks across her face, right before she stomps in the puddle, soaking both of us.

"Hey!" I laugh, even though my jeans are now cold and wet against my legs.

"Whoops! That kind of backfired." She laughs, shaking her wet leg out. "I pictured that turning out way differently in my head."

I swoop in and take advantage of her brief moment of remorse, pressing my lips down on hers. My hands are at her waist, drawing her in. She smiles against my lips and her fingers cinch into my jacket, holding me close. I can feel my reserve tanks filling with pure bliss.

She pulls back and gets in the car, still grinning. It's a five-minute drive to my house. Jess waits for me on the curb before we walk in together.

"Ma, we're here," I call to her while Jess and I kick off our shoes. Mom's at the kitchen table with her laptop open, glasses on.

"Hi," she greets us, still tapping on the keyboard. She looks up and smiles at Jess. "Hi, Jess."

"Hi." Jess waves. "Thank you for the coupons!" she says.

"You're welcome! Did Lucas tell you Wednesdays are double-coupon days? You might want to wait until next week to use them."

Jess nods, wide-eyed and eager to please. I feel guilty watching her try too hard to make my mother happy. I projected Jason and Reggie's drama onto our relationship for no good reason.

Mom refocuses her attention on her laptop.

"What're you working on?" I ask.

There's something in the way my mother's sitting that's different. Shoulders squared, eyes focused . . . and she's tapping like a boss on the keyboard. Papers are fanned out on the table next to her. She glances at them, then back to her screen.

"My company—my old company—offered me a freelance job. And I said yes. I mean, why not, right?"

Watching her work again fills me with a mix of pride and happiness, and not a small amount of relief. It's the closest thing to normal I've seen from her in a while.

I take Jess by the shoulders and steer her toward the basement door. "We'll get out of your way. We're going downstairs to watch a movie."

Mom looks up from her keyboard with a strained smile. "Okay. But I'm doing laundry down there, just so you know," which is a mom warning for "don't do anything you don't want me catching you doing."

My family has a huge DVD collection. Downstairs, Jess plops down in front of the storage bins cross-legged, as excited as a kid in the toy store.

"Oh my God!" She holds *Young Frankenstein* up and waves it in the air like she struck gold. "This! We have to watch this first!" But she's not done. She makes piles of movies she wants to watch next time she comes over. I like that she's planning on coming back again, and by the number of movies she's putting aside, she's planning on coming back a bunch of times. Some of the movies are old as dirt but classics: *The Birds, The Graduate, The Exorcist.*

She stops when she gets to *Roman Holiday.* Her finger traces the cover and her smile dims. I crouch down next to her.

"What?" I ask.

"Nothing," she says. Then she shrugs. "My mom and I used to check out movies from the library all the time. She loved Audrey Hepburn. This one was her favorite." She turns it around to show me, then she puts the movie back in the bin. I take it out and place it on top of the pile of movies she's put aside to watch another time.

"We should watch it, then," I say.

She scrunches up her nose and shakes her head. "I don't think so."

I put my hand on her shoulder and squeeze.

"Why don't you take it home to watch with your mom?"

She bites her lip and thinks about it.

"Maybe."

The metaphorical door closes, slamming in my face. That's all I'm getting. Jess hands me *Young Frankenstein* with a smile. I pop it in and we set up camp on the couch.

I have to give her credit; Jess can switch gears faster than anyone I know.

By the time Gene Wilder stabs himself in the leg with a scalpel, Jess and I are in full make-out mode. I stretch out on the couch, taking Jess with me, and pull the blanket over us . . . just in case. My hand skims underneath Jess's shirt. She rolls her eyes to look up the stairs.

"It's okay," I murmur in her ear. "I'm watching out."

I kiss her ear and tug on her earlobe with my teeth. She gasps and hitches her leg around my hip, pulling me closer. Soon, we're both pressing into each other and I'm wishing so hard my mother would have to go to the store for something, anything, because this would be so much better if we could peel off a few layers of clothes.

The door opens and we both bolt up. I hold the blanket across our laps, smoothing it down and trying to act normal.

"I'm coming to check on the laundry!" Mom announces in a commanding voice.

Mom looks between us on the couch, both of us trying to pretend nothing was going on, but by Jess's messy hair and swollen lips, I think it's obvious what we were up to.

Mom opens the dryer, peeks in, then shuts the door again. She pushes the start button and walks by. "Needs a little more time," she says, pointing to the dryer. At the foot of the stairs, she adds, "I'm just going to keep the door open, okay?" Mom's not really asking, she's telling. Jess's cheeks flame.

As soon as we hear my mother's footsteps crossing the floor over us, I pounce on Jess again.

"Your *mom*!" She shoves at me.

"Kiss quieter!" I tease. She rolls out from under me onto the floor. Then she shoves a throw pillow in my face.

"Maybe you'd rather kiss *this* instead!" She laughs. I fall back on the couch and stare at the pocked ceiling tiles.

Jess tries to take the blanket from me, but I hold on.

"Give me a minute." I close my eyes and scour my brain for anything that will get this situation under control. Remembering the time some drunk guy walked out of the Blarney Stone and puked on my sneakers as I was walking by usually does it.

"That's quite an impressive tent you've pitched, Mr. Rossi," I hear Jess say. "Your talents are being wasted at Enzo's. You should get a job at Dick's Sporting Goods." She snorts at her own joke.

I groan. "You're not helping."

Later that night, I drive Jess home. The porch light to her house is off. I wait for her to get inside safely, but I can't help but wonder what's waiting for her, what she wants to hide from me.

Jess

> If one more idiot promposes in front of me, I'm going to scream.
> I'm about ready to put a No Promposal Zone sign on my locker.

> Too late. Andrew just arrived, hair looking extra crispy today.

A string quartet lines up in the hallway next to Sarah's locker. Risa organizes the cello between her legs.

"I can't be late for chem," she warns Andrew, who's holding up his promposal sign.

WHAT'S BETTER THAN A QUARTET?
A DUET!
ME AND YOU @ PROM, BABY!

It's really the "baby" part that makes me throw up in my mouth a little. That and the fact that Sarah is still dating him after he got all aggro with her in the hall.

Prom is ten days away. All the stragglers who waited until the last minute are scrambling to line up their dates.

"*Jess!*"

Aisha rushes down the hallway calling my name. Aisha is always rushing from place to place. She's one of those overachievers who's involved in every club.

She skids to a stop in front of me.

"Please tell me you didn't come up with this one." I point across the hall to Andrew's sign.

Aisha presses a hand against her chest, her silver rings sparkling against her brown skin, trying to catch her breath. Then she looks at the promposal sign and lifts her lip in distaste. "No way, Andrew is a douche. I refused to even accept his money. Are you and Lucas going?"

I laugh just picturing us going to prom. Our big date was going to Key Food for double-coupon Wednesday so I could cash in the coupons his mom gave me. "Uh, no. We're not really prom people."

I think of all the prom pictures posted on the school website. The orange spray tans. The fake nails. Girls squeezed into dresses too tight, guys hoping they can figure out how to get girls out of those tight dresses. Blowing all that money on hair, makeup, limos, tuxes. All that pomp and circumstance, and for what? One night? I'd rather spend prom night at the beach alone with Lucas.

She takes a deep breath and lets it out quickly. "Okay, two things. One!" She holds up her finger. "No one's running for class treasurer next year. Like, zilch, nada." She makes a zero with her fingers. "Would you do it?"

My head snaps back in shock. "Why me?"

"Why not?" she pushes back.

"No, seriously. What makes you think I'd want to do it?"

She lifts a shoulder. "'Cause you're good at math?" When I roll my eyes at that, she adds, "Jess, don't read too much into it. I'm asking *everyone*. No one wants to do it. It's not a tough job and it'll look good on your college applications. No one's running against you, so it's not like you have to campaign or anything. Just think about it."

I shrug. Fine. I'll pretend to think about, even if I doubt I'll be filling out any college applications next year.

Aisha pushes her dark curls over her shoulder and scratches at her chin while poring over an open notebook in her hand.

"Okay, next . . . I'm working on the 'In Memoriam' section of the yearbook," she begins. Her eyes are glued to her notebook; otherwise she'd see how her words flatten me. "We want to do one for everyone we lost that night who would've graduated this year." Her voice is careful, delicate. Well intentioned. It doesn't stop the hallway from shrinking or my fingers from tingling.

"If you have a baby picture of Ethan to bring in that would be great, and a list of his favorite things so we can personalize it."

Her voice drowns out in the vortex of noise around me. Laughter that's too shrill. Lockers that clang like they're mic'd. Someone runs by and yells, right in my ear. I flinch.

Aisha's arm wraps around me in a hug, suddenly, out of nowhere. Or maybe she's been talking longer than I realized.

"You okay?" she asks, and I lie and nod.

Aisha leans back, and her eyes well up. "It doesn't get any easier, does it?" she asks, as if she has personal experience, as if she knows what it's like to lose your brother.

When she walks away, I have the vague recollection of her giving me a homework assignment to bring in pieces of Ethan's life so years from now people can point to his page in the yearbook and feel sorry for him, for us.

The bell rings, striking through me like a thunderbolt. The hallway empties, sucking all of my space, all my air, everything I need to survive.

I race down the hall to the bathroom, shutting the door behind me.

Once I'm safely locked in a stall, I pull my phone out of my back pocket to flip through old pictures of Ethan and Marissa. It helps, but only a little. My heart is still racing like a helicopter propeller about to take flight out of my mouth.

The bathroom door flies open and Charmaine's and Domie's booming voices bounce off the cinder block walls.

"You need to get your ass to church more, Domie! You got the devil in you! You need Jesus in your heart!"

"Jesus, Jesus, Jesus," Domie replies.

It's the cavalry coming to the rescue. My legs feel like jelly, so I wait on the toilet, listening. The window opens with a groan. I hear the spark of a lighter and the skunky smell of weed wafting around the small bathroom.

"Hey, Red! You want?" Charmaine holds the joint between her fingers under the stall. I accept it and take a hit, letting it sit in my lungs. Then I take another one before coming out.

"How'd you know it was me?" I pass the joint back to her.

She laughs and takes a hit, then passes it to Domie. "You're the only person I know whose baby feet don't touch the floor when they're sitting on the toilet," she squeezes out tightly, trying to hold the smoke in her lungs.

Domie cracks up. So do I. The joint passes around a few more times. The ghosts that sit on top of my chest every minute of the day blur and fade into the backdrop.

Lucas

The dismissal bell just rang. Jess walks by my side, her feet sluggish, as we worm through the throngs of sun-starved students all trying to squeeze out of the building at the same time, like carbonation exploding out of a shaken soda bottle.

"I'm soooo tired." She yawns hugely. Her eyes are bloodshot.

"Did you get any sleep last night? You practically look wasted," I say, and laugh. Until she shrugs and nods. "You're wasted?"

"Maybe?" she says, which I've learned is Jess's reluctant yes. "I may have run into Domie in the bathroom earlier. She may have had some weed."

"During school?" I ask, scratching the back of my head.

"Yeah. I was in a funk. She was there. It seemed like the right thing at the moment. Except I forgot about my APUSH test. I either aced it or tanked. I'm not sure yet." She laughs it off. I mean, getting stoned is okay, I guess. It's not for me. It tightens my lid instead of loosening it, makes me uptight, angry, paranoid . . . all those things I'm trying to quiet down, not jack up.

"So . . . what were you in a funk about?"

"I dunno," she says, staring off into space.

I blow a stream of air in frustration. Pumping her for information is getting exhausting. But a new wave of optimism washes over me as soon as we're out the door. It's a beautiful spring day. Warm air rushes up against our skin. School will be over next month, graduation, and then we'll have summer before my classes start at Queensborough Community. Weekends at the beach, bonfires, barbecues. I can pretty much handle anything when the weather is nice. Maybe Jess and I will go camping, get out of here for a few days.

We walk to my car, parked on the street. She hops in the passenger seat and lowers the seat back as I get in and turn the ignition.

Closing her eyes, she mumbles, "Sleepy."

"Should I take you home?" I ask.

She opens one bloodshot eye and glares at me. "What? No! Drive!" She gestures in front of her toward the windshield, egging me to get a move on.

"Where to?" I ask, pulling away from the curb.

"Surprise me," she says with her eyes closed.

"I thought you don't do surprises."

"I'll make an exception today." She lets out another huge yawn. "I'm just going to take a quick power nap. Ten minutes, tops," she says, and almost immediately starts snoring.

She's in such a deep sleep, I decide to get out of Queens and do something different. I drive an hour east, then north until I hit the state park my parents used to take us to when we were kids. Jess wakes up as I pull into the parking lot.

Stretching, she turns her head to look out every window. Green foliage greets her at every turn. She faces me with a questioning look.

"Do you know you snore?"

She wipes the back of her hand along her mouth. I don't want to point out she drooled also. "Now you know all my dark secrets," she says. "Where are we?"

"A state park on the North Shore. We're mixing things up today."

We get out of the car and walk until we reach the water. I find us a secluded spot on top of the sea cliff, where we have a view of the Long Island Sound. Jess parks herself in my lap, arms looped around my neck, in our little private oasis overlooking the beach.

Pushing her hair behind her ear, she then presses her lips against mine, soft at first, then more urgent.

But I have questions. So many. I pull my lips away from hers.

"So when we were walking to the car you were telling me how—" She kisses the corner of my mouth. "You and Domie—" She plants another kiss on my lips. "Why'd you—" Kiss. "Are you trying to shut me up?"

"Is it working?" she asks, kissing me again.

"Kinda." She smiles against my lips but I pull away just far enough so I can get the words out. "But seriously. Why'd you get stoned at school?"

She leans farther away, eyes narrowing to scrutinize me. "Why are you judging?"

"I'm not. I mean, I'm not trying to. It's just . . . you don't drink, but you smoke weed? I'm just trying to figure it out."

With her arms still draped around my neck, she takes a deep breath through her nose and scans the tree awning overhead. "I don't drink because alcoholism is a thing in my family. But weed helps cut the edge."

"But, you're still self-medicating," I tell her, because I learned all about this in therapy.

Her arms undrape from around my neck. "What's the difference? You pop a pill from the pharmacist. I smoke weed. I don't do it every day and it's not like I can't get through life without it. I mean . . . are you seriously bugging out about this?"

"No . . . I'm not bugging out," I argue. "Just . . . look, if it's a casual thing, fine. But if you're using it to deal with day-to-day life, then yeah, it's a problem."

She huffs and slips off my lap. She's mad at me for caring?

I shoulder-bump her.

"Hey."

"Hey," she repeats, plucking rocks off the ground to avoid looking at me.

I bump her again. "I just give a shit, Jess. Is that so awful?"

She shakes her head and bounces the rocks in her hand. She sighs. "No. It's not. I think you're the only one who does lately."

I reach my arm around her and she gives in and leans against me. "It's not you anyway. Aisha came up to me today. She's working on the 'In Memoriam' section of the yearbook."

"Shit," I groan.

"Yeah. The bell rang. All of a sudden, I felt like I couldn't breathe. Everything felt too tight. And when that happens, I hope to God I find Domie in the bathroom to make it go away."

I nod. "I had a full-blown panic attack with Pete at Five Guys. Loud noises can do it to me. I just about passed out. Poor Pete had to mop up my mess."

I tear a dandelion out of the ground that's gone to seed and blow. The seeds float away, except for one. It lands in Jess's hair. I pluck it out, rolling it back and forth between my fingers, trying to work up the nerve to say what's been on my mind.

"I don't know how else to say this but to just say it," I hedge. "But I'm worried about you."

Her head jerks back in surprise. "Me? Why?"

It hurts not to eye-roll at that. "Why? Because there are obviously things going on in your life you're not talking about. And I'm pretty sure what you're describing is because you're bottling it all up."

She glances away, following the lethargic trek of the fluffy seeds.

"Okay," she says, and then pauses. She squeezes her eyes shut and her entire face clenches. "Okay," she says again, like she's about to jump off a high diving board and is trying to muster up the courage. "So, my mom." She stops and swallows, followed by a sniff. Then she swipes at her eyes. "This is why I don't talk about it." She tries to laugh but it's choked off by a sob.

"Jess. You have to start somewhere."

She nods and sniffs some more.

"It's like she died that night too. With Ethan." The words come out strangled. She buries her face in her hands and cries. Muffled between her fingers, she says, "You asked for it!"

"Hey, give me a little more credit." I nuzzle in closer to her ear. "This doesn't faze me. I *want* to know."

She nods and cries some more. "I know," she admits. "I don't know why this is so hard."

I hug her tighter. "I can't tell you how many times I bawled through my therapy sessions."

It takes her a while to be able to talk again. Finally she sits up straighter. Fisting her sleeves, she wipes her eyes. "It started when my dad left us. She stayed in bed for days. And we needed her, you know? He didn't just leave her. Our dad left us too."

She takes a ragged breath and blows it out. "She went back to work a few days later, but she wasn't the same. It did something to her. She *just* pawned off her wedding band and engagement ring a few weeks ago . . . the night I blew off going bowling. She was a mess; I couldn't leave her. Even though we really needed that money, I don't think she wanted to sell them. I think she's still waiting for my father to come back."

She swipes under her eyes. "When Ethan died, she used up all her bereavement days, her personal days, sick days, vacation days. . . . Then she took a leave of absence. When twelve weeks were up, she told her job she wasn't coming back. She was getting unemployment for a while until Social Security set up appointments for her to come in and she didn't go. So we stopped getting those checks. Then she stopped taking her antidepressants because she said they weren't helping. And in the past couple of months since she went off them, she's only gotten worse. She doesn't even want to get out of bed most days.

"So basically, everyone's gone." She ticks off on her fingers. "My father. Ethan. Marissa. My mom. Even the people who didn't die aren't here for me anymore where I need them. Everyone's either a ghost or ghosted on me."

"Hey. I'm not going anywhere."

She nods, raking the ground with her fingers. "I know." But I get it. I'm not enough. She wants and needs her mother.

"They're not all bad days," she adds. "Some days she tries. I've been trying to get her to go back to the doctor, or get a new one. She won't go though."

"What about you?" I ask.

She turns to me. "What *about* me?"

"Don't you think you should talk to someone?"

She opens her mouth to huff with irritation, jutting out a hand. "I *told* you. We can't afford it."

"Mrs. Walker is free," I say. When she doesn't say anything, I add, "Look, if you were sick, you'd go to the nurse, right? Same thing."

She nods, and stares at the ground. "Yeah, okay."

"I just want to help. You know that, right?"

She looks up at me. "You help me every day. You give me something to look forward to."

Jess wipes her face with her sleeves, then takes my hand and pries my pinch apart. The seed of the dandelion is still there, slightly smushed. She closes her eyes and blows. When she looks up at me again, she smiles. "See? Wish granted. You're still here."

She lies back and tugs on my shirt until I join her. Jess digs an elbow into the ground and props her head up on her hand, then reaches over me and plucks another dandelion out of the ground, this one still a tight yellow bud, and runs it down my nose.

I don't for a second take for granted that Jess opening up to me today wasn't a huge deal. We're moving forward. Communicating. Getting through this, together. It's time to think ahead, make plans where ghosts aren't invited or welcomed.

"So, here's something that'll make you laugh," I say, wrapping my fingers around her wrist as she drags the yellow bud down my nose. She bops me on the nose with it. "Prom's coming up soon."

She tilts her head as if she didn't hear me correctly. "Prom?"

"Next Sunday."

"Yeah? So?"

"We should go."

She stares at me for too long. My heart skips a beat waiting for a reaction from her.

Her eyes, still swollen from crying, narrow in a look I now am very familiar with.

"Prom?" she repeats, the hint of a laugh in her voice.

"Why not?" I ask. "It'll be fun."

She flops back into the crook of my arm. "Your idea of fun is drastically different from mine. Maybe boxing should have been my first clue."

I roll onto my side to face her. "I didn't think I wanted to go either, but the idea grew on me."

"Like mold." She lets out a groan of surrender. "Fine. We'll go. Only because you're graduating and I don't want you to regret not going to your prom. But I have conditions. One: No limo. They're stupid. Two: No corsage. They're cheesy as hell. Cheesy in a *bad* way. And three: Absolutely under no circumstance are you to prompose to me. I mean it. That is a deal-fucking-breaker."

"You drive a hard bargain, Jessica Nolan. But you're also a cheap date, so no arguments here."

Jess

When we're parked outside my house, Lucas plucks a piece of grass from my hair, then leans in for another kiss that turns into a long breathless one. I push him away, gently.

"Leo's gonna be mad."

"He's always mad." Lucas finds my lips again.

"What time were you supposed to be there?" I ask against his lips, looking over at the clock on the dashboard.

"Seven," he says, his lips traveling down my chin.

I'm in no rush to go inside, but I don't want him to get in trouble. I push him away. "It's seven twenty. He'll blame me for holding you up."

I turn around to lean over my seat, grabbing my backpack from the floor behind us. His hand travels up the back of my leg.

I swat at his hand. "Don't start something now."

"We could keep driving," he offers.

Back in my seat, I position my bag between us like a lion tamer wielding a chair. "Go burn it off, champ. Punch bags, jump rope, chase chickens . . ."

"Chickens are only in Rocky movies." He tries to wrestle my backpack away. We both laugh.

"Whatever. You train like Rocky, even though you're never going to actually fight."

He stops laughing. "Yeah, about that." He props his arm on the windowsill and rests his head in his hand, closing his eyes. "There's an amateur competition coming up that I might do."

I pause. He's joking. He's got to be. "Right." I laugh. When he doesn't say anything, I ask, "Lucas, what are you telling me?"

He exhales heavily. "Okay, yeah . . . I'm doing it. But I haven't told anyone yet."

"What? Why?"

He shrugs, his jaw set. "To see if I can."

"To see if you can kick someone's ass? Because the alternative is having *your* ass kicked!"

"Why do you think I've been training so hard?" he counters. "Don't you think people who train in any competitive sport have to test their skills at some point?"

"I just thought you were doing this to burn off steam or stay in shape or something. I don't know. I honestly never thought you were itching to hurt someone!"

Both of his hands squeeze the steering wheel. "It's not about hurting someone. It's a sport. Every sport is about fighting and winning."

I steeple my fingers over my face and shake my head. "I don't get it."

He takes a breath and tries again. "Boxing isn't an all-out

punching match. It's a game of chess. You have to control your mind and your body while always being one step ahead of your opponent. You know that feeling you described having today in the hallway? What your body went through today was 'fight or flight.' Everything raced, your heart, your breathing, your blood pressure. When you're boxing, you have to do the exact opposite, calm your heart rate down, relax yourself mind, body, and spirit so you can see what is happening in front of you. . . .

I purse my lips in disapproval. "So when's the fight?"

"Next Saturday," he says, clutching the steering wheel as if he's physically bracing himself for my response.

"So the day before prom." He stares back but his silence is my answer. "Well, that'll make for some fun prom pictures, you looking like your face went through the wood chipper."

He laughs, even though I'm not joking. "Why are you assuming I'll lose?"

I grab the door handle to leave.

"Don't be mad," he pleads.

I huff. "I'm not *mad*." I don't think. "If you thought I was going to be thrilled about it, you would've told me sooner, right? Just give me some time to wrap my head around it. I hear what you're saying. But my mind keeps showing me pictures I don't want to see."

I walk around the front of the car. He rolls his window down. "Jess?"

I lean in. "Look, you can't blame me for feeling this way. I've grown to really like this face of yours. I don't like the idea of someone messing it up." I kiss him good-bye.

He waits for me to get in the house before driving to the gym.

The living room lamp is on when I walk in the house. The hallway to the bedrooms is dark. On the coffee table, there's something new. My parents' wedding album.

I flip through the pictures, most of them painfully hokey. Mom in her wedding gown, holding a bottle of perfume up, pretending to get ready for her big day.

"I didn't even wear perfume." Mom had pointed to the picture a few years ago when we were still a family who believed in happily-ever-afters. "The photographer made me do it. Look, I'm practically squirting it in my ear!"

There's a picture of Dad at the church waiting for Mom, his hair still thick and wavy, combed away from his face. The photographer had him check his watch and mop his brow with a handkerchief. "Pretend you're afraid Nicole's going to leave you at the altar." As if. Mom was already three months pregnant with Ethan. They had their reception at a VFW hall. Mom's maid of honor, Maureen, decorated it for less than one hundred dollars with plastic tablecloths, streamers, and paper plates from Party Central. They got a keg from the beer distributor and a sheet cake from Costco.

I can't help but see the wedding pictures through my mother's lens and her sadness becomes mine, again. Reminders, every time I look around. They're always there to ground me just as I'm starting to feel like the worst is over.

LUCAS

Jess doesn't bring up the boxing match again, so I leave it alone. But she does come with me after work the next day to get fitted for a tux. There's a place a few blocks down from Enzo's that's been around forever, Marvin's Tuxedo Rental, next door to the Everything 92¢ Store. Way to squeeze out the 99¢ store competition.

The bell chimes as we walk in. Jess closes her eyes and takes a whiff, her shoulders lifting as she fills her lungs.

"Mothballs and cigar smoke. Oh my God, this is exactly what I imagined a tuxedo store would smell like!"

We walk around, checking out the styles on the mannequins. Jess's face lights up at the all-white tux. She stands behind it and places both hands on the mannequin's shoulders. "I *insist*!"

I shake my head at her, playing along. "Nope. No way. It's powder blue and ruffles or nothing at all."

She pretends to weigh her options, lifting first one hand, then the other. "Powder blue or birthday suit. Hmmm . . . I think that's a win-win for me."

I turn around before she can see how my body just weighed in on the matter. I need to get things under control before I get fitted.

A stooped old man comes out from behind a curtain, a tape measure looped around his neck like a loosened tie. The thick lenses of his glasses give him an owlish look. This must be Marvin.

"Hello, hello," he greets us with an openmouthed grin. "Don't tell me, let me guess!" He raises one withered hand to stop us from speaking while pressing the other to his forehead, pretending to read our minds. "You have a prom coming up and you need a tux." His eyes pop open. "Am I right?"

Jess grins. "Yep! Does this one come supersized?" She squeezes the shoulders of the all-white tux.

I shake my head. "She's kidding," I tell Marvin.

"I am not!" Jess protests, but Marvin follows me across the store as I put my hand on another mannequin, this one in a white jacket with black pants. I turn to Jess. "My nonna would've said this one was snazzy."

She rolls her eyes. "My bad. All this time, I thought the look we were going for was ludicrous."

Marvin claps his hands and laughs at us, as if we're the most charming and delightful customers he's ever had. I'm afraid his dentures are going to fall out of his head at how hard he's grinning.

"Yes, this one *is* snazzy. And very popular. When's your prom?"

"Next Sunday," I say.

"Oh." Marvin laughs. "Waiting to the last minute, huh?

Okay, let's take some measurements. Young lady, would you like to join us?"

"I'd *love* to." She claps and skips across the store to us.

I turn to look at her. "Who are you and what have you done with my girlfriend?"

"Alien prom pods have taken over. Now that I know what tux you're going with, I know the perfect dress."

"Oh. Dress, huh? Can you rent one of those too?" I ask. I obviously forgot that Jess doesn't have a whole lot of money to buy a prom dress.

"Even better. Don't worry. It'll be a surprise."

Now I'm worried. "*Ludicrous* surprise, or . . ."

"Ludicrous only works if the two of us are in it together, and since you went rogue without consulting with me, I'm obligated to go snazzy. It'll be fine, trust me. Your nonna would approve."

Marvin takes me to the back of the store and has me step up onto a platform to measure me. Then he runs the tape measure between my legs to get my inseam.

"Have you ever been here before?" Marvin looks up at me, compelled to make small talk from between my legs.

"Uh, no. Never had an occasion."

"Huh." Marvin writes down a number on a piece of paper, then wraps the tape around my waist. "Phew. Look at you. You work out or something?"

"Yeah. I box," I say, a little embarrassed by Marvin's overexuberance.

"Oh-ho! A boxer, huh. We got us a Muhammad Ali here." He

loosens the tape from around my waist. "I had another fella about your age come in about a year ago. Had your build, exactly." He writes a number down on a piece of paper. "Wasn't a boxer though. Football player."

Oh no.

"Was getting married, he said. Arms up."

I raise my arms but barely. They feel like they're made of lead.

"A *little* higher," he says.

He was standing right here, right where I'm standing, looking at himself in the mirror. His whole life with Reggie ahead of him.

My chest feels too tight. I stare at my reflection in the mirror. It distorts. The blurry white ghost of Jason stares back at me, watching me get on with my life, without him.

I take a breath but it stalls, never making it all the way to my lungs. I try again and it stutters. My body is falling apart, and I'm watching it happen in the mirror like a car accident I can't tear my eyes away from. I'm outside my body looking in.

"Lucas?" Jess is standing next to me. "Are you okay?"

"I need air," I gasp.

I hop off the platform and my knees start to buckle under me. I pull myself up. Jess takes me by the arm to steady me.

Once outside, I lean against the wall, feeling as if my esophagus cuts off each breath. I slide down until my butt hits the sidewalk. People walk by and watch, staring at the big guy sitting on the filthy cement where dogs pee, where drunk people puke, where germ-ridden shoes step every day. Jess gets down on her knees next to me.

"It's okay," she says, but she's scared, I hear it.

I can't stop my body from doing what it wants to do. I press the heels of my hands into my eyes. Tears squeeze through anyway.

"Oh God."

It's never going to go away, never going to get better.

Jess sits across from me in the booth at the diner down the street, sipping a cup of tea. She insisted on herbal tea and toast for us both, like this is a twenty-four-hour bug that will go away on its own with plenty of fluids, bland food, and rest.

Staring at me over her cup she breaks the silence. "Told you prom was stupid."

It's the first laugh I've had in half an hour. Once I could stand up on my own, we came to the diner next door, where I popped a Xanax and waited it out.

I stare out the window watching the mash of foot traffic. Mothers in stretchy pants push strollers on their errands. The Q114 bus drives its regular route. A car rolls by, windows down, music blasting so loud the thumping of the bass rattles through the diner windows all the way to my molars.

Everyone's just going about their business, and here I sit, feeling small and damaged, afraid to look in Jess's eyes and see if something changed when she looks back at me.

I stare down into my cup. "I'm really embarrassed."

"What? Why?"

I jerk my head to the side, outside the window, refusing to look up. "For that. For what happened."

Jess sighs. "Please don't be. I'm just happy you're feeling better."

I pick up a sugar packet and flip it back and forth. "I think you were right though," I admit.

She takes a sip of her tea, then reaches for a wedge of my untouched toast. "I'm always right," she says, peeling back the top of a strawberry preserves tub. Slathering it on the toast with her teaspoon, she says, "Which part am I right about this time though?"

I tear the packet open and pour it into the tea. Maybe it just needs a lot of sugar.

"About prom being stupid. Why bother?" I say.

She crunches into the toast and chews, taking a deep contemplative breath through her nose.

"I changed my mind. I want to go now," she says. I look up in surprise. There's a dab of strawberry preserves in the corner of her mouth that if we were anywhere else any other time, I would have leaned over to kiss it off. Or maybe she doesn't even want to kiss me ever again after she watched me curl into a ball on the sidewalk.

"*Now* you want to go."

She nods. "Now we *have* to."

"Why?"

She sighs and reaches across the table to take my hand. She props it up to thread her fingers through mine.

"Because we need it. We need to start doing things again. Embarrassing, cheesy, fun . . . all of it. Because we can." She shrugs, like I'm supposed to understand what that means. "Besides," she adds, "I'm not kidding. The dress I'm thinking of? Holy crap, I'm going to look *amazing* in it. Just wait, you'll see."

A smile takes over my face. "I can't tell if you're being sarcastic or not."

She tilts her head and makes wide eye contact with me, her face completely deadpan. "*When* am I *ever* sarcastic?"

I rub my forehead and laugh. "Who, you? You're *never* sarcastic."

Between our snorts and giggles, and the Xanax, I start to feel better.

Jess

> **Remember the bridesmaid dress you wore to Brittany's wedding?**

> **You said it made you look like a giant string bean? Well, thank you in advance, or maybe thank you after the fact. By the time you get this, I'll have already worn it to PROM! I'll give you a second to let that settle in.**

> **It's like Invasion of the Body Snatchers over here! What's happening to me?!**

After work on Sunday, Lucas drops me off at Marissa's house.

Marissa's home is a post-Sandy, modern-construction monstrosity that sits snugly on the edge of the Norton Basin. When they bought the house, Mr. Connell said, "If you're going to spit in the eye of nature, might as well do it in style!" Style to him meant topiaries at the front entrance trimmed to look like swirling ice cream cones that spit in the eye of nature every day just by existing.

I ring the doorbell. Beethoven's Fifth chimes. It never failed to crack Marissa and me up. This is actually how Mr. Connell made his money, selling doorbells with different chime selections. Turns out there really is no such thing as a bad idea; people pay a lot of money to have "The Star-Spangled Banner" greet their guests on the Fourth of July.

The door opens to Mrs. Connell's beaming face.

"JESS!" She folds me into a tight hug. *This isn't awkward at all,* I think to myself. I can count on one hand how many times Mrs. Connell has ever hugged me: At Ethan's funeral. At Gino's. And today.

She finally releases me. "I can't tell you how happy it makes me to see you."

"I'm sorry about last time, at Gino's," I apologize before walking in. "Sometimes I just really miss her in weird ways." I shrug and swallow the knot rising up in my throat, hoping she doesn't want to explore in any greater depth my understatement of the century.

Mrs. Connell waves my apology away. "Jess, it's fine. I understand, trust me. Come *in*!" She takes my hand and tugs me over the threshold.

Walking through the foyer, I can feel Marissa's absence like I'm a human barometer and there's been a shift in the atmosphere. Even Mrs. Connell's overabundant enthusiasm can't mask the aching emptiness of the house without Marissa.

Liam sits on the couch in the den playing his Xbox, ignoring me, as if the doorbell didn't announce my arrival to probably half the block.

"Hey, Nugget. What's up?" I call over to him.

Silence.

Mrs. Connell lets out an exasperated huff. "Liam. Don't be rude. Say hello to Jess."

He mumbles something I assume is a coerced greeting.

Mrs. Connell waves for me to follow her. Inside the kitchen, she opens the refrigerator and pulls out a glass pitcher of lemon-infused water. She sits at the table and pours each of us a glass.

"Why is he so mad at me?" I whisper, careful that the vaulted ceilings don't carry my voice throughout the house.

"He misses both of you," she says, her face pained. "Marissa went away; then you did. He's young, Jess. He doesn't understand that this is hard for you too. In his mind, the only reason why you ever came here was to see Marissa. He feels left behind."

I actually know exactly how Liam feels. It's not easy being the one left behind.

I sip my water. Really tasty water, actually. Lemons really elevate water's game.

Mrs. Connell stands up. "Come on. Bring your water with you. Let's go get that dress."

I follow her upstairs. Once we cross the threshold into Marissa's room, Mrs. Connell gestures for me to take the lead. I know Marissa's room, and her closet, almost better than she does. In the back, I find it. The emerald-green bridesmaid dress she wore as part of her cousin's wedding party. Spaghetti straps with a low

V-neckline. Simple, easy. Totally me. When I texted Mrs. Connell to ask her if I could borrow it, she was thrilled it was going to get at least one more wear.

"It might need to be hemmed." She eyes it as I hold it up by my ears to keep it from dragging on the floor. "Can your mom do it?"

"Yeah, sure," I lie. I'll figure it out. I mean, it's a free dress. I can take it from here.

She takes the dress and holds it for me to admire it. "This will be stunning on you. Are you going with the boy you were with at Gino's?"

I nod. "Yeah. Lucas."

"Lucaaas?" She raises her eyebrows and stretches out his name, letting me know she needs more.

"Lucas Rossi."

"Oh," she says, barely a breath of air but with so much underlying subcontext. Then her head tilts to the side like people do when they're expressing their condolences. "The Rossis. I know the family."

Enough said.

"Well . . . that's just . . . that's really wonderful that you two found each other. It really, really is."

I wonder how many reallys it will take for her to really believe it. Because it sounds like the exact opposite, like she doesn't think Lucas and I together is all that wonderful.

I take the dress back and hold it carefully so that it doesn't drag on the way downstairs. Liam's still on the couch.

Pointing to him, I ask Mrs. Connell, "Is it okay if I hang out with Liam for a bit?"

She smiles and squeezes my arm. "It would be really nice if you did."

I flop down on the couch next to him and grab the other remote. "Want to start a new game?"

I have to give him some credit; he tries to hold on to his grudge. But his excitement at having a second player wins out.

I play with Liam for a couple of hours, until I know we're okay again. I can't have Liam be mad at me. He's practically my other brother.

Mrs. Connell orders in pizza for us. We eat, and Liam and I play more Xbox until there's an impossible glare on the screen. When I look outside, the sun is setting over the Norton Basin. I've been here for longer than I realized.

Since it's going to be dark soon and it's a long walk, Mrs. Connell drives me home. Liam sits in the back seat catching me up on what feels like everything that's happened to him in the past year. He barely stops to take a breath before launching into another story about the horrors of sixth grade.

When we get to my house, Mrs. Connell stares at the darkened stoop as I unbuckle.

"How's your mom doing, Jess? I haven't seen her in a while."

I grab the handle to escape. "She's fine," I say over my shoulder. "Well, you know. Not *fine*. Just . . ." I've run out of words to lie for my mother.

"Why don't I come in and say hello." She turns the ignition off and takes the keys out.

"No," I say quickly. Rudely, I realize by the shocked look on her face. "She's asleep. Truth is, she sleeps a lot." There, that's not a lie.

"Is she sleeping too much?" she asks carefully, probing for information like a professional.

"Probably," I say. "I mean, it's grief. Everyone deals with grief differently, you know? There's no right or wrong way or length of time to grieve. That's what her psychiatrist told her."

Mrs. Connell nods, slowly. "Yes, that's true. Grief is compli-cated. But at a certain point, it could be more than just grief. I'm glad to hear she's in therapy though."

I gave her that impression, I realize. I open my mouth to cor-rect her, to tell her that my mother quit therapy months ago. But then this conversation would keep going and I might have to allow her to come in. I picture my mother in her thin nightgown and greasy hair. The bills spread out across the dining room table. The empty refrigerator. Having just come from the Connells' house, which overflows with excess, so much that they have to put lem-ons in their water because it's too bland without it, I can't stand the thought of letting Mrs. Connell inside.

With the beautiful green dress in hand, I wave them good-bye and find my key to let myself in.

Inside, I make my way in the dark, laying the dress carefully over Mom's recliner before reaching for the lamp on the side table, turning the light on.

I walk down the hall to my mom's room to check in on her. She's not in bed.

I pan around her bedroom and find the bottle of Zoloft is on her nightstand. I pick it up. It's empty.

"Mom?" I call out, quietly at first, then louder. "MOM?"

"Jess?" Her voice is weak, coming from the bathroom. I find her in front of the toilet, shivering, sweating so much her night-gown is plastered to her body. There's vomit everywhere.

With trembling hands, I dial 911.

> **My mom tried to commit suicide.**

Select All. Cut.

> **My mother took a bottle of pills to kill herself.**

Select All. Cut.

> **I'm in the hospital with my mother. She tried to**

Select All. Cut.

> **I'm not going to be at school tomorrow. I'll explain later.**
>
> (Delivered 11:58 p.m.)

LUCAS

You are a woman of mystery. What's there to explain? Are you home sick?

(Today 7:17 a.m.)

Hellooooooo? If you're sick, let me know if you need anything.

(Today 11:33 a.m.)

Reg said she got pretty much the same text I did. Now we're both worried. I'm coming over.

(Today 2:35 p.m.)

I start with our meeting spot: Jess's bedroom window. The screen is still where I left it, behind a bush. Tempted as I am to just go in through her window to look for her, I can't cross that line. I press my face against the glass pane to look around. There's no sign of Jess. I have to try the front door.

It's strange, but ringing her doorbell almost feels like a bigger breach of her family's privacy than sneaking through her bedroom window. It's the first time I've ever rung her bell. Does her mother ever answer the door? I press my ear to the door to listen for foot-steps, anything.

No voices, no footsteps, nothing.

I walk along the porch to look through the living room win-dow. There's a sliver of space between the drawn curtains that allows me to peek inside. The house is dark. Her mother could be sleeping. But where's Jess?

What if something happened to both of them? What if they're both lying on the floor unconscious from carbon monoxide poi-soning? What if someone broke in and is holding them captive?

Screw it. I go back to Jess's bedroom window and slide it open. As soon as I'm in, I shut the window behind me, then pull the blinds down. It's too dark and quiet in the house. This isn't good. I have the same nervous feeling I did when I was looking for Mrs. Graham, terrified I'm going to find something I am not going to survive finding, except multiplied times infinity.

Creeping carefully out of Jess's bedroom, I see the door across the hall is open. The queen-sized bed is unmade, the blankets rumpled. Her mother's room.

Next to it is a closed door. My guess is this is Ethan's room. I open it just to make sure no one's unconscious in there. It's just Ethan's stuff. Even though we ran in different crowds, I feel the familiar knot of grief in my throat. I close the door behind me and head down the hallway.

Hanging over the recliner in the den, there's a long green dress covered in a clear dry-cleaner bag. This must be the dress Jess is wearing to prom. I hold it up by the hanger. She wasn't being sarcastic; it's really pretty. I reach under the bag and rub the soft thin fabric between my fingers, as if it can somehow fill itself with Jess's body just by touch, by wish.

Behind me, the dining room table is covered in bills, stacks of them. I lift a few off the table, some medical bills stamped "OVERDUE" from months ago. Stupid comments I made to her come back to slap me in the face. *"Insurance covers it."* I'm such a fucking asshole.

I dip into the kitchen for a quick look, clues, anything to help me find Jess. There are empty tubs of yogurt and cottage cheese turned upside down in the dish rack to dry. Flies swirl and land on a chicken salad sandwich on the kitchen table. Mrs. Alvarez is always bringing over food, Jess said. Maybe this was for Mrs. Nolan or was supposed to be Jess's dinner when she came home from Marissa's house last night. Though judging by the flies and yellowed crust of mayo around the edges, the untouched sandwich has been here for a while.

On the way back to Jess's room, I peek in the bathroom. No one here. The shower curtain is closed though.

Shit shit shit! I don't want to find anyone collapsed in there! But I have to look. As I'm pushing the curtain aside with my finger to reveal an empty tub, I see it. The pink toilet seat and pink tiles around it are splattered with vomit. Lots of it. Dread rises in my stomach, coming up as bile in my throat. One of them got violently sick last night.

I run out the front door to find Mrs. Alvarez. She'll know. I march up her stoop and ring her bell.

She pokes her head out the door.

"Hello, Lucas."

I almost don't recognize her without her wig and lipstick. She looks tired. Really tired.

"Hi, Mrs. Alvarez. I'm sorry to bother you. I'm just worried about Jess. Do you know where she is?"

She nods. "Her mother's sick. She's been in the emergency room with her since last night. I was there for a while, but . . . I'm old. I needed to come home and take my medicine and lie down for a bit."

The vomit around the toilet. Was it a stomach bug? Food poisoning?

"Is her mom okay?"

The question just makes her look even more tired and sad. "Jessica will call you to explain when she's ready."

I stand on her stoop staring at her, trying to decide if I can ask her more questions.

She reaches over and squeezes my arm, then shuts the door.

I come home from work a little after seven. I only went because I knew Pete wasn't going to be able to handle it alone, with Jess out and Joe gone. I head upstairs before dinner and try calling Jess again. Still nothing.

I come back downstairs, not wanting to be alone.

"Any word from Jess?" my mom asks as I take my seat at the kitchen table.

I shake my head. So far all I've told her is what Mrs. Alvarez told me.

Mom tsks and sighs. "It must've been an awful bug for her to be admitted to the hospital. By the way, I called Marvin and gave him your measurements. Your tux will be ready in time for prom," she says over her shoulder as she washes dishes in the sink.

I picture Jess's green dress left hanging over the chair of her dark, empty home. This is what happens when the universe isn't done torturing you yet. I have no idea if we're even still going to prom.

Holding up a soapy wooden spoon, Mom says, "Maybe you should go down to the gym to work out, try to get your mind off of it for a little while. Sitting around worrying doesn't help anyone."

I rub my hands down my face to hide my grimace. If she knew about the boxing match on Saturday, she'd hide my keys again, my sneakers, my clothes . . . anything to stop me from going. The fight is the only thing that should be on my mind this week. But Jess is taking up way too much head space, and not in the usual good way.

Mom takes the casserole out of the oven and puts it on top of the trivet in front of me. "Help yourself," she says, then heads back to the sink to wash some more dishes.

"Don't you want to sit down and eat with me?" I ask. I could really use some of her smothering today.

She stops midswipe with a soapy sponge. Then she dries her hands on a dish towel and joins me at the table.

"I'll wait for your father to eat, but I'll keep you company. How's that?"

I nod and blow on the clump of saucy ground beef and noodles on my fork.

We're silent for a bit, Mom holding her chin up on her hand, watching me inhale the food.

"It's good," I tell her, and she smiles.

The kitchen clock ticks, counting our seconds of silence. I hardly ever notice how loud it is except at times like this.

"So . . . what aren't you telling me?"

I look up at her in surprise and her lips edge up in a small, satisfied smile. I clear my throat before I choke on that last bite. Mom sits up straighter and folds her arms on the table.

"You read minds now?"

She lifts a shoulder. "Mother's intuition."

Everything that has been steadily building up inside of me is ready to blow. All I can see, think about, are the piles of bills, the vomit, the flies. The silence from Jess.

"I broke into Jess's house today," I admit, staring at my plate.

"You *what*?"

"I was worried about her. All these what-ifs were coming at me. I just wanted to make sure she was okay."

"Was this before or after you asked her neighbor?"

"Before," I confess.

"Maybe you should have rung Mrs. Alvarez's bell *first*?" she says, her voice rising a few octaves.

"Yeah. I guess."

She huffs. "So what happened?" she asks. She's reserving judgment for now. I appreciate that.

"There was vomit all over the bathroom. She must've gotten really sick. I didn't know yet if it was Jess or her mom."

She wrinkles her nose and waits, I guess knowing there's more to the story.

"Mom . . . there were *so* many bills on the table. *Overdue* bills. I mean, Jess has pretty much said things were tight. But those bills stressed *me* out."

Her hand goes up to her cheek. She groans. "That poor girl. I kind of picked up on something when she came over for dinner. She sounds like she's on her own over there." She sighs and shakes her head. "But you knew this. So what else is bothering you?"

Staring at my phone all day waiting for it to buzz with a call or text from Jess is messing with my head.

I twirl my fork in circles on my plate. "I feel like, if this were *me*, I would've called her so she wouldn't worry. You know? It feels like she's . . . I don't know . . . shutting me out. And that makes me an asshole for making this about me, right? I mean, I *know* this isn't about me. But it's eating at me in ways that it shouldn't and I hate that! I hate that I'm even thinking about *me* when *all* I should be worried about is *her*!"

Mom squeezes my forearm. "You're right, it's not about you. And Jess is *not* you. She's not going to behave or react the same way you do. Especially if she's gotten used to doing things on her own out of necessity. And breaking into a girl's house because she's not confiding in you enough is not okay, Lucas!"

"I was worried," I say, with less conviction this time. I sink in my seat and rub my hands down my face. "I just wish she'd call me."

Mom groans, then gazes out the kitchen window, her eyes lost, watching something I can't see. "You're both so young. The world shouldn't be this hard for you yet." She lets out a tragic, world-weary sigh.

Her eyes well up as she becomes lost in her own thoughts, her own nightmare. She picks up a napkin off the table and dabs at her eyes before her tears can spill. I wonder if she sees Jason in the backyard, the way I saw his image in the mirror at Marvin's.

When she looks over at me, she says, crumpling the napkin in her hand, "What would the wise Dr. Engel have to say right now?"

I pretty much know what Dr. Engel would say. Grief is uncomfortable. What I don't know is what my mother has to say, mostly because I haven't been entirely open with her lately.

"I kind of want to hear your take on this," I tell her.

That makes her smile. She turns the napkin in her hand, then folds it into squares.

"Did you know your father and I broke up twice when we were dating?" she asks, dabbing under her eye with the edge of the napkin to salvage her mascara.

Is she implying that Jess and I might break up? If so, that's *not* what I want or need to hear right now.

"Uh, no?"

She nods. "Once in college. And once right out of college."

"Why?" I ask.

She shakes her head and smiles wryly. "For reasons you don't really want to know. But we worked through them. Here's what we learned." She leans closer. "We had to make it work between us because we didn't know how to *not* be together."

I inhale, deeply, unevenly, allowing her words to sink in.

"Every couple hits some hurdles in their relationship." She reaches for my water glass. "Learning how to get over them together is how you grow. You and Jess have more challenges than any couple your age should have to deal with. But if you're meant to be together, you'll find a way. Even through all of this." She sweeps her hand around her, because *this* is the shattered world we—and Jess—were left with.

Lifting my glass, she chugs it all down. "Crying makes me thirsty," she gasps when she's done, then laughs. "I'll get you another one." She stands up and I watch her refill my glass at the faucet.

"Ma?"

She turns from the sink.

"How's your project going?" I point to her laptop, closed on the counter.

An eager, excited expression crosses her face. She leans her hip against the counter. "Really well! I can't wait to show them my concepts."

She lights up in front of me.

"It's okay to go back to work if you want." I feel like she needs to hear this from me, to let her know I'm okay. "I'm really doing a lot better now. You know that, right?"

She looks down at the glass of water in her hand and nods. "Maybe I will," she says. Her voice sounds hopeful, to my ears at least. "Maybe sooner than I thought."

I've been so afraid of talking to Mom about Jess, life, Jason, life after Jason. . . . Right now, I am so incredibly grateful to the universe for giving me this mom to talk to.

Jess

It doesn't even matter that you won't see this. I'm actually glad that you're not here for this. I'm not in a good place. You don't need that on top of everything you're going through.

I went outside the ER entrance to try and call Lucas. While I was out there, ambulances were pulling up. So many people who were scared. Who wanted to live.

I didn't end up calling Lucas. I'm having a hard time saying those words out loud. "My mother tried to kill herself." What's that say about me? That I'm not enough for her?

I swear I can practically hear you screaming at me! Yes, I'll tell him! Soon. Eventually. Just not yet.

Me again. Who else has the stamina to keep a one-sided conversation going this long?

One of the doctors met with me and Mrs. Alvarez. He asked us how long this has been going on.

He thinks it's something called complicated grief disorder. Big red flag he said was that this has gone on longer than six months.

He said it's a treatment-resistant depression, which doesn't sound so hot, I know. But the beast has a name and, in a weird way, that helps.

The therapy and meds she was on weren't the right kind. There's a different kind of therapy she can do. It was hard to keep track of everything he said, but the big headline is they think they can help her.

If all this happened so Mom can finally get the help she needs, then okay. We hit rock bottom and someone's giving us a ladder to climb out of this rotting, stinking hellhole.

^^^ How Jess expresses optimism and resiliency in the face of adversity.

Lucas

Jess is lying on her belly under the blankets, her hair messy, face flushed, curled up in the nook of my arm. Her chin is propped on that sensitive area, right above the armpit, the point of her chin digging into a ligament. It should hurt, but surprisingly I feel nothing.

My finger traces the freckles that dot along her shoulders, continuing under the blanket, plotting a constellation along her back.

Wait. Is she naked under there?

She's rambling, one long run-on sentence, not even stopping for a breath. The words are gibberish, but it doesn't matter because her smile is electric. I squeeze her tighter and tighter against me, trying to become one with her. The arm that's wrapped around her is falling asleep, but I'm afraid one false move will shut her down.

Finally, she stops talking and gnaws on her lip, looking up at me with these big doe eyes. That did it. This is definitely a dream. Jess doesn't do that doe-eyed thing. But I let it keep rolling, because, you know, she's naked and I kind of want to see where this will go.

I pull her up closer to me, so we're nose to nose. Her body is pressed up next to mine, her skin warm; her eyelashes brush against my cheek.

"Jess, remember at the beach on Thursday?" I nudge my nose against hers, inhaling her breath on my face.

She smiles again but this smile is spooky. Everything about my experience with dreams—my pounding heart, my rapid breathing—tells me this dream is changing, veering far off course from the outcome I was rooting for.

"You said everyone you know is a ghost," I press on. Why am I picking at that scab?

"None of this is real, Lucas." Her eyes go flat, dead, like all the characters in *The Polar Express* that made that movie terrifyingly unwatchable for me as a kid.

"I know . . . this is a dream."

She continues as if I hadn't spoken. "We all died that night, Lucas."

To illustrate her point—because God forbid Jess is ever wrong—the blankets pull back on their own, and Jess's pale naked body rises up into the air, her arms lifting by her sides. She floats away from me across the room, her toes barely skimming my bed. Shivering from the absence of her warmth, I grab at the empty air to pull her back to me, but I'm also terrified. She's a ghost. My Jess is a ghost!

She drifts upward toward the ceiling, and then she's nothing but smoke and vapors. Gone.

My alarm clock on my nightstand reads 12:28 when my phone buzzes. May as well answer it; I've been staring at the ceiling where I last saw Dream Jess for the past hour.

I glance at the name on the screen before answering it. "Jess?"

"I'm sorry," she starts off, almost as if she's calling to apologize for turning into a ghost and leaving me an hour ago.

"Just tell me: Are you okay?"

"Yeah?"

I swing my feet out of bed and onto the floor and run my hand through my hair. "Jesus, I've been so worried. Is your mom okay?"

Her phone is ancient and has the worst reception. Her voice rolls in and out in between crackles.

"Jess . . . we have a bad connection . . . what'd you say?"

"Can you hear me? I said I'm sorry about today . . . wait . . . yesterday . . . God, what time *is* it?"

"It's twelve thirty," I tell her.

"I am the worst girlfriend!" she cries.

"There are worse," I tease. "Where are you now?"

The connection breaks up again.

"Jess . . . I'm sorry . . . what'd you say?"

"HOME!" she hollers and this time I hear her loud and clear.

"I'm coming over," I decide.

"Wait . . . what?"

"I'll be there in half an hour. Keep your window open."

I hang up, hopping out of bed and reaching for some pants at the same time.

I don't dare take my car and risk waking my parents. Just my phone, my keys, and my germ-infested sneakers, before slipping out the front door. Tying the laces on the front porch, I take off, running to Jess's house.

I slow down as I turn onto McBride so I don't alert any neighbors or barking dogs. Last thing I need is to get arrested for sneaking around Jess's house. I crouch down below the window line, hoping Mrs. Alvarez isn't one of those old people who can't sleep.

Jess's room is dark, except for a lit candle on her dresser and the phone in her hand casting a pale glow on her face. I poke my head in first so I don't startle her and then pull myself in. She shuts the window behind me and pulls down her shade. The candle is vanilla scented; her bedroom smells like a dessert factory.

One look at her and I know I made the right decision coming here. The stress of the last twenty-four hours is all over her face.

"Hey." I pull her into my arms. She squishes her face into my chest. I pull her over to the bed and we both sprawl out.

"You okay?" I ask, breathing in the scent of her hair, and then I recognize it. Honeysuckle. I'm hit with a memory of Jason and me plucking its flowers off a shrub in early spring, removing the pistil from the center, and licking its nectar. It was hardly a drop, barely enough for a bee or a hummingbird, but it tasted magical.

"You being here helps, a lot actually. Thank you."

She reaches behind her, grabbing a pamphlet off her night-stand. She holds it up for me to see.

Complicated Grief Disorder
Recognizing the Signs

She points to the bulleted list of symptoms. "Everything. Every symptom here my mom has." She takes the flyer from me and shakes it. "When I came home yesterday and found her . . ." Her voice shakes. "She threw up most of the pills. Thank God they made her sick. Otherwise, it could've been so much worse. The doctor said she could've slipped into a coma if the pills were fully absorbed."

I close my eyes. The vomit splatters in the bathroom. Her mother tried to commit suicide and Jess found her. It's so much worse than I thought.

"I spoke to a doctor at the hospital. A psychiatrist. He said my mom's going to have to do the work but they've had some success with a type of psychotherapy with patients who have this kind of grief disorder. He told me what everyone else said, you know, losing a child is the most difficult loss to process. But then he said, 'But that doesn't make it any easier on you'—meaning me—'does it?'"

She reaches over again to grab a card off her nightstand. "I came home with all kinds of goodies." She hands me the card, pointing to the name on it. "That's the woman who runs a support group for teens who have lost siblings. She wants me to go."

I recognize the address. It's in the same building where I see Dr. Engel.

"Are you going to do it?" I ask, hoping she'll say yes.

Jess nods. "Yeah. I am. If my mother's going to put in the work, so am I." She glances up at me. "Can't hurt, right?"

I smile down at her. "It helps," I tell her. "I can come with you if you want. Or not. Up to you."

She gnaws on her lip. "Let me go to one on my own first. Maybe I don't want you to know every dark secret inside of me. Could be a real turnoff." She laughs softly, but there's a flicker of insecurity in her eyes that tells me that's something that actually worries her.

"A social worker met with me and Mrs. Alvarez. When she found out about our situation here, she made calls and gave us a list of things to do. Since we own the house, there's a lot of equity we can tap into. Mom can get a line of credit with the bank to pay off the bills. When she's ready, she can go back to work to pay it off. And we qualify for Medicaid. So yay, us. We'll have health insurance too."

She plucks at my T-shirt but doesn't look me in the eye.

"I feel like an asshole," I admit.

She looks up at me. "*You?* Why?"

I shake my head. "Jess, I said some stupid things. I didn't realize how bad things were."

"That's because I didn't tell you everything," she says, trying to make me feel better.

"I know that. But *why* didn't you tell me?"

She takes a breath and runs her hand through her hair. "I didn't want people to know, to judge us. Especially you. Your family is so perfect—"

"*Perfect?* My family is so not perfect!"

"Well, they seem pretty perfect to me, okay? I was embarrassed. And I didn't want you to feel sorry for me."

I pull her closer. Her knee hooks up over my leg. "Do you know what I see when I look at you?"

She shakes her head against my chest. I push her hair behind her ear.

"One of the strongest people I've ever met."

She laughs. "Yeah. Right."

"I mean it. Give yourself some credit. You get up every day and do what you have to do. No one tells you what to do. You just do it."

She shrugs. "It's not like I had a choice."

"You did, but you're not a quitter, so it never occurred to you to give up."

She rolls onto her stomach and rests her chin on my armpit. Unlike my dream, it does kind of hurt. I pull her up so she's on top of me, then wrap my arms behind her lower back.

"I have a confession to make. I broke into your house today."

"You were *here*!" she squeals a little saying it.

"I have zero regrets. I was afraid something happened to you and your mom."

She stares at me for a while, and I can't really figure out what she's thinking.

Finally she says, "Thank you," and kisses my chin.

I shrug. "For breaking and entering?"

She laughs softly and plants her hands on my chest. "For caring. For being here."

With a deep sigh, she buries her face in my chest and exhales; her breath swoops through me and I can feel it coursing through my body like a current. She folds her hands on my chest and rests her chin on them.

"By the way, I need the address of where you're fighting on Saturday."

"Why?"

"Because I'm coming."

"No . . . Jess . . . you don't have to. I know you don't want to see that."

"You know I don't take no for an answer. So forget it. I'm coming. Some things, you just don't do alone, okay? You need people rooting for you. I'm your people. And you're mine."

She runs a finger over my eyebrow, then the other. "Did I ever tell you that you have really sexy eyebrows?" she asks.

"Eyebrows?"

"Yeah. Eyebrows can go either way. They can really mess up a person's face. Yours are perfection. And this thing here." She kisses my chin. "This butt crack on your chin. It's hot. Makes you look like a superhero."

Suspended above me, she pauses, holding my gaze, her lips slightly parted. My hands run down her back.

"What now? My erotic attached earlobes? My sensual deviated septum? If weird is your thing, I have a hitchhiker thumb that's going to drive you wild!" I hold up my bent thumb.

She bites her lips, watching me.

"What?" I'm desperate to know her thoughts since they're obviously about me.

Instead, she shows me.

She presses her lips against mine and knots her fingers through my hair, holding me to her. If it were physically possible to fuse with another human being, in this moment, I think Jess and I are damn close to becoming one.

Her other hand slips under my shirt, tracing my stomach, running up my side. Tearing herself away, she sits up and pulls her shirt off and tosses it. The candle stutters in the slight breeze of her shirt flying across the room and her shadow dances along the wall in the flickering light. My hands stop moving, frozen by the sight of Jess half naked on top of me. She reaches behind her to unclasp her bra.

Shit . . . is this . . . Are we . . . tonight?

But what if *this* is just another way of Jess trying to tune out what's happened to her in the past twenty-four hours? Jess, queen of mystery and deflection, finding yet another method to repel actual feelings.

"Jess? Maybe we should wait." The words hurt just coming out of my mouth because I really want this.

Her hands freeze behind her back. She stares back at me, confused.

"Ummm . . . are you saving yourself for marriage or something?"

"No. You can thank Krista Gardner for taking care of that," I joke. "She dumped me right after."

"Sorry to hear that," she says, lying back down on top of me. She folds her hands under her chin to peer up at me. "So . . . if it's not that . . . what is it? I have you alone in my bedroom and you don't want to take advantage of this moment with me. I even lit a candle to set the mood." She giggles, but she's nervous, I can tell.

I push her hair behind her ear, then trace her forehead with my finger to erase those worried creases.

"Jess . . . I like you . . . a lot. A lot a lot. But if you're doing this because you don't want to deal with what's really going on, then we have to wait."

She stacks her fists on top of each other like a tower and props her chin on them to be more at eye level with me.

"Lucas, there are very few things I'm entirely certain of. I can't make a whole lot of sense out of anything going on in my life right now. Except for you."

She buries her nose in my shirt and sniffs. "You're sweaty and a little stinky. I'm convinced you don't own a brush because you always look like you just came out of a wind tunnel. But you're the kindest, most beautiful boy I've ever met." She kisses a trail along my jaw. "But the real clincher was tonight. Running over here in the middle of the night to be here with me is probably *the* most romantic thing anyone's ever done. Ever." She starts to slide off of me. "But if you don't want to . . ."

My hands run up the sides of her neck and cup right below her ears, bringing her down for a kiss.

"You make a compelling argument," I tell her. "You win."

Around five thirty, I sneak out of Jess's window before the sun makes an appearance and jog home. Just me and the garbage truck out on the empty roads. They honk and the guy in the neon-orange vest holding on to the back of the truck flexes his bicep at me and laughs.

The carpeting on the stairs pads my footsteps as I make my way quietly back into my bedroom. By the time I get home, I have just about an hour to sleep before my alarm clock goes off. I strip off my clothes down to my boxers and throw them across the room before pulling the covers over me. When I open my eyes again, Dad is sitting on the edge of my bed giving me the stink eye.

"Hey." I sit up. My head feels like it's been stuffed with cotton. "Did I sleep through my alarm?"

The light quality of the room is about right; still liquid gold. I look at the time. It's only 6:53. I could have slept for another seven minutes. Seven more minutes would have been nice. His eyes have me locked in his angry crosshairs.

"Mind telling me where you went last night?"

My first instinct is to deny everything. But no.

"Jess called. I went over there."

His internal conflict is written all over his face. Being the father of an eighteen-year-old must be weird. "She *asked* you to come over in the middle of the night?" He leans closer as if he didn't hear me correctly.

"No! God no. I offered. She was upset. Her mom's in the hospital," I answer.

"Yeah, your mother told me." He breathes in deeply through his nose, those enormous nostrils being put to good use to vacuum the stale air in my room. They even have built-in HEPA filters.

"Still . . . you can't go sneaking around in the middle of the night."

I nod to be agreeable, but then I stop.

"Dad. She . . . uh . . . I really like her, you know? And I can't promise I won't go to her if she needs me." I scratch the back of my head. Something about the gesture makes him both wince and smile. He's got that melancholy look on his face like when we bust out the old home movies.

"You've been doing that since you were a little kid. Anytime you got nervous or stressed, the hand went up to the head." He reaches over and tousles my hair. With a resigned sigh, he drops his hands between his legs. "You're eighteen, Lucas. I can't . . . I know I have to start letting go. You've never done anything to make me doubt your judgment."

Shit. Now I feel really guilty about the fight on Saturday.

"Just . . . text me, at least, if you do that again, so I know. So I don't worry. It won't matter if you're forty-eight; I'll still worry."

Maybe for the first time I'm getting a glimpse of a relationship my dad and I may have a few years from now.

"Does Mom know?" I ask.

He shakes his head. "No . . . but I can't keep running interference. She's your mother. You need to start talking to her."

"I talk to her!" I say, hearing the defensive whine in my voice.

"You talk. But you don't *talk*. Anytime there's a problem, you ask me to fix it," he says. "It's not just you. Both of you are dancing around it." He juts his hand out to me. "She was really happy yesterday. That you talked to her about Jess."

Up until yesterday, even the thought of Mom and me having

a feelings conversation filled me with dull anxiety. It's one thing for me to talk to Dr. Engel. I know my words can't do any harm there. But I've been afraid of saying the wrong thing and hurting my mom. But yesterday was okay. Mom did cry, but she didn't fall apart. Neither did I.

"How'd you know I was out, anyway?" I squint as the morning sun angles through the blinds directly into my eyes.

"What? And give away my secrets? No way." He picks up a dirty shirt off the floor and throws it at my face. "Clean up your room. And good luck getting through the day. You look like hell."

He laughs and shuts the door behind him. My alarm goes off a minute later.

Jess

"Don't worry, you won't fall."

As Mrs. Alvarez's ancient dining room table wiggles under my weight, I find no comfort or reassurance in her words.

"Mr. Alvarez and I used to have his entire family over every Thanksgiving. Remember? Our turkey alone used to weigh more than you do. Turn a little." She manages to say all of this with pins between her lips.

I glance down at her gray wig, grateful that she offered to alter my dress for me. The tailor I called told me it would be thirty-five dollars for alterations without even seeing the dress or knowing how much work it needed. Thirty-five dollars! I was ready to grab some electrical tape from Enzo's for a quick, no-fuss, do-it-yourself hem job.

Strange how I was so turned off by anything prom-related but now . . . now I really am excited to go. I want to do normal teen-age things. I *crave* normal the way I crave salad and apples when I haven't had a vegetable or fruit in a while. I *get* prom now. The old-school feeling of really liking someone enough to want to share a rite of passage with them.

Mrs. Alvarez glances up at me. Her wig is slightly askew today. I want to bend down and straighten it and give her the biggest hug while I'm there.

"Did you know Lucas came looking for you the day you were in the hospital with your mother? He's very sweet on you. I can tell."

A smile takes a life of its own, ready to split my face in half. Mrs. Alvarez cackles around the pins in her mouth.

"I know *that* look!" She proceeds to tell me the story of when she met Mr. Alvarez at a church dance when she was forty years old. It's a story I've heard a million times before. But it's okay. She's lonely. So am I.

"Everyone thought I'd never marry, don't think I didn't hear it every time I turned around. I was too picky, I was going to be a spinster, I wasn't getting any younger . . ." She waves her hand in the air dismissing all those harsh words from decades ago. "And then I met Mr. Alvarez. He was twenty years older than me and already collecting social security. But who cares? I didn't! It was too late for us to have children. But not too late to fall in love."

When she inserts the last pin in the hem, she stands back to admire her handiwork. The smile on her face tells me she's pleased.

"Oh, Jessica. You look lovely." Her hands flutter to her cheeks.

"I don't know why everyone says you look like your father. I see your mother's delicate cheekbones. Classic beauties, both of you."

I step off the table onto the chair. Mrs. Alvarez offers a hand to help me down; I take it to be polite, but if I fall, there's nothing she can do to stop me. Once I'm back on the ground, her eyes drop to my chest. Her scowl tells me this does *not* please her.

"You're showing too much."

I look down at my chest. "It's fine."

She waves her hand in front of her own chest. "Jessica. You have to leave a little something for the imagination!" Reaching over for the straps, she lifts them up. "Let me take these up a bit."

I turn around so she can't see my blush thinking about last night with Lucas when we didn't leave anything for the imagination.

She pins the straps in the back.

When she spins me around again, she looks at my chest with a pleased expression. "Better. You can get dressed now."

Mrs. Alvarez's sewing room has a twin bed and an old Singer sewing machine. I take the dress off, then readjust the pins in the straps to drop them back down a little. I may not have much cleavage, but I also don't need to look like a seven-year-old at my prom.

When I'm done, Mrs. Alvarez comes in and hangs the dress back up.

"Are you going home now?" Her voice is steeped with disapproval. She doesn't like that I'm staying in the house alone. I love Mrs. Alvarez, but I don't want to sleep in her sewing room.

"Not yet. I'm going to try out that support group the doctor told me about. *Then* I'm going home. I'll call you when I get back so you don't worry. Deal?"

She pats my arm. "All right, then."

I reach over and straighten her wig, just a little. Then I throw my arms around her and squeeze.

When I let go, she cups my chin. "I love you like a granddaughter, Jessica. You're never alone as long as I'm here. You know that, right?"

I clear my throat so I don't cry in front of her. "I know."

I do know. But it helps to hear it. More than she can imagine.

LUCAS

Leo's walking around the heavy bag as I get my last workout in.

"Weigh-in's at eight. Be there on time."

I nod, working the bag.

"Don't forget the body." Leo dances around the bag with me. He's been giving me last-minute pointers since I got here. "Check your bag tonight. Remember your mouthpiece."

Panting, I say, "I've been having anxiety dreams about that. Showing up and getting my teeth knocked out because I forgot it."

"Triple-check your bag, 'kay? Next . . . get some sleep! I have guys who spend the night on the computer looking for tips. Or shadowboxing all night 'cause they're too jacked up. I'm telling you . . . go to bed! And no messing around with your girl. It drains the fight out of you."

"Seriously?" I pant. "I thought that was a myth."

"Not a myth. Gimme a round of snapping punches."

I nod, lowering my head to the bag for a round of quick jabs. My arms are burning, but I know there's still more gas in me to keep going.

"Who's coming?" he asks.

"You?"

"What about your girlfriend?"

I shake my head. "I'm trying to talk her out of it."

He's quiet for a little bit. "She should come. Some moral support, you know?"

I keep punching.

"What about your folks?"

"I didn't tell them."

He shoves the bag at me. *"The fuck not?"*

I dodge the bag. "They don't need to know," I argue.

"Why not? 'Cause they might not let you fight?" he challenges me.

"I'm eighteen. I don't need their permission."

He simmers silently, breathing through his engorged nostrils like a fire-breathing dragon. "Water. I want you drinking all day today. Then two hours before the match tomorrow you just sip. Same with food. One punch to the gut and you'll hurl all over the ring."

I might hurl even on an empty stomach. Just the thought of entering that ring for the first time makes my stomach clench.

After the heavy bag, Leo calls Kenny over to meet us in the ring for mitt drills.

Finally, Honor comes in to spar with me. We strap on our headgear and Leo helps me with my mouthpiece.

Dancing around the ring with that smug-ass grin of his, Honor taunts me, "Did your girl get a chance to kiss that cute face of yours good-bye?" Honor makes kissy noises. Kenny shuts him up by shoving a mouthpiece in.

Leo snaps his fingers in front of my face so I have his undivided attention. "Guy you're fighting is a southpaw. So's Honor. This is good practice. Let's go."

Honor's not one to take it easy on me, but I know his moves by now. I have no idea what I'm in for tomorrow.

I hear Jess's worried complaint bouncing around in my brain. *"I don't get it."*

As my stomach clenches and swirls with prefight nervous muck, I'm not so sure I get it either.

Jess

On my way to pick up my mother.

Enough said.

Our reunion at the hospital is far from a fairy-tale mother-and-child reunion.

As Mom wraps her arms around my neck in a hug, her hospital wristband scratches the skin by my ear. An involuntary shudder runs through my body. I think Mom notices, because she pulls away and looks down at the tiled floor, ashamed.

We don't speak much on the cab ride home, maybe because I jumped up front with the cabdriver and let Mrs. Alvarez sit in the back with Mom.

I can't even look at her, let alone talk to her. What's there to say? She tried to leave me. Didn't she think for a second that I lost Dad and Ethan too, that she's not the only one who's been hurting all this time? Didn't it even occur to her how killing herself would mess me up—even more!—for the rest of my life?

When we pile out of the cab outside our house, Mrs. Alvarez shoos us up our front stoop.

"I have a roast chicken ready for you. Let me go get it. You go on in."

I lead the way, focusing on the steps, my key, the doorknob. Anything to avoid looking at my mother.

Inside, Mom rubs her arms as if she's cold, even though the house is warm and stuffy.

My gaze pans around our house, double-checking to make sure I haven't left any triggers out in the open. I hid the bills so they wouldn't be the first thing she saw when she walked in. I scrubbed the toilet and bathroom tiles twice to get rid of any sign of vomit.

She walks through the living room and turns right toward the bedrooms.

Here we go. Back to her bed.

But she stops outside the bathroom and looks inside.

"I'm sorry, Jess," she says.

I'm not sure what exactly she's apologizing for, but I say, "It's okay," anyway.

Hugging herself, she probes me with her eyes as if she's trying to see where it hurts. Everywhere, I want to tell her. It hurts everywhere.

"I didn't get sick," she says, so suddenly it feels disjointed from this moment.

"Huh?"

"The pills didn't make me sick. Mrs. Alvarez told me that's what you thought."

She watches me for a second, letting that sink in, I guess.

"I was lying down in bed after I took them. Across the room, on my vanity, I saw the flower you made me out of yellow duct tape, from when you and Marissa went through that craze where you made everything out of that tape. I had a duct tape wallet. A duct tape bracelet. Remember? You made the flower for me for Mother's Day." She pauses, waiting for me to understand. Understand *what*? "I saw it and . . . I went to the bathroom and made myself throw up."

When I still haven't said anything, her hand flutters to her mouth. Then she gestures to me. "*Jess.* I made a mistake. I didn't really want to die. I could never do that to you."

It's enough to make me walk over and hug her. It's a start.

LUCAS

I shut the alarm clock five minutes before it goes off.

Even with Leo's warning to get some sleep, I had anxiety dreams all night. I showed up to the fight barefoot, hoping no one would notice. Next dream, I couldn't figure out how to get through the ropes into the ring. The crowd laughed at me as I got all tangled up and landed on my face on the mat.

Tugging a T-shirt on, I walk over to my desk and flip open my laptop. The file is up from last night.

March 27 Broke up a fight at school; guy was getting physical with his girlfriend.

January 18 Gave a homeless guy my sandwich.

November 7 Helped a woman load a case of water in her car at Key Food.

August 4 Gave a guy a jump start.

The list goes on and on. So many random acts of kindness, so many good deeds. But did any one of them really make a difference? Is the world a better place now because of them? Am I a better person for breaking up a fight at school or feeding a stray cat? Better than the person I was before that night?

I keep searching for meaning, a reason why my brother's bed is empty every night and mine isn't. I wish I could go into this fight feeling like I know why I'm doing it. But I'm not sure of anything anymore.

The smell of eggs and sizzling bacon greets me as I walk downstairs. English muffins are heating up in the toaster oven.

"I made you breakfast," Mom calls over her shoulder from the stove with a cheer in her voice only she can muster at this hour.

"You didn't have to do that," I tell her, watching her work two frying pans.

She shrugs and smiles up at me. "You're getting up so early to work on a weekend. How could I not?"

There's that pang of guilt again ringing through my body like the electronic bell at the gym. I could tell her now that I'm not going in early to do inventory but going to my first boxing match in Brooklyn.

But I don't.

"Can I get it to go?" I ask her.

"Sure! I'll make you an egg sandwich. How's that?" She takes the muffins out of the toaster and opens the drawer with the aluminum foil. Watching her hustle around the kitchen, knowing what she gave up for me—and for herself, and for the family, I'm sure—fills me with the breathless unconditional love I had for her when I was really young.

"Ma?" She turns around and I wrap my arms around her, squeezing her so hard I lift her off the ground. "I really love you. Okay?"

"Lucas!" she squeaks. When her feet are back on the ground, she says, "I don't know what that was for, but thank you!" She pulls my head down to kiss my cheek, then goes back to making me a ginormous egg sandwich.

I touch my headgear with my glove to reassure myself that it's there. Then I lift my lip up around my mouthpiece. Without totally grabbing my crotch, I twist a little to feel the jockstrap in place. I'd like to keep my brains, my teeth, and my balls intact. Nothing too awful can happen with those three bases covered.

"You're ready for this," Leo says to me in my corner of the ring. "You're here to show everyone what you learned. And to prove to yourself that you got this."

He's in my corner with me, in every way imaginable. No matter what happens to me today, I am grateful to him. He's been such an important part of my healing process, some days I think he gets what's going on inside my head even more than Dr. Engel.

The gym has some folding chairs lined up around the ring. This isn't a pro match. There's no fancy seating, no boxers' wives in furs and jewels. Just friends and family milling around, hoping for the best.

I find Jess right away off to the side, her red hair making her stand out in the crowd. When she sees that I see her, she gives me two "you got this" thumbs-up. I know she's not loving the idea of me in the ring right now, but I appreciate the show of faith. Pete's next to her. He throws both arms up in victory, prematurely. I hope he didn't just jinx me, but I take it for the vote of confidence that I know I always have from him. I'm glad Jess brought him. I just hope I don't embarrass myself too much in front of them.

"How're you feeling?" Leo asks.

Panic swells in my bowels. "I think I need to go to the bathroom."

"Too late." Leo slaps me on the back. "Let that urge fuel you to get this over with fast!" He laughs at that. I try to find an extra ounce of breath to laugh with him, but I don't have even a gasp to spare.

The ref calls us into the center of the ring to introduce me to my opponent, Tony. Physically, we're equally matched. But he looks to be a few years older. I hope that doesn't mean he's had a few years of training on me.

Tony smacks my gloves with his, a boxer handshake. Then we go back to our corners and wait for the bell.

There it is.

Tony comes at me, fists ups. I meet him in the center of the ring with some feeler jabs, while keeping an eye out for his right hand. Circling him, I hold center ring. Everything Leo taught me comes into play. Touch him before committing to power punches. Let him know I can reach him, hurt him. Make him cautious instead of trying to knock me out.

I throw fast jabs. His hands drop and I hook him. I dance around, finding new angles, new openings. He is nowhere near as prepared as I am.

The bell rings and we go back to our corners. Leo's waiting for me with a huge grin.

"Nice," he says, gushing praise coming from Leo. "You're doing good out there. Stick with the plan."

I turn to find Pete and Jess in the thin crowd. Jess jumps up and down and claps for me. Cupping her hands around her mouth, she hollers, *"Yay, Lucas!"*

Leo smacks my back. "Aren't you glad she came?"

I roll my shoulders. The verdict's still out on that one—we'll see how I finish. The bell rings and I'm back in the ring.

I connect with an uppercut to Tony's body, but I drop my defense. Tony counterpunches hard to my jaw. The impact sends me flying against the ropes. He comes after me. I'm not controlling the space anymore; Tony is.

A rapid-fire assault of fists comes at me and all I can do is block. He gets a solid punch into my ribs and I fold over like a rag doll. My guard drops and he punches me in the head. The ring spins.

I don't see Jess but I know she's there, watching all this. I hear Leo's words to me that first day in the gym.

"What's going to keep you going when you think you got nothing left?"

Now I know. Jess.

I'm not going down in front of her. I won't. I find the resolve to stand up and keep fighting.

Shaking it off, I spring off the ropes and come at him. Chin down, tight guard, I whip out a bunch of shots. I get a solid uppercut into his ribs—ha! Stings, don't it? His guard drops and I'm on him before he has a chance to figure out what just happened. I get him with a three-hit combo and I keep on pummeling him as he backs away. He throws a punch and I slip it, then follow it with more counters. He backs away and opens himself up. I throw a straight right that hits him square in the forehead. He falls backward onto the mat.

The bell rings.

I go back to my corner while Tony pulls himself up.

One more round.

Leo eyes me. "Feeling okay?"

I nod and dance around. "Yeah!"

He smiles. "Okay. Guy's getting gassed. This is the last round. He's gonna give it his all. The only time you stop punching is to let him miss. Go after him with everything you got. Don't leave nothing behind. Let those punches fly. Strong finish. Show the judges you're the winner."

The bell rings and we're off.

I go after him with punches that have been ingrained in me from the gym. No thought, just the automatic combos I practiced with Leo, Kenny, and Honor. Fists are flying. If he's connecting, I barely feel it. I step aside and swing a big left hook.

Tony goes down. The ref crouches over him. Tony shakes his head, nah. No more. He's done.

The bell rings. It's over.

Jess

"Come back! You're not going to hurt me," Lucas says, but I don't believe him.

Lying on the blanket at our spot overlooking the Long Island Sound, I put several inches between us for safety.

"I'm not touching you again until you stop saying 'ow.'"

He reaches for me and I scoot away.

"I only said 'ow' once. Just watch my ribs, that's all."

I exhale, flapping my lips noisily, and turn to face him. My hand slips under his shirt, skimming against his soft skin. I graze his left ribs. "Here?"

He nods.

I trace across his stomach to his right ribs. "Here?"

He shakes his head.

I trace lower, above his belly button, watching his face. "Here?"

He shakes his head. A smile forms on his face.

I dip lower, just above the line of his jeans.

His grin splits his face in half as he shakes his head. I bury my head in his chest and snort.

"You have the goofiest grin on your face!"

He laughs. "I wanted to see how far you'd take it."

I curl up into him. I know he's in more pain than he's letting on. I overheard Leo telling him he got whacked in the head more than he realized. Lucas also has a fat lip, a swollen nose, and bruises starting to form on his chin and all along his arms from blocking punches.

"How are you feeling, otherwise?" I ask, gently skimming his ribs over his shirt with my fingers.

"Oddly euphoric," he answers, staring up at the trees overhead "It's over. I did it."

"And you knocked that guy out."

"Not out. He had his headgear on. He just didn't want to get punched anymore. Turns out it was his first fight too."

"Think he'll box again?" I ask.

He shrugs. "Maybe."

"What about you?" I glance up at him. He watches my face, measuring my reaction.

"Would you mind if I did?"

The dappled light through the tree awning plays like music along his eyelashes, picking up the muted blue in his eyes. How is this gentle giant of a boy the same person who pummeled a stranger in the ring for fun? It's still hard to wrap my brain around this. I'm trying, for him.

"I don't love it. I don't want you to get hurt. But it seems like it really helps you, so . . . it's up to you. How serious are you about it?"

He juts his bottom lip out, then winces and lifts his fingers to his bruised mouth. "I don't think I want to go pro. But I'm not ready to quit just yet either."

A seagull squawks, reacting to the scent of food. We picked up lunch at a diner near the boxing gym and brought it here. Lucas also had an egg sandwich his mom made him, which we split. There's nothing left of our picnic but balled-up aluminum foil and empty to-go containers.

Pete went back to Enzo's and Reggie offered to work my shift today. They even called Joe in to work off the books so we could take the day off together.

Lucas twirls my hair around his finger. "The first day I walked into the gym, Leo asked me why I was here. It freaked me out because it's something I've asked myself every day since Jason died. Why him and not me? But what he really wanted to know was what was going to make me get up every day and give it everything I got. What was my motivation, you know? I thought boxing was just going to be about getting stuff out. But it's more. Stepping into the ring today, I felt it."

He pauses to look at me. "First of all, I knew I was not going to let myself get clobbered in front of you. You being there was some serious motivation."

I huff. "Glad I could be of assistance."

He smiles and plays with my hair, fanning my nose with a strand. "I also proved something to myself. Jason and my dad, they were both football legends. I finally have something that's mine, that I'm good at. I felt in control in there. The opposite of helpless."

I pluck a blade of grass and twirl it in the air in front of my face. "It's not easy to watch you get beat up. Or watch you punch someone else. But you were really holding your own. I didn't realize how good you were."

His scoops me into his arms. "Does it make you horny, baby?" he imitates *Austin Powers*, one of the movies I added to the pile in his basement. But when he rolls over onto his side with the bruised ribs, he winces and groans out loud.

"Not even a little!" I shove him away. "So maybe think about *that* before you get into the ring again."

I sit up to look at the beach down below. A fishing boat buzzes along the horizon like a lazy bumblebee. Lucas sits up next to me, carefully, holding his ribs as he does, then wraps an arm behind my back.

I brush my finger along his bruised lip.

"Wanna hear something funny?" he asks, his eyes warm, glowing.

"Last time we were here and you said that, you asked me to prom. I'm not sure I'm up to any more of your 'funny' stories."

He laughs. "This one's good. You'll like it. Remember that time you covered for Pete and you didn't bring food with you?"

I chuckle, remembering. "Yeah. And you kept trying to shove a slice of pizza down my throat."

He nods. "Yeah, well. You asked me about my fat lip. You reached your hand out and I thought for a second you were going to touch my lip. Well, more like hoped. And right then, I knew, dang, I like this girl."

I smile and touch his lip again, gently. "Yeah? Like this?"

He holds my hand on his lips and gently kisses my fingertips.

"What're you going to tell your parents? When they see your face?"

"The truth," he says, planting another kiss, this one on my wrist. Still holding my hand, he says, "I'm really glad you came today."

His eyes are so earnest and wide. I could swim in them all day, all night. "I wouldn't have missed it."

Threading his fingers through mine, he takes a deep breath, filling his lungs, then exhales just as deeply. "I just wanted to tell you . . . to let you know . . . that I love you. Okay?"

A surge of happiness blasts through me. It tingles, effervescent bubbles coursing through my blood, all the way to my fingertips, my scalp, my toes.

"Okay." I grin. Shock drains the light out of his face. "Wait!" I shout when I realize the wrong word popped out of my mouth. "I mean . . . I love you too." It comes out in a rush of giggles. Lucas pulls me closer so our lips are almost touching.

"Your lip!"

"Totally worth it," he says, and kisses me.

Lucas

"I'm home." I hang my keys on the peg and kick off my shoes. The house smells warm and savory, like my parents just finished dinner.

"We're in here," Dad hollers from the den.

I follow the sound of the explosions coming from the speakers. Mom and Dad are watching *Guardians of the Galaxy* . . . again. Dad loves anything Marvel, and I'm pretty sure Mom has a thing for Chris Pratt.

The den is dark except for the TV. Good. Neither of them will be able to see my fat lip or bruises. For a second I think I could let this go, at least until tomorrow. But no: it's time.

"Hey, guys . . . can I talk to you for a minute?"

Dad aims the remote at the TV and pauses the movie. "What's up?"

Cracking my knuckles, I say, "So, I didn't actually go to work today." My stomach clenches and cramps with nerves. This conversation scares me more than getting into the ring with Tony.

I pause long enough that Dad feels he needs to prod me along. "So . . . where were you?"

"Boxing," I say.

"At the gym?" Mom asks, confused.

"No, at a match," I admit.

Mom flops back against the couch cushions. "Are you *serious*?" she asks, her voice rising a few octaves.

Dad turns on the table lamp by his side. They both stare at my face, Dad silently, his eyes unreadable—angry, upset, I can't tell. Mom's gasp is enough reaction for both of them.

"LUCAS!" Mom is off the couch and inspecting my face with two hands, turning me this way, that way.

"I'm okay. You should see the other guy!" I try to break the ice with a joke. There's no cracking through Dad's frigid stare without a chisel.

"So you *lied* to us?" Dad says in a hurt voice. I *did* hurt him. We had a moment on Tuesday. I could have told him that morning when he was in my room.

"I didn't want to tell anyone. I just wanted to do it."

"Because you knew we'd say no!" Mom adds.

"It's something I needed to do. I'm sorry I didn't tell you."

Dad shakes his head and gets up off the couch. He walks into the kitchen and grabs a beer from the fridge. Mom sits back down rubbing her temples as if she's suddenly overcome by a migraine.

Taking a deep swig as he comes back in again, Dad lowers the beer bottle and shakes his head again. "I don't know, Lucas. I think I gave you too much credit the other day."

"What happened the other day?" Mom asks, craning her neck to look up at him from the couch.

Dad points his beer at me. "He snuck out Monday night to meet Jess."

"Dad," I protest. "You know that's not all of it."

"Snuck out?" Mom looks at me as if she no longer recognizes me. "In the middle of the night?"

"It's not like that," I assure her. "It was the night Jess's mom was in the hospital. And I went to see her."

She throws a hand over her eyes. "Lovely." Then she turns to Dad. Or rather, on Dad. "You should've told me."

Dad snaps back. "What would it have changed? You would've gotten upset and—"

"Hey, guys," I interrupt them, and wave my hands in the air. "I'm right here. Anything you want to say, you can say to me. We need to be able to talk to each other, right? So, let's talk."

I give Dad a meaningful look, reminding him about our conversation the other morning.

He takes a swig of his beer.

Hunched over, I stare at the carpeting under my socks and tug my fingers until my knuckles pop. "Ever since Jason died, I've been trying to make sense of why I'm here. Why I'm here and he's not. Why the universe would take the brother so obviously better at everything."

"Lucas! That's not true!" Mom cries.

I nod and shrug. I feel the pressure of tears building up inside of me. I swallow them back down and clear my throat. "Part of me gets that. And part of me doesn't. And that's the part I'm struggling with. And then there's the other part of me that thinks it's my fault that he's gone."

When I look up, both of them look so stricken by my admission that my eyes start to prick and I know I'm going to end up crying if I keep going. I'm pretty sure one or both of them will too.

But I want them to understand. So I tell them about my Random Acts of Kindness list and how I've spent every day since Jason died trying to prove my worth, the reason for my existence.

"It's not that I feel you guys think that," I make sure to clarify. "I realize the only person I've been trying to prove this to is myself."

Mom cries; Dad's eyes are staring into mine with fierce protectiveness.

When I'm done, Mom jumps up and hugs me like she's never going to let me go. Dad comes in and wraps us both in his arms. It reminds me of how Jason shielded me with his body when those gunshots rang out, only this time I feel the love, not the guilt.

Back in my room, I open my laptop. The Random Acts of Kindness file is still open. I close it and drag it to the trash. Then I empty the trash. A running tally can't define me. It doesn't prove that I deserve a seat at the table with the rest of the world. But it helped me get through this year.

I open a blank document and start writing my term paper. I think I know now how to approach this. I had it all wrong. It was never about forgiving the monster. The power of forgiveness begins with forgiving yourself.

Jess

Shoes! How did I forget shoes for prom?!

I press my hands together and close my eyes, wishing for a miracle. Maybe my fairy godmother will show up with a pair of glass slippers. When I open my eyes again, I'm still barefoot in my prom dress. I'm going to end up going in my Converse. If Lucas wasn't so set on looking *snazzy*, it would be a perfectly reasonable option in my opinion.

I look at the time on my phone. Four thirty. Lucas is coming in an hour.

Careful not to wake my mother, I tiptoe into her room. Her closet opens with a loud squeak.

"What are you doing?" she asks in a sleepy voice.

"Sorry," I whisper. "I was hoping maybe you had a pair of shoes I could borrow."

She's sleeping, but the doctor told us the new medicine may make her drowsy for a little while, until she gets used to it. This nap is doctor-approved.

Turning on her bedroom lamp, she gazes at me in my prom dress. She doesn't say anything for a few moments. But her smile says enough.

"You look so pretty, Jess." She stands up and pushes my hair away from my face. "I have a pair of shoes that will work." She reaches in and pulls out a pair of strappy silver sandals. "Don't even ask how old these are. They're from some wedding I went to years ago."

She puts them on the floor. I slip one foot in and she holds my elbow so I don't tip over. Then I slip the other foot in.

"How are the heels? Too high?" she asks, looking down at the shoes and up at my face.

"They're fine." I wobble. "Well, maybe I should do a few practice laps before Lucas comes."

She nods, then looks at my hair. "I used to be pretty good at doing hair. You want me to pin it up for you?"

I bite my bottom lip so I don't cry. "Yeah? Maybe?"

She sits me down in her vanity chair and brushes my hair. The yellow duct tape rose taped to a straw stands between the mirror and me. It's always been here, but I never really paid attention to it. I want to believe a piece of me was always here with her, reminding her of my existence, even when it felt like she was shutting me out.

In our reflection, I see a mother helping her daughter get ready for prom. Like a portrait with no backstory, we look perfectly normal, like we haven't been to hell and back this year.

She shows me a few options. "I can do a French braid for you, or a chignon."

"That. I like that." I point to the little knot she's holding at the back of my neck.

Mom smiles and nods in agreement. "I agree. Perfect with that dress."

While Mom bends over, focusing on my hair, I watch her movements in the mirror, recording her as if through a lens; with a little editing and cropping, I can treasure this moment forever. Her hands are busy at work, her focus intense. At one point, she pulls a little too hard and I wince.

"Oh, honey. I'm sorry." She massages the pained section with her fingertips. Memories of my mother getting me ready for school come flooding back. Every morning, I was scrubbed, brushed, and fed. Cared for. Old memories piece together with this one as she grabs bobby pins from the tray on her vanity, pinning my hair in the right places to keep it from falling out.

It feels as if the storm is passing. The sea and sand around us calm and recede.

Maybe I understand now why we stay here on our fragile sandbar, why we make ourselves vulnerable.

Because we're resilient. We rebuild. It's what we do.

LuCAs

I park the car across the street from the catering hall.

"Don't get out yet." I scroll through Spotify until I find the playlist I made for tonight. "Cue the music."

Frank Sinatra's "New York, New York," comes on and Jess's shoulders shudder with laughter. Her hair is piled into this low knot at the back of her head, exposing the long sexy length of her neck, and all I can think of right now is that I want to kiss it.

So I do.

As the big-band orchestra belts out Sinatra's anthem to New York, the limos start pulling up in front of Johnny's Catering Hall on the Water. A parade of spray-tanned promgoers piles out, one limo at a time.

"Okay, ready to play a new game? Who's Snazzy and Who's Ludicrous. I'll start." I point out the window at Aisha and Ron Daudin walking up the steps together.

"Snazzy," I decide.

"Snazzy," Jess agrees. "Holy crap. Aisha looks awesome."

Andrew and Sarah are next. "Ludicrous," we both say at the same time, then fist-bump.

Peachy and his date, Miranda, are next. "Snazzy."

Jess shakes her head. "She's Snazzy. He's Ludicrous. I'm glad you didn't go all-white tux after all."

We're split right down the middle, when there's a knock on the window.

Pete bends down to look in the car, then feigns a look of outrage, pointing to my tux, then his. We're matching.

I roll down the window. He leans in. "Dude, I know imitation is the greatest form of flattery, but come on. Have some pride. Hi, Jess. You look ah-mazing."

"Thank you. So do you!"

Pete tugs at his lapels and grins.

Jess does look amazing. With that dress . . . that *dress* . . . and her hair up, she looks like a movie star from one of those old movies.

Gwen leans over Pete's shoulder and waves. "Hi!" Pete's arm wraps around her waist. Ha! I *knew* they weren't going as just friends.

"Meet you in there?" Pete points across the street. I nod.

I turn to Jess and lean in for a quick kiss. "All right. We didn't come here to sit in the car all night. Let's do this."

Jess

Andrew's hand freezes just as he's shoveling a jumbo shrimp in his mouth. He does a double take, his eyes traveling up to Lucas's bruised face and split swollen lip.

Lucas catches his eye and points to me. "She did it."

I elbow Lucas, forgetting about his bruised ribs. "OW!" he shouts, louder than necessary, I think. Then he points to me again. "See what I mean?"

As we make our way through the audacious catering hall, Lucas holds my hand. Huge murals of dolphins swimming and diving around what must be a Mediterranean island by the white-washed buildings overlooking the sea take up the entire back wall. Long banquet tables are covered with elaborate displays of cheese platters, fruit, seafood, carving stations. Lucas heads straight for the food and loads two plates.

"Is that all for you or should I get my own plate?" I ask, looking over his arm.

"I'm bad, but I'm not that bad. Melon?" He points to the fruit display that's shaped to look like a lobster. I nod and he tears off a melon skewer antennae.

We sit at a table with Pete and Gwen. Aisha and Ron join us.

Peachy walks over, fist-bumping everyone around the table before sitting down with us; he's already lost his date.

"Yo, man, you get mugged or something?" he asks Lucas.

"You should see the other guy," Lucas says.

"We're going to have to put that on a card for you to hand to everyone who asks," Pete says. He tosses a cheese square in the air and catches it in his mouth.

Peachy persists. "Yeah, but seriously. What happened?"

So Lucas tells them every last detail of all three rounds of the match, how he was so scared he wanted to call it off and run to the bathroom, how he nearly lost it in the second round, but by the third round the other guy was gassed and Lucas was able to get some hooks in to knock the guy down.

Pete, Ron, and Peachy are riveted. Gwen and Aisha grimace.

"Jess? Did you go?" Gwen asks.

I nod, slowly. "Yeah. He's not even embellishing." Lucas shoulder-bumps me and grins.

The DJ gets right into it, pumping the music so loud it makes talking impossible. That's probably the point. Swarms of people rush the dance floor.

"Come on, let's dance." Lucas takes me by the hand and tugs me toward the wildly gyrating crowd. I pull away.

"It's going to be ugly," I warn him. "Cleanup-in-aisle-six ugly."

"I never said *I* was any good. I just want to dance." He puts his hands on my hips and walks backward holding on to me until we reach the dance floor.

We find our groove together, laughing and touching more than dancing. Pete takes Gwen by the arm and tangoes in between us. "Coming through," he announces.

Lucas takes my hand and twirls me. "See? You got this." He reels me back.

"Just don't let me fall. These heels are a bit higher than I'm used to."

With his hand on my waist, I know without a doubt he'd never let me fall.

Close to my ear, he whispers, "Careful. People might actually think you're having fun."

"Can't let that happen." I laugh.

He spins me out again. The song ends and a slow song comes on. This is more my speed. Lucas takes my hand and pulls me closer, inch by inch, until I am leaning fully up against him. I don't resist. Not like I ever could resist Lucas.

Lucas

Of the eighteen people who died that night, five of them would have graduated today. Graduation gowns and mortarboards are placed over their vacant chairs, in alphabetical order. All around me, shoulders heave and people try to wipe away errant tears, especially when Mr. Klein calls on us for a moment of silence before they start handing out the diplomas. Ethan would have graduated today. I'm glad Jess is sitting with my parents. I know they'll take care of her.

Even though Jason graduated two years ago, I still feel him here today, especially when they call my name—*our* name—to accept my diploma. It feels like a baton is being passed to me. Jason made it this far; now it's up to me to take it from here and run with it.

As I walk across the stage to accept my symbolic rolled-up piece of paper from Mr. Klein (the real diplomas will be mailed to us), I squeak out a tiny bubble of a fart, barely audible over all the commotion, but *definitely* toxic. Steak and onions last night. I grin for the cameras in the audience but really I'm thinking, *Smell you later*. It's totally juvenile, but something Jason and I would've laughed about together later.

After the ceremony, everyone in the auditorium pours outside the school. Mom, Dad, and Jess find Pete and me. Mom takes her phone out to get some pictures, but she can't stop crying.

"Lucas and Pete, squish together. Closer. Pretend you like each other," she says, dabbing her nose.

I groan; Pete grins. We wrap our arms behind each other's backs. It's ninety-seven degrees today and our robes are navy, trapping the heat against my body like an insulated thermal bag. I haven't stopped sweating since I got dressed. The sun beats down on the cement and brick; buildings block any relief of a breeze. There's no tree in sight, no sliver of shade to save us. Summer in the city is in full swing.

Pete turns to whisper in my ear, "I'm totally alfresco under this robe."

Mom takes the picture just that second, capturing my look of grossed-out shock forever.

"Jess, you get in there now," Mom orders.

Jess hops over and squishes in between Pete and me.

"Careful," I warn her through my forced smile. "Pete's going commando."

"Smart move," she says, and smiles. Mom takes the picture of the three of us.

Pete sees his family and waves. Pointing first to Jess, then me, he says, "Bonfire, tonight. Meet you guys there." Then he runs off to have his picture taken with his parents and his grandma. One strong gust of wind and Pete's going to flash his Bubbe. I pray to the weather gods for this one graduation gift. Please!

Jess hands my mom her phone. "Mrs. Rossi, would you mind taking a picture on my phone please?"

Mom takes a picture on Jess's phone and hands it back. Jess immediately looks at it, her thumbs tapping.

"What are you doing?" I ask.

"Sending it to Marissa," she says, typing a text.

Reggie pokes her head through the crowd, her eyes darting between my parents and me.

"I just wanted to give you a quick hug." She slips through the crowd to make her way over.

My parents haven't seen Reggie since right after Jason died. At first it was just because they were dealing with their grief, but really I think they've been harboring some misguided resentment toward her. And Reggie, sensing she was persona non grata, stayed away.

But now Mom and Dad exchange looks as Reggie, making good on her word, hugs me quickly and tries to escape. Shooting those nonverbal married couple looks, Mom nods to my father in agreement and takes those first hesitant steps. "Hi, Reggie."

Reggie turns around, looking sad.

"Hi, Mrs. Rossi." Even her voice sounds younger, insecure around my parents.

Mom opens her arms. "We've missed you," she says.

Their small talk starts off strained, but then starts to warm up.

Within minutes, my parents invite Reggie to come to dinner with us. And they're not taking no for an answer.

All around us, people are laughing and crying. In another year or two, there won't be clusters of empty seats at graduation, or an entire "In Memoriam" section in the yearbook. They'll move on and try to forget about that night. There'll be another thing that will rock their world, maybe another storm, another war, another monster. But this will be history.

Life is either about moving forward or looking back. We're moving forward again, but we'll never forget what's back there behind us. We can't. Because if we forget, it could happen again.

Jess

The late-August heat makes its way into the garage, suffocating us like a wet blanket.

"Jab with your left, then come at it with your right! Keep moving!" Lucas says, punching the air every time my fist makes contact with the bag. We've been at it for fifteen minutes and I'm exhausted. But I see now why it helps Lucas so much. All of that anger has a place to go.

Lucas convinced his parents to let him hang a heavy bag in the garage so he can train at home in addition to Leo's gym. He's only had one other fight since the one back in May. His bruises are turning a putrid shade of yellow, even two weeks later. But he won that one too.

Three months have passed since the day I found my mother crumpled on the bathroom floor. Since then, Mrs. Alvarez has become even more of a regular fixture in our home. If Mom was noncompliant before, now she does whatever Mrs. Alvarez tells her, including taking her antidepressants every day and seeing her therapist twice a week.

Glimpses of my mother from before are coming back. Therapy is like having to reset a broken bone; in order to heal properly, it has to hurt a little first. Her therapist had me come in to talk about our life together, before and after Ethan died, to help my mother reengage with her life and her relationships. There were a lot of tears, from both of us, especially when I told her, "I know it's not your fault. But I lost you too when I lost Ethan. You left me alone." I've been keeping up with my peer support group too.

My shattered life is coming together again, piece by piece.

We live our lives like survivors, weaker in some places, but stronger in others. Scarred, but healing. Just a few months ago, I couldn't imagine anything beyond trying to get through the day. Now I'm thinking about my future, a path unfurling for the first time with a glimmer of hope. Today, Lucas and I are going to look at colleges upstate together. If for some reason we don't get into the same school, we'll figure out how to make us work. We've been through worse. Every day we're stronger, closer to being whole again.

Lucas wipes the sweat from his brow with his forearm. "You take a shower first. Let's try and hit the road by ten." He tosses back a glass of water.

I pick up my phone off the floor. There's a new text:

ARE YOU SERIOUSLY DATING LUCAS ROSSI????

All I can text back is: !!!!!!!!!!!!!!!!!!!!!!!!!!!!
"Who are you texting?" Lucas asks.
"Marissa." I stare at the screen with a huge grin on my face.

By ten o'clock, we're on the road, heading north, leaving Queens behind.

Windows open, I dangle my hand out to feel the breeze weave through the web of my fingers as we cross the Whitestone Bridge. My hair blows around me, the sun splashes down on my face.

Lucas takes my left hand and squeezes, little compressions that remind me that I'm here, I'm alive. I'm still fighting.

A Note from Amy Giles

In publishing, an author has one last chance before a book goes to print to make changes. At best, I'd hope to catch a few embarrassing typos. It never occurred to me that I'd need to update my author's note to address the Parkland shooting in Florida that killed seventeen students and teachers on Valentine's Day, 2018.

I wrote the first draft of *That Night* in 2014. It was not written in reaction to Sandy Hook or Aurora or any particular mass shootings in recent history. It was written out of grief and despair that these events keep happening. But with this recent shooting, there appears to be a new force challenging our lawmakers, our elected officials, the status quo. From this most recent heinous crime, students have become the most vocal advocates calling for action. New gun law activists—some still too young to vote, but not for long—are shouting at the top of their lungs, "Never again!" Your voices are the ones that will affect real change. You will succeed where we have failed.

That Night is a work of fiction. Rather than focus on the shooting at the Balcony, I wanted to turn the lens to focus on the victims who survive this kind of tragedy, the "walking wounded." I wanted to tell a story about what life is like for them a year later, after the cameras and reporters leave. For Jess, Lucas, Mrs. Nolan, Mr. and Mrs. Rossi, and Marissa, their lives will never be the same, whether they suffer from grief and loss of a loved one, anxiety, PTSD, and/or clinical depression. The repercussions of gun violence extend well beyond the reach of a bullet.

While this story is an invention of my imagination, we've seen that the real world can be equally, if not more, terrifying. From lockdown drills at school to the nightly news, to the most recent Parkland shooting, the world can become too much to bear alone. If you're feeling scared, overwhelmed, anxious, depressed, please talk to someone about it. A parent, a teacher, a counselor at school. Anonymous, confidential, and free hotlines across the country are also available anytime you need help.

If you or someone you know is feeling suicidal, call 911 immediately.

National Suicide Prevention Hotline
(800) 273-TALK (8255)
Twenty-four hours a day, seven days a week
TTY–Hearing and Speech Impaired: (800) 799-4TTY
Text ANSWER to 839863

National Hopeline Network
(800) SUICIDE (784-2433)
(800) 442-HOPE (4673)
Twenty-four hours a day, seven days a week
www.hopeline.com

TeenLine

Teen-to-teen counseling

(310) 855-HOPE (4673)

(800) TLC-TEEN (852-8336)

6 p.m. to 10 p.m. PST

Text TEEN to 839863

www.teenlineonline.org

Crisis Call Center

(800) 273-8255

Text ANSWER to 839863 Twenty-four hours a day, seven days a week

www.crisiscallcenter.org

National Mental Health Association Hotline

(800) 273-TALK (8255)

Twenty-four hours a day, seven days a week

www.nmha.org

National Institute of Mental Health Information Center

(866) 615-6464

8 a.m. to 8 p.m. EST, Monday through Friday

www.nimh.nih.gov

National Alliance on Mental Illness (NAMI) Helpline

(800) 950-NAMI (6264)

10 a.m. to 6 p.m. EST, Monday through Friday

www.nami.org

Substance Abuse and Mental Health Services Administration (SAMHSA) Helpline

(800) 662-HELP (4357)

Twenty-four hours a day, seven days a week, English and Spanish

www.samhsa.gov

Boys Town National Hotline

For teens (boys and girls) and parents

(800) 448-3000

Twenty-four hours a day, seven days a week

www.boystown.org

Speak Up

Safely and anonymously report suspected gun violence threats

(866) SPEAK-UP (773-2587)

Twenty-four hours a day, seven days a week

www.bradycampaign.org

Acknowledgments

It takes a team effort to write a book.

I would like to thank my agent, Alexandra Machinist, for championing this book in its earliest stages. My unflappable editor, Jessica MacLeish, who put so much time and energy into helping me take this book apart and piece it back together. Thank you to the ever-warm and gracious Rosemary Brosnan for welcoming me on to your team. A debt of gratitude goes out to everyone at Harper who had a hand in shepherding both of my books into the world.

Thank you to Kelvin Dickenson, Chris Cassatto, Sean Cooper, and Erin Beaty for helping me get into the mind, body, and spirit of a boxer. For more reasons than I can list here, I am eternally grateful to Julie Hochman, LCSW, whose enormous heart, skill, and talent have helped countless teenagers find their way. Thank you to Anne Myrka for allowing me to pick her brains about pharmaceuticals and drug safety, but above all else, for being a friend and kindred spirit.

To the people of Far Rockaway: thank you for allowing me to settle into your peninsula on the Atlantic. I may have taken a few liberties, but I tried to stay true to your location and vibe. Your community is no stranger to tragedy, and I apologize for adding an additional fictional one. In writing this story, I wanted Lucas and Jess to personify and honor your resiliency and strength of character that I so deeply admire.

And last, but always first, thank you to my heart, my home: Pat, Maggie, and Julia.